ENTRAPPED

THE ROGUES SERIES BOOK 3

TRACIE DELANEY

Copyright © 2020 Tracie Delaney

Edited by StudioEnp

Proofreading by Katie Schmahl, Jean Bachen, and Jacqueline Beard

Cover art by *Tiffany @TEBlack Designs*

All rights reserved. No part of this publication may be reproduced, stored in any retrieval system, or transmitted, in uniform or by any means, electronic, mechanical, photocopying, recording or otherwise without prior written permission of the author.

This is a work of fiction. Names, characters, places, and incidents are either the products of the author's imagination or are used fictitiously, and any resemblance to actual persons, living or dead, business establishments, events, or locales is entirely coincidental.

BOOK THREE IN THE ROGUES SERIES

If I wrote an autobiography of my life right now, I'd call it "Blackmailed by the Billionaire".

Ruthless, callous, and self-serving are the nicest words to describe the powerful CEO who wants what's mine.

He'll use any method at his disposal to emerge victorious—including coercion.

Okay, fine, I'll concede defeat, but as his interest pivots I spot the opportunity for payback.

And hell, I'm gonna take it.

A NOTE TO THE READER

∼

Dear Reader,

Thank you so much for choosing Entrapped when there are so many other books out there you could have picked. I am having such a good time with these ROGUES. Garen, in particular, was brilliant to spend time with, although be warned, he is very much the anti-hero, so if you're looking for a warm and fluffy man to cuddle up at night with, reading this novel might result in disappointment :-)

Catriona gives as good as she gets, though. Maybe not in an obvious way, but believe me, she makes her point. The two of them together are absolute dynamite.

I hope you enjoy reading Catriona and Garen's story. I'd love to hear what you think about Entrapped once you're finished reading, either by leaving a review, or by joining my Facebook reader group Tracie's Racy Aces. Can't wait to chat to you over there.

In the meantime, flip the page. Garen and Catriona can't wait for you to join them.

Happy reading.

Love,
Tracie

BOOKS BY TRACIE DELANEY

The Winning Ace Series

Ace - A Winning Ace Novella

Winning Ace

Losing Game

Grand Slam

Winning Ace Boxset

Mismatch

Break Point - A Winning Ace Novella

Stand-alone

My Gift To You

Draven

The Brook Brothers Series

The Blame Game

Against All Odds

His To Protect

Web of Lies

The Brook Brothers Complete Boxset

Irresistibly Mine Series

Tempting Christa

Avenging Christa

Full Velocity Series

Friction

Gridlock

Inside Track

Full Velocity Boxset (Books 1-3)

ROGUES Series

Entranced

Enraptured

Entrapped

Enchanted

Enthralled

Enticed

1

Catriona

"One, and two, and three." I rapped my black dance cane on the floor in time to the music, with Ammaline, one of my most talented students, responding to each tap. "And plié. Arms up, bend at the elbows. That's it. Good girl. Lovely positioning. And jeté. Wonderful."

Ammaline flashed me a broad grin, my compliments providing exactly the right amount of motivation. She blossomed under praise, although I only gave it when it was earned. Telling the kids they were doing brilliantly when they weren't wouldn't do them any favors in the long run. That didn't mean I was *ever* cruel, only constructive. The sad fact remained that ninety-five percent of the girls who attended my classes wouldn't make it as chorus line dancers, let alone prima ballerinas. This was a tough business, and only the very best had a chance at making it.

Ammaline, though, was my star pupil. I had high hopes for her. She'd attended my ballet school for three years now, ever since she and her mother moved to Vancouver from Banff, and during that time, I'd watched her morph from an awkward teenager into a young woman with true promise, if seventeen counted in the 'young woman' category.

Last week, she'd received an invitation to attend the Royal Academy of Dance (RAD) in Battersea, London. Within the month, she'd leave these shores and start her new life in England. My pride in this girl knew no bounds, and while I'd miss her terribly, her future lay elsewhere. I'd taken her as far as my knowledge extended. To move to the next level, she needed higher-quality teachers than me.

Ballet had been my whole life. My grandmother had started this school when she emigrated from her native Ireland to Canada many decades earlier, and she'd instilled her love of dance into me. At one time, I'd dreamed of becoming a prima ballerina and dancing for the Royal Ballet. Then a nasty ankle break at the age of sixteen put an end to my hopes and dreams. Since I couldn't dance professionally, I did the next best thing and followed my grandmother into teaching.

Grams moved into our family home to raise me and my brother after our parents were killed in a car accident thirteen years ago. I was twelve at the time, my brother barely two. I honestly don't know what we would have done if my grandmother hadn't stepped in to take care of us. These days her age had started to catch up with her, and she needed extra support in the form of a walker. Despite her disability, she still took a keen interest in the dance school. Every evening, she'd demand I update her with the events of the day, relaying the smallest detail each of the kids' achievements. She wasn't shy at sharing her opinion either, especially if she disagreed with me on a point of principle.

"Hi, Miss Landry," an unwelcome voice behind me called. "Has it been a week already?"

I looked over my shoulder, frowning at the intrusion.

Standing in the entranceway to my studio was a man who'd grown familiar to me over the last few weeks, the usual large envelope clutched in his hands, the cream coloring with the recognizable crest stamped along the seal.

I sighed. *Here we go again.*

Glancing up at the clock on the wall, I realized Ammaline's lesson was almost over. Finishing a couple of minutes early wouldn't do her any harm. "Let's call it a day, Ammaline," I said. "Very well done. You're improving by leaps and bounds at every single lesson."

She beamed with pleasure, reaching for a towel with which she dabbed at her face and neck. "Thank you, Miss Landry. Is it okay if I take a shower before leaving for home?"

I nodded, gesturing to the rear of the studio toward the changing area. "Of course. I'll be here for a little while longer. Take your time."

I waited until she disappeared and the sound of running water reached me, then I turned my attention to the man casually loitering just inside the main doorway.

"Back so soon?" I spoke in an icy tone, even though it wasn't his fault he'd been sent to do someone else's dirty work. *Don't shoot the messenger.* Wasn't that the phrase? Regardless, he got the cold shoulder. Served him right for working for an asshole of a boss.

"I have another offer for you." He held the letter in the air like a trophy.

I pointed to a small area off the studio that doubled as my office. "You can put it on the desk in there."

He made a face. "Sorry, I need a signature. You know how it is."

I rolled my eyes and let out an irritated huff. Striding across the wooden floor of the ballet studio, I snatched the letter from his outstretched hand and scrawled an illegible signature on his electronic device.

"Thanks," he said, heading for the door with a grin and a wave. "See you next week, or maybe sooner."

I waited until he left, then flipped him off. I stared at the crisp, expensive envelope for a good sixty seconds, then entered my office and flopped in the chair behind my desk. The space overflowed with paperwork as it always did at this time of the week. Friday afternoons were for admin, and today was only Tuesday. Until Friday came around, every scrap of paper had to wait its turn. Including this one.

I tossed the latest arrival on top of the pile, then changed my mind and buried it inside the top drawer instead. *Out of sight, out of mind.*

I slammed it shut. The warped wood caught on the lip of the desk. I ground my teeth as I wrenched it open, then rammed it shut with considerable force. Why wouldn't the damned man get the message? Maybe the time had come to take his unsolicited offer, roll it into a tube, and shove it up his ass. On the three previous occasions his lackey showed up, I'd sent a polite note declining the offer and reiterating that my dance school wasn't for sale. It was evident to me now that Mr. Jerkoff Billionaire had no intention of giving up on his quest. The fact that most of my neighbors had already capitulated to his disgustingly bloated offers to purchase their businesses didn't help my cause, but this studio meant far more to me than bricks and mortar. It had soul, heart, and so many irreplaceable memories.

Dad standing on the sidelines watching, his face shining with pride the first time I managed en pointe without falling over.

Mom clapping so hard, she almost took the skin off her hands when I earned a rare "Not bad, Catriona," from my grandmother after I'd mastered the challenging fouetté, a pirouette performed with a circular whipping movement and a raised leg to the side.

The comfort I found in the tired wood paneling where I'd carved my name—earning a fierce scolding from my grandmother—following my parents' untimely death.

My grandmother hugging me so tightly when the realization hit me that the damage to my ankle meant I'd have to give up ballet.

"Bye, Miss Landry." Ammaline poked her head around the door to my office, her face scrubbed clean of perspiration, her still-wet hair pulled back into a severe bun on top of her head.

"Ammaline," I scolded with a shake of my head. "It's cold outside. You really should dry your hair before walking home."

She shot me a grin and gestured dismissively. "It's fine, Miss Landry. It's only ten minutes."

"Well, don't dawdle." I smiled fondly at her. Sometimes I found it hard to believe I was only eight years older than her. I felt about eighty years older.

"I won't. See you Friday."

She gave me a final wave, and left.

I waited until the click of the door reached me, then I opened the drawer and removed the thick, cream envelope. I tapped it against my desk, wondering what this latest offer would entail.

With a resigned sigh, I slid my fingernail underneath the seal and opened it. I removed a single sheet of matching cream paper, and a whiff of cologne assaulted my nostrils. I closed my eyes and breathed in the masculine, and undoubtedly expensive, scent. Garen Gauthier, local billionaire businessman and all-round arrogant prick wouldn't think of gracing his too-handsome face with some cheap cologne. One bottle by his favorite designer probably cost more than my entire year's taxes on the income from this place.

I scanned the typewritten letter, ignoring the majority of hyperbole, searching for the financial offer I knew was somewhere on the page. When I reached the particular section, my eyes widened. I quickly ran the figures through my head. He'd increased his offer. Significantly. Another thirty percent by my reckoning.

Hmm. I'd bet the increased offer had something to do with the amount of capital he'd already sunk into buying up the businesses on this prime piece of real estate in downtown Vancouver. He intended to replace these independent ventures with yet another hotel in a chain that was growing in size across North America. His narcissistic attitude meant he confidently assumed every single business owner would be only too happy to sell out for the right number of zeroes on the check.

And then he'd met me. Well, not *met,* exactly. No, I hadn't had the pleasure of meeting Mr. Gauthier. He sat in his ivory tower while his minions did his bidding, buying up all but two businesses.

Mine, and Jeff's, the butcher's shop two doors down.

I wonder if Jeff's had another offer?

Making a mental note to ask him tomorrow—he didn't open on Tuesday's—I gathered my things, including the offending letter, locked up, and set off for home.

Halfway there, though, I changed my mind. Maybe it was time I told Mr. Gauthier directly to his face that he was wasting his breath—and his expensive letter-headed paper.

My business wasn't for sale, and neither was I.

2

Garen

My phone dinged with a text. I gave it a cursory glance, reading the banner across the screen.

Offer delivered and signed for.

I picked it up and unlocked it, opened the message, then hit call.

"How was it received?" I asked, tapping my pen against the desk.

James, my executive assistant, chuckled. "This time she only said 'fuck off' with her eyes. She might be coming around."

I laughed, even though there was nothing funny about this situation. Huge amounts of cash had already gone into this venture, and I wouldn't allow one stubborn woman to stand in my way. Maybe the time had come for me to employ more... coercive methods.

"The butcher signed, though. I just got the paperwork through."

A tight smile lifted my lips. That meant she was the only one still holding out. Should make things easier.

"Good." I cut the call without any warning. Not that James would care. He'd worked for me for two years and had grown used to my curt manner. At least he didn't spend half his time crying at his desk like his four predecessors. I tore through executive assistants almost as fast as I tore through women. The former usually resigned. The latter I dumped after three or four dates before they got any silly ideas of something longer term.

I didn't do relationships.

In my experience, women were too needy, always demanding validation or attention. Don't get me wrong, I liked female company as much as the next guy, but only as a means to an end. I was a twenty-nine-year-old virile man. I needed sex almost as much as oxygen. That didn't mean I wanted the baggage that came with the orgasms.

A tentative knock at my office door brought my head up. "Come in," I barked.

The door opened slowly, and a young girl peered inside. I vaguely recognized her as one of the recent group of interns. Daisy? Poppy? Daffodil? Some stupid name or other.

"Yes," I snapped when she stood there, frozen to the spot as if by simply entering my office, she'd turned into stone.

"Um, Miss... Miss Calderwood n-needs you to s-sign this, Mr. Gauthier," she stammered, her face blooming with color as nerves took over.

"Well, don't just stand there." I held out my hand for the manila folder she clutched so tightly her fingers had turned white. "Give it to me."

She tottered over on a pair of heels she clearly couldn't walk in. I raised my eyes heavenward. Who the fuck was she trying to impress? She looked like Bambi on drugs, staggering her way across my office.

As if to prove my point, she'd almost reached me when... Splat! Over she went, face-planting right in front of my desk. The folder of papers scattered everywhere, and she let out an "Oomph" as the air was knocked from her lungs.

"For fuck's sake," I muttered, getting to my feet. I crouched in front of her, slipped my hands under her armpits, and hoisted her to her feet.

She bobbed and weaved, reminding me of a punch-drunk boxer, then found her balance by gripping my upper arms. The horror of what had happened hit her fast. Her eyes widened, and then her head bowed as she took in the mess strewn around her feet like confetti.

"Oh God, I'm s-sorry Mr. Gau-Gauthier," she wailed, dropping to her knees, her arms flailing as she scooped up bits of paper and shoved them back into the folder. "P-please don't fire me. I really n-need this job."

I stood there, watching her desperately try to recover the situation. A gentleman would have helped.

I wasn't a gentleman.

"Next time, I suggest you wear sensible shoes when visiting my office," I bit out, taking the folder from her trembling hands. "That way, you might have a chance of staying upright."

I strode back around my desk and sat down while whatever-her-name-was blushed bright red and tucked her chin into her chest, eyes on the floor. Her elevated breathing was the only sound in the otherwise quiet space. I could tell she was trying to get her shuddering breaths under control—and failing miserably.

I expelled a sigh, drawing a sob from the intern. I raised my eyes to find her furiously blinking to prevent her burgeoning tears. Had to give the girl credit where it was due. Lesser women would have dissolved into hysterics by now. Maybe there was hope for this one yet.

I scrawled my signature on the bottom of the marked pages. "What's your name?"

"Tulip," she whispered.

That's right. Fucking Tulip. What kind of idiotic parent names their kid Tulip?

"Okay, Tulip, I'm going to give you some free advice, so listen up. This is a place of work, not a nightclub. When you finish your shift today, pay a visit to the mall on your way home and buy yourself a pair of sensible fucking shoes. I do not need one of my interns breaking their leg on my watch. Got it?"

Relief that I hadn't fired her swept across her face. "Yes, Mr. Gauthier," she said, her nodding reminding me of a spring-loaded bobble head found in tacky gift shops. "I absolutely will."

I signed the last form, closed the folder, and handed it to her. She tucked it under her arm, took two steps, then stopped and turned around to face me again.

"You're not nearly as horrible as they said you were," she offered and then, realizing she'd spoken completely out of turn, clapped a hand over her mouth as if she was trying to shove the words back in.

I gave her a blank, cold stare. "Yes, I am. And if you want to keep your job, you'd do well to listen to your coworkers."

Her face flushed with embarrassment, and then she bolted from the room, closing the door behind her.

I smiled.

That was fun.

My desk phone rang, and I picked it up. "Gauthier."

"Mr. Gauthier, it's Shana in reception. I have a Miss Landry here. She's demanding to see you, sir, and won't take no for an answer."

Oh, but this will be more fun.

I tapped a few keys on my keyboard, and an image appeared on my screen showing a view of the lobby of my building. I'd never met the Landry woman, preferring to leave the dirty work to the likes of James, but as she came into view, I realized I'd made a mistake not handling this myself.

Catriona Landry was nothing like I expected. For some reason, the fact that she ran a ballet school meant I'd pictured a woman in her fifties, tall, thin, with gray hair scraped back into a bun and a pair of half-moon glasses perched on the end of her nose.

Instead, what filled my screen was a beauty with dark, wavy, waist-length hair and creamy smooth skin. She wasn't dressed in anything fancy, just jeans and a tangerine sweater, but dang, I'd like to explore her body. Slim hips, a firm ass, tapered waist, and tits that were the perfect handful.

I moved my mouse, zooming closer into her face. She bent her head and looked right into the camera, almost as if she knew I was watching. Her eyes were a stunning green, and swirling in their depths lay an indignant rage.

My cock hardened. *Hello, Miss Landry.*

"Sir, are you still there?"

I went to answer her, but the words wouldn't come. *What the fuck? I'm never tongue-tied.* A warmth crept up the back of my neck, and I palmed it, feeling dampness there. I swallowed, pulled myself together, took a deep breath.

"I'm here," I replied. "Tell Miss Landry I'm busy."

I hung up and waited for the receptionist to relay my message. Catriona's head snapped back, and she cut her gaze to the camera in the corner. Her hands curled into fists, and then she spun on her heel and strode outside.

I raced to the window, catching sight of her as she disappeared down the street. She walked with graceful, precise steps and a straight back, her fluid hips swaying with the kind of natural sensuality that couldn't be faked as she weaved through the pedestrians.

A smile touched my lips, the brief moment of awkwardness

long forgotten.

From now on, the only person dealing with Miss Catriona Landry is me.

3

Catriona

Too busy? Too busy! The damned gall of the man. I'd give him too busy when I laid my hands on him. What a complete prick. Who the hell did he think he was? Why did rich people always think normal world rules didn't apply to them?

I stomped down the street toward the bus stop. If he thought this was the end of it, then he was sorely mistaken. I'd tried the polite approach, and it had fallen on deaf ears. One way or another, I'd get an audience with Sir Stuck Up Gauthier and drive my message through his thick skull.

In fact…

An idea took hold. I circled around and returned to his tall, imposing, glass-fronted building. He must be inside. The receptionist had spoken to him directly. All I had to do was wait for him to leave and then accost him in the street. So what if I embarrassed him? It'd serve him right, and maybe, just maybe, if I rammed my point home hard enough, he'd realize I couldn't be bought and he'd back off.

A little voice inside my head murmured something about a pipe dream.

I ignored it.

I took up residence under the awning of an Italian restaurant that gave me a perfect view of the front of Gauthier's building. I waited and waited, my eyes locked on the sliding glass doors, scared to even blink in case he slipped by unnoticed. The cold ground seeped through my shoes, and I fidgeted, shifting from foot to foot, my irritation mounting the longer I hung around with no sign of him.

Oh, hell. I hadn't thought to let Grams know I'd be late.

Fishing my phone from my purse, I dropped her a quick text. I asked about Aiden, my heart twisting as my mind turned to him. He hadn't been well these past few weeks and on Monday he'd finally undergone some tests. Waiting for the results was killing me. God only knew what it was doing to Aiden.

Grams replied to say she'd keep some dinner warm and to travel safely, and that Aiden was asleep on the couch, but she'd managed to get a bit of food into him, thank goodness. He'd scarcely eaten in days, his already too-thin body losing weight he couldn't afford to shed. I tried to swallow any panic that threatened to consume me until we knew exactly what we were dealing with, but most nights I lay awake staring at the ceiling and imagining the worst.

If anything happened to Aiden... I couldn't bear to think of it. After our parents were torn so cruelly from us, to lose him as well would probably kill my grandmother, leaving me all alone.

I shook my head. *Stop those thoughts, Catriona.*

A sleek black limousine with blacked-out windows and blinding headlights glided to a stop in front of Gauthier's building. I straightened, my heart rate ramping up. This had to be his ride. I glued my eyes to the entranceway, waiting for the man himself to appear. A uniformed driver alighted from the vehicle and opened the rear door, then stood at attention as if he was one of the Queen's royal guard.

I snorted a laugh.

A full minute passed, and then Gauthier strode outside, briefcase in hand and a jet-black pea coat buttoned up as a defense against the stiff wind swirling down the street. Canada only had two months of good weather in an average year, really. July and August. Apart from those times when the warmth of the sun bathed your face, and the days went on forever, our weather consisted of chilly, cold, bitter, and fucking freezing.

I'd filed today's weather under 'chilly'.

"I'd like a word, please, Mr. Gauthier."

He paused mid-step and twisted his head in my direction. At first he frowned, and then recognition smoothed his features. Gesturing to his driver to wait, he stood there, waiting for me to go to him, one perfectly shaped eyebrow curved in query.

Prick.

"Have you been out here all this time, Miss Landry?" he asked. "I'm honored."

"Don't be," I replied, riffling through my purse for the offending offer letter. "I came to bring you this." Three strides took me to him. I thrust the cream envelope against his chest, suppressing a tremor as I came into contact with the taut muscles lying beneath his outer clothing.

His hand closed over mine, and the tremor morphed into a full-on shudder. I slid my hand out from beneath his, leaving him holding the envelope.

"You could have mailed your acceptance," he drawled, a sardonic curve to his lips that meant he knew very well I hadn't accepted his offer. "Rather than coming all this way."

My jaw flexed, teeth gnashing together. "Aren't you business types supposed to be smart? You know damn well I haven't signed that agreement, just like I didn't sign any of the others."

My chest rose and fell too fast, oxygen battling for access to compressed lungs. "And don't insult me by adding more zeroes to your next offer. It doesn't matter how much money you offer me. The answer remains the same. No. Got it?"

His gunmetal-gray eyes bored into mine. My knees wobbled at the fierce determination swirling in their depths. This man was used to getting his own way, and he wouldn't take kindly to losing. Well, too bad. He'd have to deal with it.

"Everyone has a price, Miss Landry," he murmured, his eyes on my lips as he said it.

"Not me." I shoved trembling hands into my pockets. "Face it, Mr. Gauthier. You might have gotten almost all the other business owners to sign, by fair means or foul, but I will never sell my business to you, and neither will Jeff."

His eyebrows drew inward toward the bridge of his nose. "Jeff?"

I breathed through my nose, my nostrils flaring. "The butcher."

"Ah." His wry grin grew in size. "Sorry to be the bearer of bad news, Miss Landry, but…" He canted his head, and his flat cold stare reminded me of a shark's eyes. Lifeless, deadly.

A despairing flush of heat swept through me. *No.* Jeff wouldn't sell, not without telling me. Would he?

"You're lying," I gritted out.

"While I'm not averse to lying to get my own way, on this occasion I'm not. Your friend, Jeff, signed earlier today." He put the envelope I'd thrust at him in the inside pocket of his coat. "See, he's a smart man. Knows when he's beaten. You, on the other hand," he ran his gaze up and down my body, "You, Miss Landry, might need a different kind of persuasion."

A bolt of fear hit me right in the gut, and I glanced around to make sure there were people in the vicinity.

"Is that a threat?"

He moved forward, his far superior height looming over

me, despite my five-feet-eight-inch frame. "No, Miss Landry." He paused and ran his tongue along the underside of his teeth. "It's a promise."

He whirled around and climbed in the back of his limousine. The car glided away. I stared until I lost sight of it, and even then I didn't move, unease gluing my feet to the ground.

Garen Gauthier wasn't a man to trifle with. I'd yanked the tiger's tail, and now he was on the hunt.

With me as his prey.

4

Garen

I twisted in my seat and peered out through the blackened rear window, watching as Catriona Landry shrank smaller and smaller until she disappeared completely. I faced forward once more, my lips curving upward. What a little firecracker. I had a colossal urge to add fuel to the flames and see which of us escaped unharmed.

Slipping a hand into my coat pocket, I withdrew the cream envelope. I lifted it to my nose, smelling a faint trace of her perfume. Unpretentious and beautiful, just like her. I opened the flap and removed the letter inside, even though I knew exactly what it said. I turned over to the signature page and laughed.

She'd written 'Hell to the fucking no' right across the bottom.

The tips of my fingers traced the indentation on the reverse side of the contract. She must have scrawled those words so deep and with such rage, the nib of her pen had almost ripped the paper.

My smile widened. *Oh, Catriona.*

I returned the letter to my jacket pocket and spent the rest of the trip to my house in Shaughnessy Heights thinking about the dark-haired, tall, graceful, green-eyed beauty with a plump mouth made for fucking. I hardened inside my pants as my mind threw up an image of Catriona on her knees sucking my cock.

Then again, right this second, if I put my cock anywhere near her delicious mouth, she'd likely bite it off, such was the venom I'd seen fizzing in her eyes. I almost rubbed my hands together in glee. For me, the fun was in the chase. Once a woman capitulated, and I'd fucked her a few times, the attraction wore off pretty damned fast, and I'd move on to the next. The problem was I had a very low boredom threshold driven, according to doctors my parents had taken me to in my teenage years, by an I.Q. in the top two percent of the country and a mild form of ADHD.

Maybe Catriona would keep my interest slightly longer than most. I hoped she fought me tooth and nail. The harder the better as far as I was concerned. The thought of conquering her, of watching her submission, Christ, I could get off on that for days.

My driver-slash-bodyguard nosed the car through the gates of my home and swept up to the front of the house. He glided to a stop, killed the engine, and climbed out. I waited for him to open my door.

"Will you need me again tonight, sir?" he asked, standing back to give me room.

"No, thank you, Darryl," I said. "See you in the morning."

My housekeeper opened the door, smiled in greeting, and held out her hand for my briefcase.

"You're late," she said. "I kept your dinner warm."

I chuckled under my breath as I walked inside. Margo had been with me for years, and I didn't know what I'd do without her. She reminded me of my mother; strong, assertive, direct, didn't take any shit. I needed that. My life was too full of people who bowed to my every whim. With my parents living on the other side of the country, Margo was the one who ensured my feet remained firmly planted on the ground.

"You're a marvel, Margo." I leaned down to kiss her weathered cheek. "Marry me?"

She blushed and shoved at me. "Go away with you, crazy man," she said, bustling off in the direction of the kitchen.

I followed, and my stomach growled with hunger at the smell of freshly baked bread and a casserole. I'd skipped breakfast and only managed half a sandwich at lunchtime. The expansion plans the ROGUES board had sanctioned for the hotel chain—my baby—resulted in insane amounts of work. I regularly pulled fourteen-hour days. Add to that the scheduled workouts with my personal trainer, screwing the latest woman I'd met, and snatching a few hours' sleep, it didn't leave a lot of time for very much else.

Margo heaped a serving of beef casserole into a bowl and set it down in front of me. I tore off a hunk of bread, dipped it into the gravy, and shoved it into my mouth. My eyes closed as I savored the rich flavor.

"God, Margo, you're a genius."

She fetched me a beer from the fridge and unscrewed the top. "I know." She placed the bottle on a coaster then picked up her purse and set the strap diagonally across her body. "It's time I went and got Frank his supper. Man's incapable of buttering a slice of bread, let alone cooking a meal."

"Give him my apologies for making you late," I said. "Next time I'm late getting home, just go, Margo. You don't have to wait here for me."

She shot me a mothering look. "Someone has to take care

of you. You work too hard, Garen. Hopefully, one of these days, you'll meet a good woman and she can take my place."

"Not likely," I muttered.

Margo rolled her eyes. "Come now," she said. "You don't want to die a lonely old man, now, do you?"

I chuckled. "I'm twenty-nine."

She patted her gray hair, then tucked a stray lock back into her messy bun. "I was twenty-nine once. Feels like five minutes ago. Time passes, young man, and before you know it, poof, your knees have given out, your hips ache, and it takes a monumental effort to roll out of bed in the morning."

I shook my head at her. "You're a bundle of joy this evening, Margo."

"Mark my words," she said, making a beeline for the door to the hallway. "Don't let the grass grow under your feet."

She left before I came back with a retort. Not that I had one ready. For some unknown reason, these last few months Margo had started nagging me about settling down. Every time I went on a date, she metaphorically dusted off her wedding hat, only to put it back in its box a week later when I'd dumped my latest conquest.

Note to self. Do NOT mention Catriona.

I finished the casserole, rinsed my bowl, and slid it into the dishwasher. After wrapping the bread, I grabbed another bottle of beer and trudged upstairs to my bedroom. Shucking my clothes, I jumped into the shower and let the hot water wash away the grime of the day.

My mind turned once again to Catriona Landry. Somehow, I had to get her to sign over her property to me. Without her property, I couldn't build the hotel and while the money already sunk on this venture wouldn't make a dent in ROGUES' profits, for me, it wasn't about money.

It was about *winning*.

I dried off, left my hair damp, and downed a third of my

beer while staring out the window. Solar lights illuminated the pristine back yard, the lawns and borders tended to by green-fingered gardeners, their aim to provide a relaxing space that I never found the time to enjoy.

Maybe Margo had a point. Perhaps the time had come to consider whether I still wanted to be playing the field in five or ten years.

I laughed.

What was I thinking? Of course I did. Marriage, kids, soccer dad stuff was for other men, not for me. I'd leave the parenting and shit to my best friend, Oliver.

Speaking of which…

I slid under the covers and grabbed my iPad from the nightstand. A quick glance at the clock showed it was half past midnight in New York. Oliver might be asleep. Then again, he might not.

I tapped the FaceTime app and called him.

He answered, bleary-eyed, his hair mussed up. "Hang on," he whispered.

I got a view of his carpet and hallway as he left his bedroom and went downstairs to his study. His face appeared again. "You know what time it is, right?" he groused.

"Yeah. Sorry I woke you."

"No, you're not," he said with a grin. "What's up?"

"The butcher signed," I said.

His face broke into a shit-eating grin. "Great news. And the ballet studio?"

I tongued my teeth. "Almost."

Oliver inclined his head. "On a scale of one to ten, what number is 'almost'?"

I shot him an evil wink. "She thinks it's a one. I'm pretty confident in a nine."

He rolled his eyes, used to my unfaltering ways. "So she's still holding out? What if she's determined not to sell?"

"She'll sell," I insisted.

"I hope you're right."

"Buddy, I'm always right." I hesitated, wondering whether to tell him about my earlier impromptu meeting with Catriona. Then again, Oliver and I didn't keep secrets from each other.

"I met her tonight. She showed up at my offices and accosted me as I left."

"Accosted doesn't sound like a woman on the verge of signing a contract."

"She's fucking hot, man. When she flayed me with her tongue, I could barely walk, my dick got so hard."

Oliver laughed and then immediately frowned. "I thought she was an older woman?"

"I thought that, too. I left James to deal with the face-to-face stuff, and he'd hardly notice, would he? For one thing, she's got the wrong equipment for his tastes."

"True," Oliver replied, and then he groaned. "Poor woman. Does she know what she's in for?"

"Not yet. But she will."

"I hope you're right. There's a lot at stake."

My lips thinned, and I narrowed my eyes. "Trust me. The next time we speak, the ink will be nice and dry on the contract."

And Catriona Landry will be naked in my bed.

5

Catriona

I stepped off the bus at the end of my street and, on sore feet, made my way home. A single light shone from the first floor of our little house, and a gap in the curtains allowed me to peek inside. Grams was sitting in her rocking chair knitting, and I could just make out Aiden propped up against a plethora of cushions watching TV. My heart squeezed tight. I loved these two people so much, and I'd do anything within my power to ensure their happiness and wellbeing.

I inserted my key in the door and stepped inside.

"Catriona, is that you?" my grandmother called out.

"It's me." I poked my head inside the living room and grinned. "Who did you think it was?"

"I hoped for Ryan Reynolds," Grams said, a wicked glint in her eye. "That boy is *fine*. Funny, too."

Aiden made a choking sound and shoved his fingers inside his mouth. "Ugh. Grams, stop. Please."

I leaned over the couch and kissed the top of his head. "How are you, little bro?"

"Good," he said, struggling to sit up, which caused another twinge of despair to settle in my gut. The sooner we got these tests back from the doctor's office, the better. "You're home late, Cati."

I lifted his feet, sat, and put his feet back in my lap. "Yeah, I had a few errands to run."

"What kind of errands?" he asked, his brow furrowing in worry.

I hadn't told him of the businesses selling out from under our feet. I didn't want to burden him, especially given his recent health challenges. But Grams knew. It was impossible to keep anything from that wily old woman.

I shot her a quick glance. Her surreptitious shake of the head told me she hadn't mentioned anything. He must just be picking up on vibes or on my body language. I forced my shoulders to relax.

"Nothing for you to be concerned about. Just a few bills and stuff."

"Oh." He let his head flop back, the brief conversation seemingly exhausting him. "We ate already."

"I know. Grams told me when I texted her earlier. It's okay. I'm not hungry."

My grandmother shot me a look, then put her knitting to one side and heaved herself into an upright position. "Girl needs to eat to keep up her strength," she said, hobbling into the kitchen.

"I'll go help Grams," I said to Aiden.

I followed my grandmother, propping my shoulder against the doorjamb as she busied about dishing up the meal she promised she'd keep warm. I nibbled my lip, wondering whether to tell her about Jeff now, or leave it until Aiden had gone to bed. I should have known keeping anything from her was an exercise in futility when she turned her emerald eyes on me, so like Mom's and mine, and jerked up her chin.

"Out with it, girl."

I heaved a sigh. "Jeff signed."

She didn't appear surprised in the slightest, greeting the news with a brief nod. "Man's got a family to feed. Can't blame him."

"*I've* got a family to feed," I said angrily. "But selling to that... that... bastard isn't the answer."

"Language," Grams chided, her Catholic roots coming to the forefront.

I'd never heard Grams swear. Now Gramps, he'd been a different story. A typical Irishman, he'd cussed regularly, and even Grams' open displeasure hadn't curtailed his swearing.

A twinge pinched inside my chest. Gramps died a couple of years after Mom and Dad. Pancreatic cancer. Poor Grams. It made me wonder whether God really existed when he allowed one woman to suffer as much as she had. Not that you'd ever know. She kept her grief tightly contained, but losing your only child and then, two years later, your husband must rip out a heart. Hell, it'd ripped mine out.

"So, we're the last?"

I nodded glumly. "Yep."

She pulled her lips to one side. "Maybe the time has come for us to let it go, girl."

"No!" I exclaimed, and then, internally cursing, I peered into the living room to see if Aiden had heard. His eyes were closed, and he looked as if he'd fallen asleep. I returned to my grandmother, lowering my voice this time. "That school means everything to me, *and* you," I hissed. "You built it from scratch, and I will *not* let him, or anyone else, take it away. It's David and Goliath, Grams. We owe it to the little guys to hang on." My shoulders bowed. "Besides, what else would I do?"

Dancing was all I knew how to do. It was all I *wanted* to do.

My students meant the world to me, and without them, I'd be nothing more than an empty husk, breathing but not really living.

She bustled over and enveloped me in a warm hug. "I just want you to be happy, that's all."

"I am happy." I moved away and pinched the bridge of my nose with my thumb and forefinger, pointlessly trying to stave off an impending tension headache. All the angst with Garen 'Thinks he's God' Gauthier had brought me to the edge of exhaustion.

"Here, eat," Grams said, pushing a plate of meatloaf and cabbage toward me. "Then go to bed. It will all look better in the morning."

I dragged out a chair, sat at the tiny table tucked into a corner of the worn but bright kitchen, and delved into the meal. My mouth watered, and only then did I realize how ravenous I was. I wolfed the entire thing and washed it down with a glass of iced water while Grams sat adjacent watching me eat. When I finished, she took my plate, washed and rinsed it in the sink, ran a towel over it to remove the excess water, then returned it to the shelf where we kept the crockery.

"Go to bed, Cati." She leaned over and kissed the top of my head. "Take Aiden with you, too. He shouldn't sleep on the couch."

I stood and wrapped my arms around her, kissing her wrinkled yet still soft cheek. "I love you, Grams. What would we do without you?"

"Be gone with you, girl," she said gruffly, removing her apron and hanging it on the back of the door. "There's life in the old dog yet."

I laughed. "I should hope so. You're only seventy-five."

Gently shaking Aiden's shoulder, I encouraged him to stand and, supporting his weight, I took him to bed. He fell asleep as soon as his head hit the pillow. I perched on the end of his bed and watched him for a few minutes, my heart squeezing painfully. Most boys his age were out with their friends, riding bikes, getting into scrapes, maybe plucking up the courage to kiss a girl or two. Not sleeping twelve hours a day, too exhausted to do anything other than eat a few morsels and keep up with personal hygiene.

I was no doctor, but something was very wrong. As I switched off his light and closed the door behind me, I vowed to call the doctor's office first thing in the morning and see if applying a little pressure couldn't move along the results from the blood tests he had done on Monday.

I changed for bed, sat at my dresser, and brushed out my hair, then tied it on top of my head in a tight bun, a routine that was necessary to keep it from knotting. I climbed under the covers. The quiet allowed my mind to work through the events of the day. I couldn't believe Jeff had sold out, and even more hurtful was that I'd had to hear the news from that bastard, Gauthier, who had taken clear delight in knowing he'd blindsided me. I didn't blame Jeff. Not really. Like Grams said, he had a family to feed, and the astronomical sums of money being offered for our businesses was hard to resist. If the ballet school didn't hold such sentimental value for me, then maybe I would have signed on the dotted line, too.

But hanging on to my memories was worth more than all the money in Gauthier's bank account. He could threaten and cajole and increase his financial offers as much as he liked. My business wasn't for sale.

Despite my determination, a shiver of anxiety took root in my gut. Garen Gauthier was a man who was used to getting his own way, and something told me his efforts to secure my business had only just begun.

6

Garen

Two days and not a single damn word from Catriona Landry.

I threw the pencil I'd snapped in two onto my desk, launched to my feet, and yanked on my suit jacket. Screw all this waiting around. I'd pay her a visit myself. Find out what was so damned special about this dance studio. Not that it mattered. Either she'd sell willingly, or I'd find some leverage to force her hand. I'd yet to meet a single individual who didn't cave in the end, either for financial reasons or simply because I found a chink in their armor and exploited it to the fullest.

Take Jeff the butcher, for example. I'd discovered he had mounting gambling debts, and I'd threatened to tell his wife if he didn't sign over the property to me. Some might call me a bastard for finding a sensitive spot and pressing down firmly. I called it business. I could have reduced the offer, but I didn't.

See, I wasn't all bad.

All I needed now was to find Catriona's weakness, and the final piece would fall into place, allowing the building of the hotel to begin. It was only a matter of time, but time was money, and when that last five percent was holding you up, it added a sense of urgency.

Darryl, my driver, pulled up right in front of the dance studio, even though it was a no-parking zone. He would circle the block until I was ready to leave, or he'd find a parking lot close by and wait for my text to come pick me up. I glanced along the row of independent businesses, all with their shutters down save for one. Part of the deal had been that as soon as they signed the contract, they closed up immediately. When others saw their neighbors selling out, it added extra pressure to their shoulders. An effective strategy and one I'd used on several previous occasions.

I entered the building via a side door. The one at the front was locked for some reason. The entranceway brought me to a narrow hallway. Voices reached me, the sounds of excited children renting the air. I groaned. Kids drove me crazy with their constant screeching and sticky fingers, and their over-exuberance about every goddamn thing.

I followed the noise and scanned around, my eyes alighting on Catriona. Dressed in a purple leotard and black tights, she was helping one of the younger children, showing her where to put her feet. I stood watching her patiently explain over the growing din of the other kids, their chattering increasing in volume with each passing second.

Should have brought my Beats noise-canceling headphones.

She straightened and clapped her hands twice, and all the kids immediately fell silent and stared at her with wide eyes and attentive expressions.

"Right, everyone, today we're going to practice the five positions of ballet. Now, who'd like to show me the first position?"

One of the girls at the back immediately shot her hand in the air. "Me, Miss Landry. Me."

Catriona smiled, nodded, and gestured. "When you're ready, Ellen."

The little girl stepped away from the group next to her and found a space in the middle of a long bar that ran the length of the room, behind it, a set of floor-to-ceiling mirrors. She held on to the bar for balance, then turned her feet outward, the heels almost touching.

Catriona clapped. "Very good, Ellen. Now, who would like to show me second position?"

Another kid's hand shot in the air, but before Catriona could gesture for her to begin, her head swiveled in my direction and her eyes locked on mine, then narrowed.

"Wait one second, Donna," she said, holding up her finger. "Girls, chat among yourselves. I won't be long."

She strode over, then walked right by me and out into the hallway, and past the changing area. Spinning around, she slammed her hands on her hips. "What the hell are you doing here?"

"I came to ask about ballet lessons," I drawled in a tone dripping with sarcasm while arching a brow. "What do you think?"

Her eyes sparked in defiance, and she jabbed a finger at the door. "Leave, now. I'm teaching."

I shoved my hands into my pockets. "I'll wait."

She leaned forward, and I caught a whiff of her perfume, the same scent that had been on the contract she'd so determinedly returned to me. Floral and delicate with a hint of lemons. I breathed in deeply. Fuck, I'd like to bury my nose in her neck, and then between her legs.

"Go away, Mr. Gauthier. You are not welcome here."

"I'm afraid I can't do that, Miss Landry."

She ground her teeth, her stormy green eyes searching mine. If she was searching for signs of compassion, we'd be here a long time.

"Fine, suit yourself. The class lasts an hour."

She shoved past me and returned to the room full of squealing children. I followed her, spotting a small office off to one side. I headed over to it and made myself comfortable behind the desk. A hint of annoyance flicked across Catriona's face when she noticed where I'd decided to wait, and then she turned her back and gave the class her full attention.

I tried to answer a few emails and read a draft contract on my phone, but concentration had proven nigh on impossible given the excited squeals of the children. By the time the parents came to pick up their frenzied charges, I feared I'd lost my hearing or, at the very least, suffered irreparable damage.

Catriona waited until the last one had filed out and then, with a weary sweep of her hand over her face, she traipsed into the office. She stood on the other side of her desk, arms folded underneath her tits, the action pushing them upward. I dropped my gaze.

Wonder if she's doing that on purpose.

She cleared her throat, forcing my attention up to her face. Not a bad exchange for her tits. She had a unique beauty. Soft skin, a perfectly formed oval face, cheekbones carved out of glass, and wide, intelligent eyes filled with challenge, the likes of which could keep me interested for a week or two.

"That's my chair," she ground out through a jaw clenched tight enough to cause a few teeth fractures.

I appraised it dismissively. "A bit soft for my tastes. I like things firm." I lowered my eyes to her chest once more.

She heaved a sigh. Hmm, did I detect a hint of resignation, or at least fatigue? Maybe I was wearing her down already. How disappointing. I'd hoped for a few more altercations. Conflict entertained me, yet these days, apart from my fellow ROGUES board members, very few people were willing to take me on. In Catriona, I'd hoped to find a worthy adversary, at least for a little while longer.

Sadly, it was not to be.

"What do you want, Mr. Gauthier?"

I rubbed at my chin, my eyes tracking her face. Now I'd taken a closer look, she did seem tired. Those dark circles beneath her eyes, and the slightly pale tinge to her skin, not to mention the bow of her shoulders, all lending themselves to a note of exhaustion.

"I think we've established that, Miss Landry." I removed an envelope from the inside pocket of my jacket and tossed it on the desk. "I've added another ten percent to the offer, but it only stands for twenty-four hours."

She stared at it but left it where it'd fallen. Her teeth grazed her bottom lip, and her green eyes dulled.

I held my breath, sensing her indecision.

Shit. She was going to cave.

I'd won.

Strangely, though, the realization didn't bring the usual flush of pleasure, the buzz of winning. Instead, an odd sense of dismay took root in my chest.

"And if I don't accept," she said, pulling my attention back to her and off my unusual, and frankly, unwelcome, thoughts.

I smiled. "Don't make an enemy of me, Miss Landry. You're not in the least equipped for the consequences."

The light came back into her eyes, and she glared at me with unveiled hatred. "Is that another threat? You should know by now I don't take kindly to threats."

I stood and came around to the other side of the desk, looming over her, using my loftier stature to add further weight to my superiority. Credit where it was due, she held her ground.

I bent my head, and the air from my breath wafted her hair. "Take it to mean whatever you wish."

I straightened just in time to catch the remnants of a tremor race through her body, her fight-or-flight instincts in full flow.

Which would she choose, I wondered?

She turned those stunning vibrant green eyes on me once more and gave me a defiant hint of a smile. "You don't scare me, Mr. Gauthier."

I licked the underside of my top teeth. "No? Then I'll have to try harder, Miss Landry, won't I?"

Leaving her with that thought, I brushed past her, making sure my shoulder touched hers on the way out. A sizzle of electricity at the brief connection brought on a tremor of my own.

Seemed as if we'd both chosen fight.

Poor Catriona. She didn't stand a chance. Still, the battle would be fun.

7

CATRIONA

Aiden and I sat in the doctor's office waiting for our name to be called. I twiddled my thumbs, and my leg wouldn't stop bouncing. In contrast, he sat still as a statue, his eyes closed, dark circles underneath a sure sign of his increasing exhaustion. He'd lost a lot of weight, too, when he could barely afford to considering he weighed next to nothing as it was.

The offer Gauthier had made last night, along with his not-so-veiled threat, popped into my head. I'd lied when I said he didn't scare me. He did, very much. Something in the man's eyes screamed *danger,* yet as much as my body wanted to take flight, my mind demanded I defend myself. Whatever he said, he couldn't make me sell my studio. He had no real leverage over me, and it was important I clung to that when his threats increased, as I fully expected them to.

I had to stay strong. For me, for Grams, and for Aiden.

As my thoughts turned to my brother, I shifted in my seat,

and my leg brushed his. He opened his eyes and gave me a wan smile.

"Relax, sis."

God, I wish I could be as calm as he was. Maybe his age allowed him to act so blasé? Or perhaps he was putting on a brave face for my sake.

"Aiden Landry."

My head snapped up, and I gestured to the nurse. I stood and held out my arm for Aiden to take. He took a step, then winced.

"Ow."

"What's wrong?" I said, panic leaching into my tone.

"My hip hurts a bit," he said, limping over to the doctor's office. "It was fine this morning."

Fear circled in my abdomen, and my legs felt weak, as if they weren't strong enough to hold me upright. I helped Aiden into the office and settled him in a chair, then sat in the one adjacent.

"Hi, Aiden," Dr. Sully, our family doctor said. "How are you feeling?"

Aiden scratched his head and twisted his lips to one side. "I'm okay, I guess."

"He's tired," I interjected. "He sleeps a lot, and just now he told me his hip was sore. That can't be normal for a boy his age, surely?"

Aiden flashed me an irritated glare but didn't correct me.

"I see." Dr. Sully glanced down at her notes. "Right, well, we've gotten the test results back from the lab, and I'd like to discuss them with you both."

I held my breath as if, by doing so, I could affect the outcome. I scanned the doctor's face for clues, but she remained blank and professional.

"The positive news is that we have found the reason for

Aiden's extreme fatigue, and the nose bleeds you mentioned last week. This would also explain the pain in his hip."

"And?" I prompted.

She glanced at my brother, then at me, then back to him. "Aiden, you have something called acute lymphoblastic leukemia."

The word leukemia exploded in my brain, sending a bolt of terror rushing through me. Oh God. This was bad.

"What does that mean?" I asked, even though I knew exactly what it meant. Aiden had cancer. And cancer was a killer. I reached for his hand which felt cold and small inside mine, but when I glanced at him, he wore a determined look, his gaze fixed on the doctor and concentration drawing his brows inward.

"Well," Dr. Sully said. "It's a rare disease, but one we know quite a lot about. I do want to reassure you that the survival rates, particularly in children, are very good. However, the current treatments are invasive and... challenging for the patient."

She was choosing her words carefully, but I knew what that meant. Chemotherapy, maybe radiotherapy. Blood transfusions, potential bone marrow transplants. Days, weeks, and months in and out of the hospital. Sickness. So much sickness.

"There is something I wanted to discuss with you. Aiden's genetic makeup is the perfect candidate for an experimental treatment that some countries are starting to explore. Fueled by emerging molecular technologies, it suggests that drugs can be targeted at the specific genetic defects of leukemia cells, resulting in a much more effective treatment plan for the patient."

Hope spiked within me. Targeted sounded good. Much more positive than the widespread scattergun approach of normal chemotherapy treatments, which meant that healthy cells were killed along with the defective cells. I was no expert, but even I knew that much.

"That's great." I squeezed Aiden's hand. "Isn't it, bro?"

He nodded in agreement, optimism bringing a pink glow to his wan cheeks.

"When can we start this experimental treatment?"

The doctor made a face. "Ah, well, there is a small issue," she said. "We don't have the treatment here in Canada yet. However, Switzerland are pioneers in this field, and I took the liberty of contacting one of the leading physicians of this therapy. I shared Aiden's results with him, confidentially, of course, and he agrees he's a perfect candidate for the program. If you're willing, and are able to afford the fees, then he's happy to treat Aiden."

"Switzerland?" I whispered. *So far away.* "How much are the fees?"

"They're not cheap," she said, scrawling on a piece of paper which she pushed across her desk to me. "This is the monthly cost. Based on Aiden's blood work, and the advice of the doctors, he'd need at least six months' treatment, three to four of which he'll need to undertake in Switzerland."

I glanced down, and the blood drained from my face. Even if I sold Mom's wedding and engagement rings and worked two extra jobs alongside running the ballet school, it wouldn't pay for one month's treatment, let alone six.

Robotically, I slid the piece of paper back, my chin high. "We can't afford this." I reached for Aiden's hand and wrapped my fingers around his. "Not even a fraction of this."

She gave me a sympathetic nod. "I understand, but I felt it my duty to at least inform you of the choices available. We can, of course, treat Aiden right here in Vancouver. We have excellent medical facilities, and I promise you he will be in the very best hands."

If Vancouver was the best place for him, then she wouldn't have mentioned the Switzerland option.

"I'll refer Aiden to the children's cancer hospital, and they'll be in touch regarding his treatment program. Try not to worry. Like I said, the recovery rates are extremely high."

Both of us were silent on the journey home. The second I pushed open the front door and stepped inside the dim hallway, Grams took one look at my face, and hers crumpled.

As for me... I knew exactly what I had to do.

Even if it cost me everything.

8

Catriona

I spent the next few hours researching everything I could get my hands on about Aiden's illness, determined that not one fact would escape my attention. To win any war, you had to know your opponent's strengths and weaknesses, and in my mind, an illness was no different.

My fevered research confirmed that Switzerland was ahead of the curve with this pioneering new treatment, the physicians there considered to be at the top of their field in this particular form of innovative remedy.

I rubbed my forehead and closed my eyes, racking my brains to try to come up with a way I could afford Aiden's hospital fees and accommodation in a country thousands of miles away, but it was pointless searching for an answer when I already knew what I had to do.

I gazed around my tiny bedroom with its crocheted bedspread made through hours of Grams' painstaking effort, and its pale-yellow walls meant to brighten and add warmth, yet I felt chilled to the bone.

Rising to my feet, I walked over to my dresser and picked up the picture frame of my parents on their wedding day. At twenty-four, Mom had been a year younger than me in this picture. The way she gazed adoringly at my dad gave me hope that goodness existed in the world.

Just not in Garen Gauthier's world.

I sighed and hugged the photograph to my chest. It was hopeless. I had to sell the studio to that vile, self-serving, manipulative, evil asshole who had a swinging brick in place of a heart, and no soul.

If only it didn't have to be him. Anyone other than *him*. But there were no other choices. I reached into my purse and removed the envelope containing his latest offer, then grabbed a pen and started calculating costs. If I took everything into consideration including flights, accommodation, and living expenses, I estimated that Gauthier's increased offer for the studio would fund around three months in Switzerland. Not six. But there was no point worrying about that yet. I needed to get Aiden started on his treatment and figure the rest out later.

As much as I wanted to be the one to go with Aiden, to sit by his bedside and comfort and support him through the difficult months ahead, I'd have to remain here and try to earn as much money as possible. That meant Grams would have to travel with him.

The thought of staying in Canada while the people I loved more than anything else in the world moved to another country to fight for my brother's life brought tears to my eyes. Why did the good people suffer and the bad ones lead a charmed life?

A tap on my door brought my head up. "Come in," I called out.

Grams poked her head inside. "I brought you a cup of tea,"

she said, entering with a steaming mug of my favorite drink. I liked to think it was my Irish roots that drew me to love tea.

I set down Mom and Dad's wedding picture and took the hot drink from her. "Thank you. Just what I needed."

She glanced at the envelope where I'd calculated the costs for Switzerland, then picked it up. "What's all this, girl?"

"I'm selling the studio," I said, the resigned tone causing a hitch to my breathing. I swallowed, barely holding on to the emotions simmering beneath the surface. "I'm so sorry, Grams. I've tried to think of another solution, but there isn't one."

"Hush now," she said, removing the mug from me before I'd even taken a sip. Setting it down on the dresser, she wrapped her arms around me. I sank against her, allowing myself a moment of weakness, and drew on her immense strength.

"It's the right decision, Cati." She drew back and cupped my face in her wrinkled hands. "I know it hurts, but even if this leaves us destitute, as long as we have each other, that's all that matters."

"Destitution doesn't put food on the table, nor pay the rent, let alone Aiden's medical bills," I said, the enormity of the situation suddenly crashing over me. "Even taking every cent Gauthier is willing to pay, it still leaves us short of what Aiden needs. That's why I've decided you have to go with him, and I'll stay here to work, and make sure you both have a home to come back to."

Grams didn't argue, just nodded, then hugged me again. "You're a good girl, Cati. Your parents would be so proud of the young woman you've grown into."

Emotion clogged the back of my throat. My grandmother was very sparing with her praise, so for her to say such a thing meant the world.

The clock on my nightstand caught my eye, and I let out a heavy sigh. "Gauthier gave me twenty-four hours to accept his latest offer. I'd better set off. There's a bus that stops not far from his building that leaves in thirty minutes. That should give me enough time to make his stupid deadline."

Grams caught my wrist. "Stay calm, Catriona. Remember, the fiery Irish spirit runs in your veins, but sometimes we need to put a cork in it. Now is one of these times. Pride comes before a fall. Don't give him the satisfaction of falling."

My grandmother was a very wise woman. I'd do well to heed her advice, even if it turned out to be the hardest thing I'd ever done.

I read over the contract once more, my heart breaking at the clause that mentioned that once I signed, I'd get two days to clear out my things, but that the business had to close immediately. A glance at my calendar showed full classes for the next week. My throat thickened. My students, *my kids*. How could I hold it together in the face of their disappointment? At least there was one saving grace: Ammaline's invitation to RAD was already in the bag. She'd miss out on a few lessons, but that wouldn't change the offer. I could talk her through some exercises she could do at home to keep her limber and supple.

But my other kids... God, this was awful. There wasn't another ballet school within a forty-mile radius, and most parents couldn't afford the time to travel that far just for a ballet lesson.

And all because that bastard billionaire wanted to add a few more zeros to his bloated bank account by stomping all over the little guy.

I took a deep, relaxing breath and repeated my grandmother's advice. *Stay calm. Don't let him get to you. Don't give him the satisfaction of knowing how much this hurts.*

Before I changed my mind, I scrawled my signature on the bottom and added today's date, then slipped the completed contract into my purse. I said goodbye to Aiden and Grams and left for Gauthier's office.

The bus ride into the city took forty minutes, and as I

alighted at the stop around the corner from my final destination, every step felt like I was wearing concrete shoes.

On arrival at the impressive glass-fronted building, I drew in a lungful of freezing air through my nose and slowly expelled it.

Here we go.

9

Garen

A sharp rap on my door lifted my head. My executive assistant, James, entered my office. I gave him a cursory glance then continued staring at my screen, reading the presentation Ryker had sent over. He wanted to use part of next month's board meeting to discuss a further expansion to the *Poles Apart* exotic dance club brand that, frankly, the entire senior leadership team had expected to fail but was actually pulling in a very healthy profit, a fact Ryker liked to remind us of regularly.

"What is it, James?"

"Reception just called. You have a visitor."

Irritated, I rolled my eyes. "Unless there's a pre-arranged appointment in my calendar for four-thirty, which I happen to know there isn't, I expect you to handle this shit. It's what I pay you for. Now get rid of them."

James' amused chuckle irked me further until he said, "Oh, I think this is one visitor you'll *definitely* want to see."

I swiveled my chair and squinted at him. "Okay, you've got my attention. Who is it?"

He jerked his chin at my curved computer monitor. "Check out the CCTV."

I clicked the mouse a couple of times, bringing up the cameras in the lobby, and a grin edged across my face. *Oh, this is priceless.* Catriona was sitting on one of the visitor's chairs, her back straight as a pole. I zoomed in. Clutched in her fingers was a stack of papers that looked remarkably like the sale contract for her studio.

This meant one of two things. Either she'd conceded defeat and signed them, or she was going to give a repeat performance and return them unsigned, accompanied by another lash of her tongue.

I shivered. Either scenario turned me on.

"Shall I arrange to have her sent up?"

I checked the time. By my reckoning, the deadline I'd given her had another fifty minutes to go before the twenty-four hours were up.

"No," I said, a plan forming in my mind, one I took great delight in. "Let her wait."

"For how long?" James asked.

"Get a message to her telling her I'm finishing up a meeting and I'll be free in around fifteen minutes."

"And will you be free in fifteen minutes?" James asked.

I shot him a sidelong glance. "No."

"Are you planning to see her at all, or shall I wait the allotted time and then get rid of her?"

"Oh no, I'll see her. When I'm good and ready."

James accompanied a grimace with a low chuckle, then nodded. "I'll get the message to her."

He spun on his heel and left, clicking the door closed behind him.

I split my screen so I could read the rest of Ryker's presentation and keep an eye on the cameras in the lobby, and scanned the rest of the document. By the time I reached the last slide, I'd decided to support the motion. The return on investment was far too good to pass up. I groaned, imagining Ryker's smug expression when he presented yet further evidence his pet project was raking it in.

Sitting back in my chair, I steepled my fingers underneath my chin and watched Catriona grow more and more fidgety. She kept getting to her feet, pacing up and down, retaking her seat, and then starting the whole process all over again. Several times she checked her watch, then glanced up at the clock on the wall behind the main reception desk. Further pacing ensued.

Once thirty minutes had passed since I'd gotten the call, she walked over to the receptionist. I couldn't hear their conversation, but I knew the point of her query.

How much longer will I have to wait?

The answer: At least ten minutes after her twenty-four hours were up which meant, technically, my offer timed out.

Yeah, I'm a bastard. I live with it just fine.

At one point, she glanced up at one of the CCTV cameras affixed in the corner, and I could have sworn, if my lipreading abilities were up to scratch, she mouthed "asshole".

I chuckled to myself. I hadn't had this much fun in ages, and I planned to stretch it out for nothing more than my own amusement.

When the clock ticked past the deadline, Catriona made another visit to the reception desk. I watched as the receptionist clearly tried to make excuses for my behavior, her hands waving about, gesturing, no doubt explaining how busy I was and that I'd be available soon, while internally cursing me for putting her in such a difficult and potentially confrontational position.

Catriona wouldn't berate the member of staff, though. No, she'd save her ire for me.

I couldn't wait.

I left it another five minutes, then buzzed through to James.

"Send her up."

I watched as the receptionist answered James' call, nodded, replaced the receiver, and then handed Catriona a visitor's pass. She motioned to the bank of elevators. Catriona strode in that direction and disappeared from view.

Standing, I stretched out my back and ambled over to the corner sofa on the far side of my office. I unfastened my jacket, sat, crossed my legs, and waited.

The door opened, and Catriona walked inside. Her gaze fell on my empty desk, and she frowned and paused mid-step.

"What a lovely surprise, Miss Landry," I drawled.

She spun around and narrowed her eyes. "Finally," she said, staring at me coldly. "I've been waiting downstairs for almost an hour."

I rose to my feet, refastened the button on my single-breasted jacket, and prowled toward her. "I'm a busy man, Miss Landry. When people turn up without an appointment, I can't simply drop everything to accommodate them."

She stood her ground, hatred burning in her eyes, the potent emotion darkening her striking irises from emerald to a forest green. "Whatever," she muttered and thrust the contract at me. "Here. You got what you wanted."

Smirking, I took it from her and flipped to the back page. As her comment indicated, she had signed it.

Let the fun begin.

I tore it in half, drawing a gasp of horror from Catriona. I let the pieces fall to the floor.

"You're too late. I told you my offer was only open for twenty-four hours." I made a point of checking my watch. I even tapped the clock face for added effect. "I make it twenty-four hours and thirteen minutes."

She gracefully dropped to her knees and gathered up the bits of the contract. I bit back a moan as blood rushed to my groin, the sight of her kneeling hardening my cock.

"I told you, I got here almost an hour ago," she declared. "I was here in plenty of time. It's not my fault you waited until now to see me."

I noted a hint of desperation to her tone that wasn't there before. Something had changed since I visited her studio yesterday, something that made Catriona desperately need to sell when she'd blocked every attempt for me to purchase her business for the last three weeks.

"It's hardly my issue that you left it until the eleventh hour to do what you should have done weeks ago."

Her gaze lowered to the floor. "What happens now?" she asked. "Is that it? The deal's off?"

There it was again. Desperation. Worry. A note of fear to her soft, lilting voice. Hell of a one-eighty from her previous entrenched position, and I wanted to know why.

"What's changed?"

She touched the base of her neck, and her head flinched back slightly. "What?"

"You heard me. I don't like repeating myself."

"What game are you playing now, Mr. Gauthier?" she bit out. "You wanted my business. I've agreed to sell it at the price offered. What more is there to say?"

I stroked my chin, then strolled past her and settled behind my desk. I knitted my fingers together and locked my gaze on her. "Here's the thing, Miss Landry. I've been entrenched in the business world long enough to know that when there is a huge gulf between two opposing parties, for the gap to narrow in such a short space of time means there's been a profound shift of some sort. I'd like to know what changed your mind."

Her lips thinned into a firm line. "My reasons are my own, Mr. Gauthier. You wanted my business, even threatened me to get it, and now you've won. Pay me what you promised, relish in your victory, and you and I never have to see each other again."

Oh no. That won't do at all.

Catriona Landry was someone I wanted to keep around for a while longer yet. The entertainment value was too good to pass up, not to mention the granite-like erection this altercation between us had given me. I didn't expect her to tell me her motive for selling, but I'd find out the reason why one way or another.

I opened a file on my computer where James had stored the different contracts for the hotel venture. Inside the main folder were sub folders for each of the businesses. I found the one containing all the offers made to Catriona. Bypassing the latest one, the pieces of which she clutched between her fingers, I opened the previous contract. I clicked on the print icon, and seconds later, the printer on my desk spat out the eight pages constituting the sale and purchase agreement.

I pushed it across the desk and placed a pen on top of the wad of cream pages.

"Sign it."

Catriona shuffled over to my desk and set down the torn pieces of paper from the other contract. She picked up the pen and the new contract and flicked through each individual sheet. When she reached page seven, where the financial settlement was laid out, she sucked in a sharp breath.

"This is not the amount we agreed upon, Mr. Gauthier."

I arched a brow. "I think you'll find it is, Miss Landry. I made it very clear to you yesterday that the enhanced offer extended for a period of twenty-four hours. That deadline has passed, meaning it is now null and void. What you see there is all I am willing to pay. Take it or leave it."

She'd shown her hand, revealed she needed the money, and

if she'd told me outright why, I might have allowed the increased offer to stand. As she'd decided to make me work for the answers I sought, I'd charge her a fee amounting to the ten percent increase I'd proposed yesterday. Regardless of my growing and, frankly, surprising attraction to the fiery woman standing before me, business was business. I never allowed my dick to rule my head. She knew the rules, and she flouted them —somewhat aided by me.

Her eyes glistened, and for one horrifying moment, I thought she might cry. Then she blinked several times, gathered her emotions, mashed them into a ball of hatred that she parked in the pit of her stomach, and scrawled her signature on the bottom of the contract, digging the pen so hard into the paper, it almost went right through.

"There. I hope this makes you happy, you absolute bastard."

I leaned forward and twisted the contract around, then pulled it toward me. "Thank you. It makes me very happy indeed."

She snorted. "You'll get what's coming to you one day, Mr. Gauthier. And I hope I'm around to witness it."

Spinning on her heel, she marched across my office, wrenched open the door, and slammed it behind her.

I pushed back my chair and stepped over to the window, waiting for her to appear on the street below. I caught sight of her, shoulders hunched, and a defeated curve to her normally erect spine. Despite that, she still moved with poise and grace, and try as I might, I couldn't tear my gaze away as her long limbs ate up the distance.

A trace of contrition took root in my gut. I killed it with a shot of bourbon.

I'd never allowed room for sentiment in business, and I didn't intend to start now.

10

Catriona

I couldn't face going straight home in the wake of that horrendous meeting with Gauthier. Instead, I grabbed a cup of tea and sat in the window of a café across the road from the bus stop. I played our meeting over in my mind. God, the man was so callous. I hated him. *Hated. Him.* How he managed to sleep at night was beyond me. Then again, he'd probably sold his soul many years ago and consequently slept like a baby.

When he'd withdrawn the higher offer, I'd almost told him to shove it. Hell, I'd come within an inch of ripping up that second contract and scattering the pieces over his head, but I couldn't do that to Aiden. While I hadn't told him yet that I'd found a way to send him to Switzerland, meaning he'd be none the wiser, *I'd* know.

But Gauthier's reduced offer meant Aiden's time in Switzerland would be even shorter now, and that piled more financial pressure on my shoulders. I mused whether I should have told him how sick my brother was. Maybe knowing a fifteen-year-old innocent boy had contracted a life-threatening illness might tug on his heartstrings. Then again, a man like that would probably use it to his own advantage in some way. *Knowledge is power.* Never truer when it came to the heinous Garen Gauthier.

I checked my watch and saw it was past seven-thirty. Damn. I'd lost track of time. I launched to my feet and jogged across the street to catch the bus. I'd just missed one, but another would be along in a few minutes so I might as well wait. The last thing I needed was to get distracted again and end up having to catch a cab home. I needed every cent I could lay my hands on. There was no room for any kind of luxuries now, not that there ever really had been.

A stiff wind raised the hair on the back of my neck, and I lifted the collar on my coat. A couple joined me at the bus stop, their arms wound around each other, their lips touching in a brief moment of intimacy before they caught me looking and broke apart. I wanted to tell them not to mind me, but that might embarrass them further, and so I averted my gaze.

Peering down the street, I spotted the bus pulling into another stop about a quarter mile away. Good. I could barely feel my feet, and my nose kept running from the cold.

What is going on with this shitty weather?

I riffled through my pocket and produced a tissue, then blew my nose. As I stepped forward to put it in the trash, a sleek limousine eased to a halt right at the bus stop, blatantly ignoring the clear signs that marked the space as busses only. When the rear door opened, my jaw dropped.

What the hell is Gauthier up to now?

"Get in," he ordered, jerking his chin at me.

"No, thank you," I replied stiffly, stamping my feet to try to get a bit of life back into them. "My bus is on its way."

"Get in the damn car, Catriona, or the deal is off."

The young couple stared at us, their eyes wide as they

absorbed the vexatious atmosphere between the two strangers, the unexpected entertainment a welcome distraction from the interminable wait for public transport.

"You wouldn't," I gasped.

He arched a perfectly shaped brow. "Is that a serious comment?"

"I've signed a contract."

"Who says?" he replied. "There were no witnesses, and you didn't take a copy. Rookie mistake, but there we have it."

I laughed bitterly. "Oh, you are a piece of work."

"Thank you."

"That wasn't a compliment."

"I know. Now get in the car before I throw you over my shoulder."

Trapped, and with no clear way out, I skirted around him and climbed into the back of his car. Even before he got in beside me and closed the door, the warmth of the cabin started to unfreeze my feet. I fastened my seat belt and rubbed my hands up and down my arms.

"I can warm you up, if you'd like," Gauthier said, his eyes glowing with mirth.

Damn man is enjoying my discomfort.

I cast a withering scowl in his direction. "I'd rather get into a coffin filled with rats."

He chuckled. "Sounds like a day in the business world."

"Where you're the biggest rat of all, no doubt."

His chuckle grew into a loud laugh. "Keep the insults coming, Catriona. I find it an enormous turn on."

My eyes flitted to his crotch. It was a pure reflex given his comment, and they barely went there. Not really. It didn't matter, though. He noticed.

And so did I.

Yep, there's a definite bulge.

Then again, as far as I understood male physiology, most

men his age got a hard-on without any form of stimulation, either physical or mental.

"Does it turn you on, too, Catriona?" he murmured, his gray eyes locking on to mine and sending a fissure of anxiety traveling up my spine. "Are you turned on simply by knowing I'm hard for you without you doing anything to instigate it?"

"No," I snapped. "I find you disgusting."

I held my breath, waiting for a biting comeback. Instead, he schooled his expression, his smirk fading into nothingness.

"Where shall I drop you?"

I shifted uncomfortably at the icy chill to his tone. "At my studio is fine." Not a chance I'd let this man know where I lived. I didn't doubt for a second he could find out my address without too much trouble if he desired, but I wouldn't gift him the information.

"*My* studio, you mean," he stated.

I winced. "The contract said I had two days to clear out my things." I shrugged. "No time like the present."

"As you wish," he murmured. He pushed a button on the center armrest and gave his driver the address, then turned his attention out of the window. For the rest of the journey, neither of us spoke, and by the time the car drew to a halt in front of the row of businesses, all of which were now closed up and firmly in the possession of the man sitting to my right, the atmosphere had become almost unbearable.

"Thanks for the ride," I muttered, eager to leave his presence. Pressing down on the handle, I had one leg out of the car when he spoke.

"Catriona?"

I twisted to peer over my shoulder. "Yes?"

"I'll be in touch. Soon."

"Don't bother," I hit back. "I'll email over my banking details. You can deposit the money directly into my account. I'll be sure to vacate the property by the end of Sunday."

I got out before he could say another word. Fumbling for my keys, I unlocked the rarely used front door—I had the students use the one to the side as that entrance took them past the changing area—and entered my beloved ballet studio for one of the last times.

The second I closed the door, locking out the cruel world beyond, I slid to the floor and dissolved into tears.

I gave myself exactly one minute to cry, to grieve for the loss of a business that had been in my family for over forty years, and then I scrambled to my feet, dusted myself off and, once I'd made sure Gauthier wasn't still loitering outside, I set off for home.

Tomorrow I'd call Dr. Sully and put the wheels in motion for Aiden's treatment in Switzerland.

In the end, that was all that mattered.

11

Garen

After a restless night's sleep, I trudged downstairs, calling out for Margo. And then I remembered it was Saturday, and she didn't work weekends.

Unlike me.

It didn't matter what day of the week it was, I always worked. Now that Catriona had finally conceded defeat and signed over her dance studio, I could put the wheels in motion to get the building of the hotel underway.

Task one: demolition.

Usually I looked forward to this part. Razing the buildings to the ground and making way for the footings of the new hotel to begin always gave me a sense of thrill, of achievement. Yet for some strange reason, this time I dreaded it.

Maybe I'd become jaded. When I'd first touted the idea of a chain of hotels with the aim to further diversify the ROGUES' portfolio, I'd relished every single build, treating each one like my baby. Vancouver would be the eighth ROGUES hotel, and I should be eagerly awaiting this one more than any of the others. Vancouver was my home. Although I was born and raised in Quebec, Montreal, where my parents still lived, Vancouver had stolen my heart. To build a hotel here should bring me an enormous sense of pride, yet the thought of flattening that row of buildings where dreams had been fulfilled—and crushed—brought me no joy at all.

Catriona.

Her name sprang up out of nowhere. That woman had wormed her way inside my head, and I'd only met her three times. I couldn't work out why she was on my mind more than she should be, or why the sight of her entering her studio last night, her shoulders bowed as if she carried the weight of the world on them was the cause for last night's lack of sleep. Whatever the reason, it wouldn't veer me from my path.

And to prove that point to myself, I fired off an email to the firm I'd hired to take on the build and instructed them to begin the preparations. I'd already secured planning consent, predicated on the butcher and Catriona signing over their businesses. Now that they had, there was nothing to stop me forging ahead.

Once I'd gotten that hurdle out of the way, I scrambled some eggs, squeezed a glass of juice, and ate my breakfast while sitting at the table that gave me a view over the manicured gardens at the back of my house. Once again, my thoughts turned to Catriona, and her unfathomable U-turn over selling her business to me. It made no difference to the outcome—I'd have gotten my way in the end, as always—but I didn't like it when information was withheld from me. Leaving any stones unturned didn't sit well, and this particular rock was no different.

I finished eating the eggs, put the plate and silverware into the dishwasher, and went to fetch my phone. I decided to call Richard Forster, the investigator I kept on payroll for a variety of reasons, and one who'd discovered Jeff the butcher's indiscretions. While I didn't think for one second the reason for Catriona's sudden willingness to capitulate would be anything along those lines, whatever she was hiding, my guy would unearth it.

I gave him all the information I had, and he promised to get back to me by Monday at the latest, although he hoped sooner. I smiled. I liked this guy. Someone else who didn't allow the weekend to get in the way of his work. There were a lot of us, as it turned out. Workaholics. Those with nothing else in their lives to distract them from their business ventures.

I ground some fresh coffee beans and made a pot of Colombia's finest, then wandered into my home office, switched on my computer, and got to work.

The next thing I recalled was the sound of the buzzer at my front gates, and only then did I realize the sky had grown dark, I'd completely missed lunch, and the pot of coffee had gone cold.

I checked the security cameras, zooming in on the unmistakable shape of a female. My pulse jolted, thinking it might be Catriona, then I peered closer and groaned. Scarlett. A woman I'd dated once and fucked twice, last Saturday as a matter of fact. A minor distraction, and one I hadn't intended to repeat.

I hovered over the intercom, prepared to reject her, but then I had second thoughts. Maybe a quick fuck, a physical release, might help me to sleep better tonight and give me the distraction I needed to jettison this unsettling feeling that had taken root since I'd dropped Catriona off last night.

I pressed the gate release and watched Scarlett smile, then slip through the widening gap. I greeted her at the door.

"I don't remember inviting you over."

She let out a girlish giggle. "Oh, Garen. I haven't heard from you all week, and I was in the neighborhood, so…" She tugged down on her top, revealing a healthy amount of cleavage.

My dick jumped to attention. Reaching out a hand, I gripped her upper arm and yanked her inside. I kicked the door closed and pushed her up against it, then slammed my mouth over hers. I wasn't gentle, nor coaxing, but the rougher I was, the more Scarlett seemed to like it. Her moans grew in volume when I yanked down her top and bit her nipple through her lace bra.

"Let's go to bed," she moaned, thrusting her chest forward.

"I'm good here." Fucking her up against the door meant I could simply open it and push her outside once I was done.

I snaked a hand underneath her skirt and found she wasn't wearing panties. "I see you came prepared." I inserted two fingers inside her.

She gasped, clenching around me, her soft keening growing in volume when I scraped my nails along the front wall of her vagina. "Christ, Garen, yes. Right there."

Fumbling with my belt, she managed to get it undone, but as she flipped open the button on my jeans and tugged down the zipper, Catriona's face crashed into my mind and my dick instantly deflated.

I released Scarlett and stepped back. She went for my zipper again, but I grasped her wrist, stopping her.

"Forget it. It's not happening,"

"What are you talking about?" she asked, her brow furrowed in confusion.

I didn't blame her. I was pretty fucking confused, too, especially as making out with Scarlett had felt all wrong, almost as if by putting my hands and mouth on another woman, I was somehow betraying Catriona.

Fucking ridiculous. Get a grip, jackass.

"I have work to do. You need to leave." I zipped myself up and refastened my belt.

Her nostrils flared, and her lips flattened. "It would have

been nice if you'd told me that before you fingered me, Garen. What kind of girl do you think I am?"

I barked out a laugh, confusion at my reaction to sex on a plate bringing on a stream of cruelty. "You turn up here, unannounced, and without panties to boot. I think we've established what kind of girl you are, sweetheart."

Her cheeks reddened, and she aimed her palm at my face. I snagged her wrist and squeezed hard.

"Not a good idea."

She yanked out of my grip, jerked the door open, and stormed down my driveway. I returned to my office, opened the gates, and watched the cameras until I was sure she'd left.

I dragged a hand through my hair. *What the fuck was that?* I'd never had my dick refuse a willing participant, right there, begging for it. Scarlett had a pretty face and a hot body, more than enough to tempt me into a fast orgasm. Catriona Landry had no place in my head. None whatsoever. I firmly believed that once I discovered her reason for selling, I'd forget she ever existed. That had to be why she was on my mind. I hated loose ends. Time to tie a knot in that one and move on. Fast.

I sent a text to Richard asking for an update. No harm in prodding him a bit. His reply came seconds later.

Working on it.

With a growl of impatience, I strode into the kitchen and opened the fridge. Margo had left me a lasagna with heating instructions taped to the lid. I followed her directions and, with a full stomach, I worked through the rest of the evening. At midnight, I crawled into bed where, thankfully, I enjoyed a dreamless night's sleep.

I awoke on Sunday morning to a clear-blue sky and a mild breeze. Feeling much more rested, I went for a run then returned home and swam fifty lengths of my indoor pool. I was halfway through a breakfast of a smoked salmon bagel with cream cheese when my cell phone rang. I answered without looking at it.

"Gauthier."

"I have news," Richard's voice came down the line, making me sit up and take notice.

"And," I prompted.

"Can we meet?"

"I'm busy today. Just email the details over."

A pause, followed by, "Ah, I'd rather not. I didn't source this information entirely legally."

"I don't want to know," I said hurriedly. "Meet me in the lobby of my office building in an hour." I never conducted business with outsiders at my home.

"Gotcha."

I finished my breakfast, dressed in a navy-blue Tom Ford suit, and a light-gray-and-white-striped tie, and headed out to my garage. Scanning the row of cars, I selected the Lamborghini Veneno that I'd had shipped over from Italy only last month. I'd only driven it once before the weather had taken a turn for the worse, but today was a nice day. Perfect weather for a sensitive Italian sports car.

Retrieving the keys from a locked cabinet just inside the entrance of my garage, I slipped into the black leather cabin and ran my hands around the perfectly stitched steering wheel. It had retained that new car smell, and I breathed in through my nose, relishing the drive ahead. Sunday morning meant the roads would be fairly empty, and I could open her up and let the power of that 6.5-liter V12 engine carry me smoothly into downtown Vancouver.

I fucking loved cars, and I loved even more that I could afford the very best. I put my insane success down to an initial stroke of luck—meeting the ROGUES guys in college and then having a gaming app we'd developed for a bit of fun go viral—and the rest from a shit ton of hard work. In the business world, if you took your eye off the ball for one second, you could find yourself filing for bankruptcy. Continued success depended only on your last deal, your last decision. Nothing that came before mattered.

I intended for my success to last a lifetime.

Nosing the car into the street where my office building was situated, I turned left and parked in the underground garage. I rode the elevator up to the lobby to find Richard waiting for me. I nodded curtly at the security guard—we only kept a skeleton staff on weekends—and jerked my head, indicating for Richard to follow me to the private elevator.

Five minutes later, we sat at the conference table with a coffee in hand, and I gestured for him to begin.

He placed a manila folder on the table and opened it. I chuckled at his old-school ways but the man got results, so who was I to argue with his methods.

"Okay, let me see. Let me see."

He thumbed through a couple of pages, and I bit down on my impatience.

"Ah, here we are."

He lifted his head and settled his gaze on mine. "The reason she decided to sell her business after resisting for so long is because her brother is sick."

A prickle of unease settled across my chest, and I sat up straight.

"How sick?"

"Leukemia," Richard said, scanning the page. "One of the aggressive kinds from what I understand, although I'm no doctor."

He removed a sheet from the file and pushed it across the desk.

I glanced down, scanning the typed page which laid out the medical findings for Catriona's brother, Aiden. This must be related to the *not entirely legal* comment Richard had made. I had no clue how he'd gotten into someone's medical records in less than twenty-four hours, and I didn't want to know.

I stroked my chin, falling deep into thought. I tried not to anticipate the answer to any problem until I had more information to go on, but whatever I'd imagined might be Catriona's reason for relenting to my demands, that particular circumstance hadn't crossed my mind.

"She's got him on one of those trial treatment programs abroad," Richard continued. "Switzerland. I couldn't find out the cost of it." He rolled his eyes. "Fucking Swiss. But I'd expect it to be a tidy sum, and if you include the added cost of accommodation and living expenses, it'll add up to a small fortune in no time."

I rubbed at my sternum, then reached into my drawer. Popping an antacid from its plastic housing, I swallowed it down with a slug of coffee. If Aiden was going to Switzerland, then did that mean Catriona would go with him?

No.

I couldn't allow that to happen.

Would not allow that to happen.

A knot formed in the pit of my stomach, and my chest tightened. Why did I care so much? What voodoo magic had Catriona cast on me that gave me this weird feeling?

I didn't like it.

"Do they have parents?" I asked.

Richard shook his head. "There's a grandmother in her seventies, but the parents died..." He paused to check his notes. "Thirteen years ago. Car accident."

I pinched the bridge of my nose. Christ, how awful. I mightn't get to visit my parents much these days, what with them being on the other side of the country, but it'd break me to lose them, even at my age. Catriona must have been very young when she lost hers. What a shitty deck of cards.

An idea nudged at me, taking hold with unbelievable

speed. One where I could get what I wanted and at the same time help a young guy who'd been dealt a dreadful hand.

Philanthropy with a personal edge wasn't my usual style. I preferred to give anonymously. But on this one occasion, I'd make an exception, for one reason, and one reason only.

Because it served my needs.

12

CATRIONA

I gazed around the ballet studio where boxes marked with thick black marker lined one wall. Behind me, in my tiny office, only the small desk, the chair, and an empty bookcase remained.

Empty.

Yeah, good word. Empty space. Empty heart. I'd put *everything* into this place, as had Grams before me, and to lose it bore a great big hole right through the center of my chest. I'd bled for my students and for myself. Dance was the only thing that brought me happiness, and after losing a chance at a career of my own, teaching others had filled the chasm. The last two days spent calling the parents of every single one of my kids had broken something inside me, and I didn't know whether I could ever fix it.

I heard the sound of someone clearing their throat and I spun around.

Oh, hell no. Garen Gauthier.

I glowered at him. "What do you want?"

"A word," he said, striding into my space.

Correction, his space.

I snatched up a broom and began furiously sweeping the floor, using the physical activity to detract me from wanting to wallop the smug smirk right off his face.

"A little pointless, don't you think?" he drawled as he propped his shoulder against the wall. "The demolition team will be here within the week."

Hot tears pooled at the backs of my eyes. "Fuck you," I muttered, then turned my back and continued sweeping.

He pushed off the wall and came to stand in front of me. "I know, Catriona."

I paused to shoot him a vicious glare, one hand resting on my hip while I gripped the broom handle tight enough to snap it.

I wish I could snap his neck.

"And what is it you think you know, Mr. Gauthier?"

He stroked his smooth, shaved chin and perused me, his steel-gray irises holding a hint of evil. Maybe evil stretched it a bit, but I couldn't think of a word more apt given what he'd done.

"I know about your brother's illness. Leukemia, right? And an aggressive form, so I understand. And you sold your precious studio to help fund his treatment in Switzerland. Tell me, Miss Landry, what would you do to save him?"

I drew in a sharp breath, pain striking me in the center of my chest. How the hell had he found out about Aiden? "Anything," I choked out, surprised by my candor. "I'd do anything to save him."

"Anything, hmm?" He raked me with his gaze, his eyes traveling from my head to my feet and back again. "Let's test the theory. If I asked you to suck my cock, would you?"

I stumbled back a step. "Wh-what?"

His lips parted, and he tongued his top teeth. "You heard me. You said anything. Is allowing me to fuck your mouth worth the blank check to secure your brother's care for the foreseeable future?"

I shook my head, my mind struggling to comprehend his words. I'd given him too much credit before. He *was* evil. A thoroughly wicked man who wanted to use my pain, and Aiden's battle, to gain pleasure for himself.

"The money I paid for this place might get you two, three months' treatment at a push. But you need more than that, don't you, Catriona?"

Shock rolled through me, and time seemed to stand still, the ticking of the clock on the wall across from the row of mirrors the only indication that the world kept turning while my life crumbled around me.

"How can you possibly know that?"

He curled his lip. "I'm a man of means." He rubbed his fingertips over his lips. "I tell you what. I'll fund Aiden's entire course of treatment, meaning you can keep the money from this place, and all you have to do is open that pretty mouth of yours and swallow my dick."

Bile crawled into my throat. Could I do it? Could I let that man put his... penis in my mouth, to come on my tongue, to have that much power and control over me?

Yes, an internal voice whispered. *Yes, you can because you love Aiden more than you love yourself.*

"Why would you want that?" I choked out. "Why would a man want to force a woman to..." I squeezed my eyes closed and swallowed past a lump lodged in my throat. "I'm sure you could get more willing partners."

"Yes, I could. Easily. But I don't want them to..." He laughed, cutting off exactly where I had, teasing at my unwillingness to say the words *suck you off*. "I want you. I want *you* to get on your knees. *Right now.*"

Silence stretched between us. I stared at the floor. My knees shook and saliva pooled in my mouth horror at the situation I found myself in.

He expelled a deep-seated sigh. "I don't have all day, Miss Landry."

I slowly lifted my gaze to find he'd moved a little closer, a confident, triumphant smirk curving his full lips upward. *The bastard.* He already knew what my answer would be. God, I wish I had the courage to bite the disgusting thing off.

"Yes." I glared at him, determined to show his actions wouldn't break me. I'd do what he wanted, and I'd show him I hated every second, that I hated him. And then, when the time was right, I'd find a way to pay him back for humiliating me. "I'll do it."

He licked his bottom lip. "Come here," he said softly, crooking his finger.

I wasn't sure whether my legs would hold me up, but somehow, they did, and I found myself standing in front of him. His feet were splayed wide, showing his arrogance, his control, his one-upmanship.

"On your knees, *mon petit chaton.*"

French was a language I excelled in, mainly because ballet had a language all its own, steeped in French history. And that meant I could translate. This fucking *creep* had just called me *his little kitten?*

Okay, then. I'd show him I had claws. Maybe not now, but soon. I'd score them down his too-handsome face. I'd ruin his good looks, make women scream for a different reason when they saw him. Then the ugly he carried on the inside would match the outside.

I slowly sank to the floor, the hard wood of the ballet studio bruising the tender skin covering my kneecaps. I steeled myself. *Just get it done. Get it over with. And get the hell out of here.*

I swallowed again, my throat raw, bile burning the tender

skin of my esophagus.

"Unzip me." His voice rasped, his excitement palpable.

I tried to control the tremble in my fisted hands, but I failed. He smiled malevolently, taking enjoyment in my revulsion, and his control. As I reached for his zipper, he grabbed my wrist, preventing me from touching him.

"Get up, Miss Landry," he ordered.

Confused, I frowned and remained in place. "I don't understand. I thought this was what you wanted."

"I'm not in the habit of forcing women into sexual acts, Miss Landry. It's not my jam. All I wanted was to see how far you were willing to go. Now I know."

Rage flushed through me, and I launched to my feet, stumbling away, putting as much distance between me and this... this... vile creature as I could. It had all been a game, one for him to test my limits.

"Why? Why would you do that?"

He shoved his hands casually into his pants pockets and shrugged, the picture of nonchalance. "In any business transaction, it's important to discover your opponent's limits. Suffice to say, yours are fairly loose." He smiled, but it didn't reach his eyes.

"You're... you're... disgusting."

"We'll see if that's still your opinion once you've begged me to push my cock between those pretty red lips of yours."

"Never," I expelled, my breath coming in gasps as shock took hold of me.

I have to get out of here.

His large frame had cut off the exit I usually used. I made a dash for the front door.

"I wouldn't leave if I were you," he drawled the second my fingers closed around the handle. "Not if you want your brother to stand a chance of beating this disease with as little pain and discomfort as possible."

I paused, my feet glued in place, my hand still wrapped around the steel handle.

"I have a proposition for you."

I glanced over my shoulder. That I was still here, and hadn't run from this building screaming sexual harassment, ceded all the power to this man. Then again, I'd already shown him the lengths I was willing to go to, as he had demonstrated so savagely.

Should I listen to him? What if his next suggestion was more heinous than his last? I almost laughed aloud. What could be worse than demanding fellatio from an unwilling participant?

Forcing me to go through with it, maybe?

My love for Aiden made me turn around and agree to listen to the man holding all the cards. I smoothed my skirt beneath my thighs and sat on one of the boxes, my back upright, hands balled into fists lying in my lap, an obvious symbol of my rage.

"Well, what is it?"

He smirked at my prickly attitude, yet his eyes narrowed as he stared down at me. He tugged on his bottom lip, seemingly deep in thought. I didn't believe that for a second. He just wanted to use the silence as another weapon to torture me with. He'd gotten my ballet studio, but that wasn't enough for him. I had no idea what I'd done to make him want to punish me, but I had no doubts that was his intention. Fear prickled over my skin, and goose bumps showered my arms. I resisted the urge to rub them.

"Like I said. I will pay for your brother's treatment and associated costs. Every cent. As long as he needs."

I held my breath, waiting for the punchline. I even leaned a little closer, a concession he acknowledged with an arched eyebrow and an even wider smirk.

"And what do you want in return?"

My body.

My soul.

My life?

"I want you to work for me."

My forehead wrinkled. I knew nothing about the corporate world. I couldn't type or take shorthand or draft a contract. I didn't know how to draw up a balance sheet or pay invoices. My whole life had revolved around dance. What job could he possibly have in mind?

"Doing what?"

"Whatever I desire."

My vision clouded, and the sound of blood rushing through my ears sent me lightheaded. This man was playing with me, toying with my emotions, yet my fear for Aiden's future led me to sit there and let him get away with it.

"Calm down, Catriona," he said, that malicious grin making a comeback. "When we have sex, it'll be because you want to, not because I've forced you into it. That little stunt I pulled was just a test. I already told you I'm not in the habit of coercing women into performing sexual acts."

I dug my fingernails into the palms of my hand. The bastard was enjoying my discomfort. Every moment of it.

And we would *not* be having sex. Not this side of the apocalypse, nor the other side.

"Just tell me what you want," I snapped, the urge to run growing larger by the second.

He sighed as if my reaction suddenly bored him. He bent down and picked up a stray paperclip, then fed it through his fingers, his eyes on me the whole time. "There are occasions I need a companion to accompany me to certain events. Business dinners, functions, meetings with local officials. Things like that. On occasion, I might have a use for you at the office, too."

"Why do you need me to attend events with you?" I asked, confusion drawing my brows into a deep frown. "Surely a guy like you doesn't lack for willing female company."

A chuckle left his mouth. "You're right. I don't lack for *willing* company. Call me sadistic, but *unwilling* company is so much more entertaining to me."

I shook my head and laughed. "Let's call this what it is. Blackmail. Aww, is that what brings you pleasure, you sad bastard? To find someone's weakness and exploit it?" I laughed harder. "You're pathetic."

Blind fury crossed his face, and I rose to my feet, ready to make my escape. Garen Gauthier was a man to be feared. And I did fear him. Not that I would *ever* allow him to see how deeply he affected me. He had all the power for now, but one day, maybe, the scales of justice would tip in my favor and, goddammit, I'd make sure I was ready to take advantage.

His anger passed as quickly as it arrived, and he schooled his expression back to his trademark flat stare. "So, do we have an agreement, Miss Landry?"

I glared, fueled by anger, my teeth aching from clenching them too tightly. "Yes."

"Excellent. I'll be in touch. Make sure you leave your phone on at all times, including overnight. I occasionally keep strange hours, and you will be expected to do the same."

He gave me a cursory nod and, without saying another word, spun on his heel and left through the side entrance.

As soon as I heard the door close, my legs gave out, and I found myself sitting on the box once more. I curled my hands into fists and made a solemn vow. Whenever this got difficult—and there wasn't a doubt in my mind it would—I'd remind myself I was doing this for Aiden.

One thing was for sure, though. My opinion about this man had been wrong.

He wasn't just a bastard.

He was the Devil.

And I'd made a deal that had the ability to destroy me.

13

Garen

"I've transferred the first month's payment to the hospital in Switzerland."

Catriona remained quiet on the other end of the phone, but I could hear her soft breathing, and my dick responded accordingly. The scene of her kneeling before me, reaching for my zipper, was one I'd masturbated to so often in the last couple of days, I had wrist ache. She hated me with a passion that flayed my skin and made me even more determined to break her, to bend her to my will.

To fuck her.

For me, bedding a woman was all about the thrill of the chase. The problem I had was that most of my potential conquests didn't even put up a feeble fight. Catriona, on the other hand, excited me far more than I'd felt in years. Maybe ever.

"Thank you," she finally responded without a hint of gratitude to her tone.

I chuckled to myself. "His physicians tell me his first treatment takes place on Monday."

She sucked in a sharp breath. "How do you know what his treatment plan is? My brother's care is none of your business, Mr. Gauthier."

"On the contrary, when I'm funding it, *everything* is my business," I stated.

"Don't be so sure," she challenged, her spunky attitude hardening me even further inside my pants.

I shifted my cock to a more comfortable position. "I have work for you to do," I said, ignoring her last comment. "Be at my office building within the hour."

I didn't have any work for her to do. What I did have was an overwhelming and worrying desire to see her. I'd figure out a relevant task before she arrived.

"I can't," she replied, her tone beseeching. "I have to pick up our passports. I have our flights to organize, I need to find an apartment to rent, and I have to shop for essentials for Aiden. As soon as I get back from Switzerland, I'll be at your beck and call, but please, I have to make sure my brother is settled first."

I liked the way she'd said "beck and call". Gave me all kinds of ideas.

"I own a private jet. It's at your disposal. I also have a house in Geneva that your grandmother and brother can use for as long as they need. And I will have one of my interns pick up your passports. As for shopping for essentials, send me a list and I'll get my executive assistant to have whatever you need sent directly to your house." I smiled to myself. "Any other obstacles you'd like to put up, Miss Landry?"

Catriona was quiet for so long, I checked to make sure she hadn't hung up on me.

"Why would you do all that for us?" she asked breathily, giving me a preview to how she might sound in the throes of passion.

Fuck.

I forced myself to focus on raindrops pattering against the windowpane and, finally, my raging erection began to deflate.

"Are you still there?"

"Yes. Someone came into my office," I lied. "You ask why? Because, Miss Landry, contrary to your opinion of me, I am not completely heartless. Besides, this way, you have no excuse to avoid the task I have for you. Now please, get your fine ass down to my office, pronto, and I will make the arrangements for your travel to Switzerland."

I hung up before her sweet voice sent my dick on the rise again, and buzzed James.

"Catriona Landry is on her way here. When she arrives, have Tulip take her down to the archive room in the basement and wait there for further instructions." I somehow withheld a snort at the intern's ridiculous name.

"Yes, sir," James replied, doing a good job of hiding his perplexity at my request. If I didn't know him as well as I did, I'd have missed the slight change in cadence.

"Also, call the airfield. Have the plane prepped and ready to fly to Geneva on Wednesday afternoon."

"Got it."

"And let me know as soon as Catriona arrives."

"Will do."

I killed the connection and sat back in my chair, rubbing at the stubble on my chin. I watched the minutes tick by, unable to concentrate on anything. Damn, this girl had gotten under my skin. I couldn't figure it out. Sure, she was beautiful, with a lithe dancer's body and eyes I could drown in if I allowed myself to stare into them for too long, but my metaphorical black book was full of women like that. Why was Catriona Landry so fucking different? The only disparity I could come up with was her abject and very obvious hatred of me. That kind of loathing drew a line in the sand that I couldn't resist wanting to scrub out.

Finally, the intercom on my desk buzzed, and I pressed the answer button. "Yes."

"Miss Landry has arrived, sir," James said. "I've sent Tulip to fetch her."

"Thanks."

I waited ten minutes, then rode my private elevator down to the basement of my building. My grin grew the farther along the hallway I ventured. The idea I'd come up with was a shitty job, and not exactly required, but given my generous offer of a private jet and accommodation, I didn't want Catriona to think I was going soft. I had a reputation as a bastard to uphold, after all.

I pushed open the door to the archiving room, a rather depressing, windowless space that I last visited when ROGUES decided to open offices in Vancouver and I was tasked by the board to find a suitable building to purchase. Most of our files were electronic these days, but there was still a necessity to keep paper copies of some specific documents, usually a legal requirement.

Tulip jumped down the moment she spotted me from where she'd perched on a box, a deferent dip to her chin. Catriona, on the other hand, greeted me with a cold stare and a very pointed check of her wristwatch.

"Mr. Gauthier," Tulip gushed, eager to please following our first disastrous encounter. "James asked me to bring this lady here and wait for you."

"And would you look at that," I drawled. "You didn't mess up."

Tulip blushed, her cheeks blooming with color. Catriona made a noise that sounded remarkably like a growl.

I suppressed a satisfied smirk, then beckoned to the two of

them and strolled over to a stack of boxes assembled on a steel, industrial-looking shelf. Lifting down the top one, I opened it.

"I need all these files scanned and saved onto the computer." I jerked my chin at the monitor and tower stack sitting on a desk covered in a sheen of dust.

Catriona's eyes widened. "I-I don't know how to do that."

"I know," I said, my eyes gleaming as I reveled in her uncertainty. "Why do you think she's here?"

"Oh, it's easy," Tulip said with far too much enthusiasm for such a mundane task. "Come on, we'll have you trained up in no time."

"And when you've finished that box, move on to the next, and then the next. You are not to leave until I return."

I swept out of the room, feeling Catriona's venomous stare burning into the back of my neck. I grinned the entire way back up to my office.

The rest of the day passed by in a blur of meetings, phone calls, and emails. By the time I lifted my head and checked my watch, I was shocked to find it was already past six. This often happened when I became embroiled in my work, and while I vaguely remembered James fetching me a grilled chicken sandwich and standing over me while I ate it, my growling stomach was more than happy to remind me that I hadn't eaten nearly enough.

And then horror rolled through me. *Catriona.* Fuck. Was she still in the basement? I strode across my office and wrenched open the door to find James' desk empty. Frowning, I returned to my office to call him, and then remembered him telling me he had a date with some guy he'd met on Elite Singles.

I dashed to the elevator, jabbing at the button several times as if that would speed the damned thing up. When the elevator stopped at the basement, I shouldered my way through before the doors had properly opened and paced toward the archive room.

I found Catriona still sitting at the computer, and next to her, six closed boxes, a seventh open to her right, and a mountain of files on the desk. She wearily glanced in my direction, the earlier fight gone from her eyes.

"Shit." I rubbed my forehead. "I completely lost track of time. I didn't expect you to still be here."

She swiveled the chair around. "You told me I couldn't leave until you returned." Standing, she stretched out her back and groaned. "Permission to go home, *sir*?"

I scraped my fingers through my hair. "I'll drive you."

Her hand shot in the air. "No, you won't."

"Please." I formed my face into one resembling penitence. Not a natural expression for me at all, but this particular situation warranted it. "Sometimes I get embroiled in work and forget the outside world exists. I honestly never expected you to spend the entire day down here. Please let me make it up to you by seeing you safely home."

She narrowed her eyes, and her lips curved into a small smile. "Apologize, and I'll think about it."

My own lips twitched in response and I lowered my chin while keeping my eyes on hers. "I'm sorry. Come on. Let's get you out of here."

She stared at me for a few seconds, then relented. Reaching down to pick up her purse, she winced. "I really need to use the bathroom before we go."

My eyes widened at a moment of clarity. "You haven't left this room all day?"

She glared at me, her fiery spirit returning, her emerald irises glistening with barely contained anger. "Tulip left, and there was no way for me to get upstairs."

I frowned, confused.

"You need a pass, jackass, and *you* didn't see fit to leave me one."

Fuck. It hadn't occurred to me. Jesus, this was a new low, even for me. If she hadn't used the bathroom, then she hadn't eaten all day either, unless she saw fit to bring food with her, which I sorely doubted.

"Follow me." I turned my back so she couldn't read the remorse stretching across my face.

I paced outside the bathroom in the lobby while Catriona used the facilities. When she reappeared, I clutched her elbow, surprised that she didn't shake me off.

"The car is right outside," I said.

Once I'd settled her inside the warm interior, I activated the privacy screen then opened the drinks cabinet.

"What's your poison?" I asked.

She closed her eyes and let her head flop back. "I'd like to poison you."

I snickered as I poured two brandies. I handed one of the glasses to her. "Here."

She reached out to take it, and our fingers brushed.

I shivered in delight.

She recoiled as if I'd held her hand to the fire.

Her reaction brought a smirk to my lips. I had a long way to go to win over this one, and I was going to enjoy every single step of the journey.

The car drew to a stop at a set of traffic lights, and Catriona's stomach growled loudly. She pressed her forearm to her midriff.

"Let me take you to dinner," I said, finding the idea of her sitting in my multi-million-dollar car without food in her belly oddly uncomfortable.

"No, thank you," she replied stiffly, then turned her head to gaze out of the window where the view just happened to be a packed Italian restaurant, the tables bursting with customers stuffing fully loaded pizza into their faces. She rubbed her fingers over her mouth and swallowed.

"They do takeout," I said. "I can have Darryl fetch whatever you'd like. For your grandmother and brother, too. It's the least I can do."

She moved her head slowly, her eyes eventually sliding to mine, a mischievous twist to her lips.

"No, *you* go. You line up and fetch pizza."

I caught on to her idea fast, a ready denial on my tongue. I couldn't remember the last time I stood in line for anything, let alone food. But refusing to do as she asked was exactly what she expected me to do, and by falling into the trap she'd set, I'd hand victory to her.

Not fucking likely.

"Darryl, pull onto the next street please and park outside Gianni's."

Darryl did as I requested.

I unclipped my belt. "What would you like?"

Her eyes flared, and she cast a sideways glance at the line of people waiting to order pizza-to-go. "You're going to stand out there in the cold and buy me a pizza?"

The disbelief in her tone brought a secretive smile to my lips. *Busted, Miss Landry.*

"Absolutely."

She bit the inside of her cheek, frowning. "Okay. I'll have a Quattro Formaggi. Grams likes a Pugliese, and Aiden's favorite is a Margarita."

"Got it." I climbed out of the car. "Be right back."

14

Catriona

I peered through the window as Garen's tall, imposing figure joined the end of the line, surprise at his unexpected actions rolling through me. I didn't know the guy at all, but it struck me as a highly irregular occurrence that he'd wait in line for anything. I bet he hadn't done anything like this since college, if even then. He had that air about him reserved for the super-rich. A click of their fingers, and their heart's desire landed at their feet.

The privacy screen deactivated, and I turned to find Darryl smiling at me in the rear-view mirror.

"What's your secret?"

"What do you mean?"

He twisted in his seat. "I've worked for Mr. Gauthier for quite a while now, and I've never seen him do anything like this."

"Like what?"

"Stand in line in the freezing cold to buy pizza for a woman."

I snorted. "Don't tell me. He'd send you?"

"No," Darryl replied. "He just wouldn't do it. He's a very... particular man, and the idea of his car smelling of greasy pizza, not to mention if any spilled on the upholstery." He made a faux shocked face, then laughed.

I chewed over that piece of information, the threads of an idea forming. A childish one, maybe, but I couldn't resist. This man had stolen something that meant the world to me.

Time for a little revenge of my own.

Twenty minutes later, he returned to the car holding three large boxes, all stacked one on top of another. He slid inside the cabin and slammed the door. Settling them in the space between us, he narrowed his eyes at the lowered privacy screen then shot a glance between Darryl and me.

"Darryl, please drive to Miss Landry's home."

His voice was cold and sharp as glass. He pressed a button on the central armrest, and the dark screen cut off the front of the car from the back once more. I withheld a wince. Poor Darryl.

"How do you know where I live?" I queried.

He gave me one of those trademark smug looks, the kind that had my fingers twitching to slap it off his face.

"Oh, Catriona."

I raised my eyes, a curt shake of my head letting him know what I thought of his unwelcome intrusion into my private life. But as the smell of pizza wafted over, my mouth watered, and the plan I'd formed while waiting for him came to the forefront of my mind.

"Which one is mine?" I asked, opening the first box.

Garen placed his hand on top, forcing the box closed again. "It'll stay warm until you get home."

I grinned. Darryl's assessment was spot-on. Gauthier

couldn't bear the idea of the smell of greasy pizza lingering as he traveled in his over-priced limo. Time to push the limits.

"It's been almost twenty-four hours since I ate anything, and that's *your* fault. I feel sick, and I have the beginnings of a headache, which always happens when I don't eat regularly. One slice, just to take the edge off."

He shot me a scowl, his mask slipping for a fleeting moment before he schooled his expression.

"You could have eaten breakfast before coming to my office, *and* you have a cell phone. You should have called me."

"I was about to cook breakfast when you phoned this morning, but since you stamped your foot and demanded I leave immediately without letting me know you intended to lock me in a basement, I stupidly imagined I'd be able to grab something to eat at some point during the day. And..." I held up my hand as he opened his mouth to interrupt. "There is no cell phone signal in the basement, so I couldn't call you or anyone else."

I felt like shouting "Gotcha!" at the expression on his face. He actually appeared on the verge of contrition. It wouldn't last long, but I reveled in the minor victory.

He furrowed his brow, rubbed it with the tips of his fingers, then slipped the third box from underneath the other two and handed it to me.

"Here. Just be caref—never mind. Go for it."

I opened the box and bent my head, breathing in that unique and oh-so-good pizza smell. Picking up a slice, I took a huge bite, the juices from the sauce and the melted cheese dripping down my chin.

"God, that tastes so good." I chewed, swallowed, then wiped across my mouth. Grease from the pizza coated my fingers and, completely on purpose, I lightly touched his pristine leather seat.

"Watch it," he barked, grabbing a handful of napkins to rub the offending mark.

"Oops, sorry," I said without an ounce of regret in my tone. "How clumsy of me."

Gray eyes met mine, a dangerous glint darkening his irises. He knew I'd smeared grease on his upholstery on purpose. I held his gaze, challenging him into an altercation. I wanted to rile him, show him he couldn't intimidate me—even if that wasn't entirely true.

A muscle ticked in his jaw, and then he wiped his hands, tucked the used napkins in the side pocket of the car, and turned his attention to the speeding scenery outside.

"Enjoy your pizza," he murmured.

He said pizza, but I knew he meant victory. *Enjoy your victory.*

I grinned, reveling in the minor triumph. "Thanks, I will."

Darryl pulled up to the curb outside my tiny house. Garen handed me the other pizza boxes.

"Thanks," I reluctantly said. "For the ride and the pizza."

He nodded curtly. "My driver will pick you up on Wednesday and take you all to the airport. Your passports will be hand delivered tomorrow. I'll be in touch if I need anything before then."

I hesitated, wondering whether I should make a small concession, then changed my mind. Balancing the three boxes on my hip, I walked to the house. The sound of Garen's car pulling away reached me, and when I glanced over my shoulder, he'd gone.

Relieved to see Aiden wolf down the pizza and drink an entire glass of orange juice, I answered Grams' questions about my day, but rather than tell her the blunt truth, I said that Garen had put me to work on a very important archiving role of crucial legal documents, which placated her somewhat.

I still hadn't divulged that our flight to Switzerland would be aboard a private jet, nor that Garen had opened up his home for us to use as long as we needed. Grams was an old-fashioned woman, and she'd instantly grow suspicious of the hidden cost of accepting such a generous offer.

As was I. But this cross was mine to bear, not hers or Aiden's. And from what I knew about Garen Gauthier, I'd pay a heavy price.

15

Garen

"James, get in here."

Five seconds later, my executive assistant scuttled into my office, iPad in hand. "What do you need?"

"The foreman of Docherty's just called." Docherty's was the company I'd chosen to begin the ground clearing before the building work on the hotel could begin. "Apparently, there's some unforeseen issue with the demolition permit. One of those damned goody-goodies from Development and Building Services has showed up on site and has put a stop to the whole thing. The foreman has asked me to go down and sort it out."

James tapped on his screen. "You have an appointment with the mayor at two this afternoon. It might be worth bringing up the issue with him?"

I shook my head. "Last resort. I don't like using my contacts for trivial matters. Experience has taught me they're less likely to apply pressure when it's really needed. Besides, that's more wasted time."

"I'll cancel your morning appointments then."

"Thanks. Oh, and can you call Miss Landry and tell her to meet me there? Maybe a little female persuasion might help the situation."

James grinned. "I'll contact her right now."

A warm feeling circled in my gut at the thought of seeing Catriona. Tomorrow she'd head off to Switzerland, and I wouldn't see her for six days. I didn't like that idea one bit, hence my request to James.

I hankered to see her more than I ever had with any other woman. With my usual dates, I mildly looked forward to the evening, especially if we were on date one or two, but by date three, boredom would set in, and by date four, if they made it that far, I usually dumped them. I swore my growing obsession with Catriona was steeped in her hatred of me. For some unknown reason, that had jet-propelled my interest. Oliver would say that I found pleasure in the chase, not the capture. He had a point, but there was something more to my interest in Catriona that I couldn't quite put my finger on. For now, I'd go along with it and have a little fun in the process.

Gathering my things, I locked my computer and headed out. "Did you get hold of Miss Landry?" I asked James.

"Yes. She didn't sound too happy, but said she'd leave home now and meet you there."

A shiver of excitement trickled down my spine at the idea of being met with Catriona in a mood. Her anger turned me on.

Darryl opened the car door as I approached, and I slipped inside. He set off smoothly into the traffic, and within thirty minutes, we'd arrived at the building site. Or what should be a building site by now, but thanks to Mr. Paper Pusher, the work hadn't yet begun.

I got out of the car and held up a hand in greeting to the foreman, then glanced around for Catriona. She was loitering outside her former ballet studio, her hand pressed to the front door.

I strolled across. "Thanks for coming."

She met my smile with a glower. "I hope this is urgent. I have a lot to do before tomorrow."

My dick twitched at her cold response, and my smile grew. "I need you to break the habit of a lifetime and try to be charming."

Her scowl deepened. "What game are you playing now?"

"No game. I got a call from my foreman. There's a small issue with the demolition paperwork, and I want to see if your feminine wiles can unblock the impasse to allow the bulldozers to move in."

Her eyes widened, and her hands went to her hips. "Let me get this straight. You want *me* to help *you* so that you can flatten a business that my grandmother started forty years ago, working her fingers to the bone to afford the down payment?" She snorted. "Fix your own goddamn issues."

She barged past me. I snaked out a hand and caught her arm. "Hold up there, kitty cat. You agreed to do whatever I wanted in order to secure funding for your brother's treatment. And I want you to do this."

"Why?" she whispered. "Why this? Do you have any idea how difficult it is just standing here knowing that soon, all this will be gone? Everything you see here, the blood, sweat, and tears that was put into these businesses, gone. And you want me to have a hand in that? You're a monster."

I moved closer and loomed over her, my eyes narrowed in warning. "Call me what you like, but remember I'm also your boss. Now paint a smile on your face and come with me, or maybe I'll recall the payment I made to that Swiss hospital."

Her mouth slackened, and she blanched. "You wouldn't."

I smirked. "Try me."

Shifting my hand to her elbow, I drove her forward, each

step feeling like a victory to me, and, undoubtedly, a penance to her. I didn't understand why punishing Catriona brought me both pleasure and pain, or why I grew more addicted to that feeling every day, but I couldn't seem to back away, even when I could see the hurt in her eyes and feel the sting of my demands flay her skin.

The foreman saw us coming and removed his yellow hard-hat, ruffled his hand over the top of his head, and made his way over to meet us halfway.

"Mr. Gauthier," he said, thrusting out his large, calloused hand, evidence of the type of work he undertook.

I shook it, then gestured to Catriona. "This is my associate, Miss Landry. Where's the problem?"

He jerked his chin in the direction where a guy in a suit holding a clipboard stood by a shop that had once been a hairdresser's. I guided Catriona over to him. He straightened as we approached and smoothed a hand over his tie.

"Mr. Gauthier?" he asked.

I nodded curtly. "My foreman tells me we have a problem with the paperwork. Considering I oversaw that particular task, would you care to explain what that might be?"

He removed a sheet of paper from his folder and handed it to me. "The date is smudged," he said, pointing as if I needed help to see the fucking date. "You can't make it out. Could be postdated for all I know."

Incredulous, I lifted my head and glowered at him. "Are you telling me that you've held up my men because of an ink smudge? Do you have any fucking idea how much a delay of an hour, let alone a half a day co—"

"What Mr. Gauthier means to say," Catriona said, cutting right across me, the unexpected interruption rendering me speechless—a damn rare occurrence. "Is that we're very sorry about this error. Could we possibly cross that out and rewrite the date if Mr. Gauthier initials the change?"

She bestowed a smile on the guy, warm and friendly, the likes of which I'd never seen, and hadn't actually thought her capable of.

Peter the fucking Pen Pusher shifted from foot to foot. "It's highly irregular."

"But not impossible?"

Catriona briefly touched his arm, and I swore she fluttered her fucking eyelashes, too.

"If you could see your way to allowing this, Mr....?"

"Trenton," he replied. "Frank Trenton."

"You'd really be helping me out, Frank. The smudge is my fault, you see." She flashed an apologetic smile that smacked of fakeness in my direction. "Mr. Gauthier trusted me with a very important task, but I'm still learning. I don't want to lose my job. If there's any way at all..."

She let the words trail off, peering at Trenton with a coy expression.

"Well, I suppose." He cleared his throat. "I suppose on this one occasion, I could allow it."

Catriona beamed. "Excellent." She turned to me, her face switching from pleasant to blind anger. "Crisis averted, *Mr. Gauthier.*"

She strode off before I could stop her. I quickly rewrote the date, initialed it, and handed it back to Trenton.

"We good?" I asked.

He peered at it, then reluctantly nodded. "This will suffice."

I had to bite my tongue not to call him a fucking time-wasting prick. Instead, I yelled over to the foreman. "We're a go," then set off jogging in the same direction Catriona had gone. I caught up with her after a half a kilometer. Damn, the woman moved fast.

"Where are you going?" I asked, marching alongside her.

She slid to a halt and jabbed a finger right in my collarbone. "Don't you *ever* do anything like that to me again."

I smirked. "Why would I not, when you're so good at it? The flirting was a master stroke."

She stared at me, incredulous. "Fuck you. That place means more to me than mere bricks and mortar. It's full of memories, of fun times and sad times. Of triumphs and tribulations. Of love and laughter. All the things a freak like *you* wouldn't understand. And yes, I know my beloved studio now belongs to you, and I know what your plans are, but to ask me to help you remove an obstruction that means in a matter of minutes, a bulldozer will smash through something that's been a part of my life for as long as I can remember, is a new low, even for you."

My lips flattened. "And yet you did it anyway."

"Because you gave me no choice!" she exclaimed. "You threatened to withdraw financial support for my brother's cancer treatment."

I expelled an irritated huff. "That was a joke. For Christ's sake, I wouldn't have actually done it."

She flexed her jaw, a nerve beating furiously in her cheek. "You are *unbelievable*."

"Thanks." I flashed her a grin that I intended to double up as an apology.

She opened her mouth, then closed it again, shook her head, and set off walking at a clip.

"Wait, I'll take you home."

"Don't bother," she threw back over her shoulder. "I'd rather crawl there on my hands and knees than spend one second in a car with you."

I watched as she rounded the corner and disappeared. Hmm. Not my finest hour. Maybe it hadn't been a good idea to ask her to help me with this particular issue, even if her reaction was completely over the top.

I spun around and headed back to my car. She'd get over it.

16

CATRIONA

By the time I reached home, I expected my anger to have receded, and my heart to beat in a normal rhythm, yet when I pushed open my front door and entered my sanctuary, anger had grown into blind rage. How dare he! And to act all innocent, as if he hadn't done it on purpose. Pah! He'd known exactly what he was doing.

Why did he enjoy punishing me? He made it pretty obvious he gained huge pleasure from my anguish, but other than originally refuse to sell my business to him, what had I done to deserve such harsh treatment?

And then, like a pin stuck into a balloon, my wrath withered and died. I had so many other more important things to give my attention to over the coming weeks and months, not least of which was ensuring Aiden got through his upcoming treatment. I hadn't underestimated how hard it would be for him. Leaving all his friends behind, moving to a foreign country for up to six months, being schooled by a tutor rather than in a classroom with teachers he was familiar with, not to mention the fear that the treatment might fail and leave him riddled with cancer.

Right, that's it. For the next few days I'd put Garen Gauthier out of my mind and focus on getting Aiden and my grandmother settled in Switzerland. I had a six-day break from the man, and I intended to make the most of it.

Yet that night when I finally fell asleep after staring at the ceiling until the small hours, my dreams were full of him and his too-handsome face, stormy gray eyes, and icy stare. The way he kept me on edge by acting like he cared one minute, then doing something cruel and callous the next.

I awoke the following morning with my eyes glued together and a head full of cotton wool. It took me a good thirty minutes and two strong cups of coffee to be able to think with any kind of clarity. Fortunately, there was too much to do to give much thought to Garen. We were due to head off to the airport mid-afternoon, and I hadn't finished packing yet.

When Darryl stopped outside my house and strode up the narrow pathway insisting he carry our suitcases to the car, Grams surprised me by holding her tongue, although she did give the car a full appraisal, then raise her eyebrow at me. Aiden, on the other hand, couldn't contain his excitement at traveling in such a luxurious vehicle, and he chattered the entire way to the airport.

I'd assumed we'd fly from Vancouver International, but when Darryl opened the back door to let us out, I realized we were at a private airfield.

"What is this, girl?" Grams hissed in my ear, taking care not to allow Aiden to hear. "What exactly is going on here?"

Given no choice but to explain, I sent her a beseeching look not to make a scene. "Mr. Gauthier offered to have his plane take us," I said. "And he's loaning his house to you and Aiden, too."

She squinted, and, running her gaze over me, moved closer. "What have you gotten yourself into?"

"Nothing," I insisted. "I told you, he wants me to work for him. That's all."

"Pfft." Grams sliced her hand through the air. "No man is that generous without expecting a payoff. You mark my words, he'll come a-knocking, and when he does," she jabbed her finger into my shoulder, "you tell him you're not for sale."

I widened my eyes as her meaning became clear. "Grandmother!" I expelled, using a term I rarely did, and one intended to let her know how furious her comments had made me. "You are out of line."

She prodded me again. "I'm an old woman, and I know what I know. You be careful, girl. I am well aware of what that boy means to you," she kicked back her head toward Aiden, "and to me. But you watch where you step."

"I can take care of myself, Grams," I said, as much to reassure myself as her. "Mr. Gauthier isn't a monster."

No, he's far worse.

"Guys, come on," Aiden shouted, already halfway up the steps to the luxurious jet. "This is amazing!"

He disappeared inside. I shot a glance at Darryl, who pointed his chin.

"Go on, Miss Landry. I'll make sure all the bags are loaded."

"Thank you, Darryl."

I took my grandmother's arm and helped her climb the steps. The inside of the jet was like nothing I'd ever seen. Thick carpeted flooring, sumptuous leather seating, a large-screen TV.

"Unbelievable," I muttered.

"Why thank you," an all-too familiar voice murmured in my ear. "I concur."

I spun around, my mouth slackening as my gaze fell on the one person I hadn't expected to see.

"What the hell are you doing here?" I ground out, hands on my hips.

Garen's trademark smirk set off a fizzing in my stomach. Goddamn the man. Every time that annoying curve of his lips appeared, my palm twitched with the desire to slap him, and the most frustrating thing was that I couldn't. A girl of eighteen might get away with such a juvenile reaction. A woman of twenty-five had to show more restraint—more's the pity.

"Why, making sure you don't trash my aircraft, Miss Landry." He bent his head, his mouth close enough to blow warm air against the shell of my ear. "Given the way we left things yesterday, and your level of hostility toward me, I wouldn't put anything past you."

And with that, he swooped around me and bestowed his most generous smile on my family.

"I'm so glad you made it. Please make yourselves comfortable."

17

GAREN

If only I could have recorded Catriona's furious expression and played it back whenever I chose. She hadn't faked her shock and rage at finding me here, and until this morning, I hadn't intended to gatecrash their trip. But then I'd woken up and realized that going six days without the ability to needle her for my own enjoyment just wouldn't do.

But more than that, I felt as if I needed to make some sort of a concession after what I did to her at the building site. I'd not yet figured out why punishing her brought such contrasting feelings of pleasure and pain. Occasionally, a memory deep in the recesses of my mind started to surface, but before I could grab on to it, it vanished, leaving me more confused than ever.

I tried to nail the precise moment when I'd found myself thinking of Catriona before I went to sleep at night and having the thought of her enter my mind the moment I awoke the next morning. I hadn't unearthed the answer yet, and, like that damned elusive memory, this, too, may permanently evade me, but one thing was certain: my life was richer with her in it.

Normally, the only thing about women that interested me was what they had between their legs, and even then, they didn't hold my attention for long. While Catriona's hand had been agonizingly close to my dick when I'd played that cruel trick on her at the ballet studio, any form of sexual contact was a long way off.

Yet still I craved to be with her. To smell the delicate, floral perfume she favored. To watch a storm brew in her emerald eyes when I pushed a particular button. To imagine stroking her lithe, dancer's body while she writhed beneath me.

A warmth spread through my groin, one I wanted to explore with the angry kitten standing in front of me. Instead, I dragged my thoughts away from Catriona while I went to say hello to her brother and introduce myself properly to her grandmother. Greeting the matriarch of the family with a visible bulge in my pants wasn't a good idea, especially as I'd already gotten the measure of her. A wily old woman with a wealth of experience in life, and one who, if the firm set to her jaw and the thin line of her lips was anything to go by, wouldn't be easy to charm.

"Aiden, great to meet you. Would you like to see the cockpit?"

Aiden beamed at me and launched to his feet from where he'd taken up residence on the couch that lined one wall of the aircraft.

"That would be *awesome*," he exclaimed.

I beckoned to Julie, my flight attendant. "Would you take him to meet the captain and show him around?"

"Of course, Mr. Gauthier," she said. "Come on, Aiden. Let's give you the grand tour."

With Aiden suitably occupied, I turned my attention to Catriona's grandmother.

"Mrs. Kelly." I held out my hand. "It's lovely to meet you."

Richard's investigations had delved into Catriona's background. Mrs. Kelly was Catriona's maternal grandmother, hence the different family name.

Green eyes, a replica of Catriona's, stared back at me, scrutinizing, and trying to read my intentions. I worked hard to keep my expression open. It wouldn't do for her to figure out my true plans for her granddaughter—namely to bed her as fast as possible and get her out of my system.

"I wish I could say the same, Mr. Gauthier, but I admit I'm very suspicious as to why a man such as yourself would find it within him to proffer such generosity for a family he doesn't know, and only crossed paths with so he could whip the family business from under their noses."

Wow. I was right about Mrs. Kelly. Astute, direct, a lioness protecting her precious cubs. I caught sight of Catriona out of the corner of my eye, a glimmer of a smile touching her lips, a keenness to see how I handled this revealed in the way she leaned slightly forward.

I decided to plump for a semi-truth. Something told me Mrs. Kelly would smell a lie at twenty paces, and I'd pay the price for any duplicity.

I took a seat across from her, and Catriona sat on the couch Aiden had vacated.

"You're right to be suspicious, Mrs. Kelly. As you so eloquently pointed out, I was both strident and single-minded in securing the purchase of your property. I'm afraid when it comes to the success of my company, I suffer from tunnel vision. I won't apologize for that. However, since meeting your granddaughter, I admit I've become rather..." I paused, searching for the right word that a grandmother wouldn't read as *horny.* "Smitten."

Catriona choked out a laugh. "Smitten? Come on."

I slid my gaze to hers, then returned my attention to her

grandmother. "I'm afraid your granddaughter isn't quite in the same place as I am but I'm hopeful that, given time, I can persuade her otherwise."

A snort came from my left. "Not a chance," she muttered.

For the first time, I saw a spark of mirth in Mrs. Kelly's eyes. "You appear to have a sizeable challenge on your hands, Mr. Gauthier."

"Indeed. However, I thrive on challenge, and I am resolute and persistent when the need arises."

She arched a brow. "Is that so?" A twist of her head brought her attention to Catriona. "And what do you have to say about this, girl?"

Catriona sat up straight. "I say that I would rather gouge out my eyes with a rusty razor blade than spend any more time than is absolutely necessary in this man's company."

I chuckled. "See, I'm winning her over."

Mrs. Kelly cackled, while Catriona's expression articulated that it was *my* eyes she'd like to use that rusty blade on, rather than her own.

"As much as I'm enjoying this exchange, we'll be taking off soon. So buckle up and enjoy the ride."

I emphasized *ride* while locking my gaze on Catriona's captivating green irises. In return, she cast a withering look in my direction, fastened her seat belt, and stared out of the window.

When I turned away with a smile, I found Mrs. Kelly with her eyes on me, a curious tilt to her head. I winked at her, drawing another bark of laughter from the old woman, which Catriona studiously ignored.

Aiden joined us, and his animated chatter filled the silence. Once we were at cruising altitude and could move around the cabin, I instructed Julie to take care of my guests and excused myself, disappearing to the rear of the plane where my office was, as well as a bedroom. I glanced inside at the king-sized bed, imagining a time when I'd introduce Catriona to the mile-high club. It would happen, I was certain of it. Or to put it another way, I wouldn't give up the chase until I'd conquered my prey. She'd relent in the end. They all did. This one might just take a little more persuading.

Engrossed in work, I lost track of time when a knock at the door brought my head up. "Come in."

The door opened to show Catriona standing on the other side, her shoulder propped against the frame.

"Sorry to disturb you," she said, not sounding in the least bit sorry. "Julie said this plane had a bedroom."

I leaned back in my chair, splayed my legs wide, and slid my tongue along the underside of my top teeth. "You've come around far quicker than I anticipated, but I'm not arguing."

She rolled her eyes and let out an exasperated huff. "Aiden is tired. He gets like that. It's his body fighting the cancer. I was hoping you wouldn't mind if he took a nap."

I grinned, enjoying this banter far more than I ever imagined. By now, I'd expected my boredom threshold might have kicked in, especially as I hadn't even gotten to first base yet, but no, I was as invested now as I'd ever been. Maybe to an even greater extent. It hadn't occurred to me that I'd find this kind of drawn-out foreplay—and I had no doubt that's exactly what it was—so fucking exciting. There was something to be said for delayed gratification, at least when it came to Catriona.

"He's more than welcome," I said.

"Thank you," she replied stiffly.

She spun on her heel, and a few seconds later returned with Aiden in tow. They disappeared into the bedroom. She was gone for a couple of minutes, then reappeared, closing the door with a quiet click. As she passed by my office, I called out to her.

"Catriona."

She paused mid-step, then backtracked. "Yes?"

"The couch converts to a bed, too. Not as comfortable, but hopefully somewhere you and your grandmother can get some sleep. Julie can fetch you pillows and a comforter."

She studied my face while tapping her fingertips against her thighs. "Where will you sleep?" she eventually asked.

I rose from my chair and walked toward her. She held her ground, even when I tucked a lock of hair behind her ear, grazing the tips of my fingers over the silky soft skin of her neck. A rush of pleasure surged through me. She hadn't pushed me away. God, I wanted to kiss her.

"Are you worried about me?"

She swallowed, then dampened her lips. "No."

I leaned in, testing the waters. "I think you are," I murmured with my lips a mere inch or two from hers. "I think you're coming around to the idea of us, Catriona."

"There is no us," she said, her breathing becoming erratic.

I swept my thumb over her plump bottom lip, my stomach clenching with need. "Not yet. But there will be."

She parted her lips, a silent invitation for me to kiss her, even if she wasn't aware of it. "Dream on," she rasped. "Whenever I think of you, all I see is the cruelty, the pleasure you take in my unhappiness, the way you reveled in my despair yesterday. You'll always be the man who stole my life, and I'll always hate you for it."

An uncomfortable feeling settled on my chest. Dammit. So close, and then she'd slammed the door on her feelings, and me. I forced a smile. "Hate is a very strong emotion, Catriona. I'd be much more concerned if you were indifferent toward me."

She stood there, a pink tinge gracing her cheeks while she tried to come up with a cutting remark. When none was forthcoming, she uttered an angry sound and stomped off.

I closed the door to my office, my balls aching for release.

Yet there was something more there than a quick fuck. A longing. I yearned to spend time with her. Each interaction with Catriona increased the strength of my desire and offered up a new and exciting experience to get close to someone in a way I hadn't before.

I shook my head to clear the unwelcome and unfamiliar thoughts. Maybe I should hook up with Valentina when we landed in Geneva. Prove to myself that the debacle with Scarlett was a one-off, brought on by tiredness rather than anything to do with Catriona.

Grabbing my phone, I found her number saved in contacts. My thumb hovered over the call button, but for some unfathomable reason, I couldn't dial. I groaned. Valentina didn't interest me. Scarlett didn't interest me. Only one woman interested me, and she was on the other side of this very thin wall, in all likelihood, deliberating on ways to punish me.

I shivered. *Yes fucking please.*

After more than eleven hours in the air, we made a brief stop in Dublin to refuel and, four hours later, we arrived at a private airfield outside Geneva. Even though Catriona assured me they were well rested, all three of them looked tired and drawn.

"It's the altitude as well as the time difference," I explained as we descended the steps to the waiting car. "A good night's sleep in a comfortable bed is all you'll need."

She gave me a wan smile. "How long is it to your house?" she asked, shooting a worried glance in Aiden's direction.

"Forty minutes or so," I said.

She waited for her grandmother and brother to get in the car, then went to climb in after them. And then she paused, one hand on the top of the door. She glanced over her shoulder at me.

"Thank you for helping him. I don't think I've said that, and I should have."

Surprised at her sudden appreciation, especially given her timely reminder on the flight of all my transgressions, I gave her a genuine smile, one not steeped in hidden agendas or innuendos.

"It's my pleasure."

18

CATRIONA

I gazed out of the window as the car wound its way through the Swiss mountains. I had assumed that traveling in luxury rather than on a commercial jet would mean I wasn't so tired, but that didn't seem to be the case. Given how exhausted Aiden and Grams appeared, I felt a surge of gratitude toward the man sitting to my right for his hospitality. If we'd had to make this trip cramped in an economy seat on a commercial flight, it would have been a lot worse.

But at the same time, an inner voice warned me to watch my step. Garen Gauthier was a man who only did things that benefitted himself, including those actions which, on the surface, appeared altruistic. I didn't buy his reasoning of needing a companion to attend dinners and the like, nor did I think his generosity was steeped in a way to get me into bed either. He was a rich, very good-looking guy who filled a suit so well, my mouth watered—not that I'd *ever* admit that to him—

and could have any woman he wanted, and probably at no greater cost than a fancy dinner cooked by a world-renowned chef. To pay the exorbitant sums for Aiden's treatment, not to mention the cost of flying us over here by private jet, and loaning his house for the duration, his motive had to be more than sex and wanting a companion on his arm on occasion. And besides, each time the ice around my heart thawed a little, he'd do something appalling and hurtful, and once again, it'd freeze over.

I was so lost in my thoughts that I didn't realize we'd stopped until Aiden shouted, "Wow".

My mouth fell open as I glanced through the heavily tinted windows. Before me stood a mansion sitting on top of a hill with a spectacular view of the glistening waters of Lake Geneva, and behind the house, the backdrop of mountains already had a dusting of snow sitting on their peaks. I had no idea how many square feet this house was, but I was damned sure I couldn't count that high.

"This is your place?"

He nodded, jerking his chin to let me know his driver was waiting for me to get out. "Come on, I'll have Lia show you to your quarters."

Quarters? It was like an episode of *Downton Abbey*, but instead of a stuffy seventeenth-century monolith, this place oozed contemporary design and style. And who was Lia? The housekeeper or his Swiss lover?

I swiped a hand over the prickles creeping along the back of my neck. If he paraded some gorgeous, buxom redhead in front of me, I'd... I'd... ugh. I didn't care what he did. He could screw her on the front lawn for all I cared. He meant nothing to me. Nothing. I couldn't bear the man. Sure, he'd played nice on the plane over, and if I closed my eyes, I could still feel the tingle caused by the tips of his fingers brushing my neck as he'd tucked my hair behind my ear and recall the butterflies swarming through my abdomen when I'd thought he was about to kiss me. But he wasn't a nice man, and I could not allow myself to get drawn into a fake persona.

My legs almost gave way when a woman in her late fifties bustled out to greet us, a friendly smile extending across her face.

Housekeeper.

Thank God.

"Welcome," she said, her arms outstretched.

Each of us received two kisses, one on each cheek, including Garen. I snuck a glance out of the corner of my eye to see how he reacted, surprised when I caught his kind smile.

"Good to see you, Lia," Garen said.

"You must be so tired after your long journey," Lia said. "Let's get you all inside and settled."

In seconds, Lia and my grandmother had their heads together gossiping as if they'd known each other for years. Aiden trailed in their wake, his mouth permanently hanging open in a state of awe, while Garen and I brought up the rear.

"This is one hell of a house," I said as we entered through the front door into a large hallway grander than a lot of five-star hotel lobbies.

"It's far too big. I bought it for the view. Come on, I'll show you."

He pressed a hand against my lower spine and steered me toward a winding staircase that led to the upper levels. Grams and Aiden were already halfway up, Lia offering her arm as assistance to Grams.

The warmth from his palm seeped through my thin shirt, and the hairs on my arms lifted in response. I should shake him off, step away, but I didn't. It felt too good.

Dangerous, Catriona. Sending mixed signals wasn't a good idea.

My reactions to him continued to confuse me. One minute I

hated his guts. This was the man who'd sent in the bulldozers to flatten my beloved ballet studio, who'd forced me to my knees and pretended he wanted payment in the form of a blow job just to show me that he was in control. Not to mention he'd left me in the basement of his building without food, water, or a bathroom for nine hours.

The next minute, I remembered that he'd offered to pay for Aiden's cancer treatment—meaning I could keep the money from the sale of the studio to help feed and clothe my family, and keep a roof over our heads—and then brought us here on his private jet and opened up his home to us.

His gentle touch on the plane and his almost-kiss meant I'd barely gotten a wink of sleep. All I could think was that he was right there, on the other side of the wall, trying to get some rest while sitting upright in an office chair, and all because he'd given up his bed for my brother, and me and Grams had commandeered his couch.

"This way," he said, urging me up another flight of stairs while Lia led Grams and Aiden off down a plushly carpeted hallway.

"Where are we going?" I looked back at my family heading in a different direction.

"The roof terrace. It has the best views." He grinned, an evil glint in his eyes. "Don't worry, Catriona. You're perfectly safe with me."

I ignored him. From what I'd gleaned so far, the more I engaged in his silly games, the more he played them.

When we reached the top of the house, Garen opened a door and gestured for me to go through. I stepped out onto an enormous terrace with views right down the mountainside to the beautiful lake below. The weak fall sunshine glinted off the water, so still it appeared almost glasslike. Nestled behind the opposite shoreline were more mountains, and the trees dotted along the slopes bore the golden colors of the season.

"Oh my goodness, it's beautiful," I said, stepping forward to take a closer peek. "I mean, we have our own wonderful scenery in Canada, but this…"

And then the strangest thing happened. Hot tears sprang up out of nowhere, my tightly contained emotions getting the better of me. It was all too much. Losing the studio, Aiden's terrifying diagnosis, the trip here. Worry over what the future held. Blinking furiously, and relieved Garen was standing behind me and therefore wouldn't witness me teetering on the edge of an emotional breakdown, I pulled myself together and put my moment of weakness down to overtiredness.

I jumped when he clasped my upper arms. His breath warmed the back of my neck, and I felt the heat coming off his body, despite the chill in the air. A tightness spread across my chest, and a sudden need to taste his lips surged through me. I leaned my head against his shoulder.

"Catriona."

Garen's voice rasped in my ear, and he turned me around until I faced him. I kept my eyes lowered to the ground, the abrupt change in atmosphere from a light teasing to something far deeper sending me off-kilter.

"Look at me," he commanded.

Slowly, my head came up. Our gazes collided, and then his mouth was on mine, hard, urgent, demanding I submit. Light-headed, I clutched his arms, feeling the power in his muscles as they bunched beneath my hands.

His tongue surged between my lips, dueling with my own as he branded me with a kiss like no other I'd ever experienced. He buried his hands in my hair, angling me, plundering my mouth over and over, like a man starved of female attention.

Except he wasn't starved of female attention. He'd freely admitted he had more than enough willing partners, but what had attracted me to him was my *unwillingness* to capitulate. And here I was, kissing him as if I'd die without his lips on mine. The man who loved to torture me, to hurt me, to punish me.

I jerked backward, stumbling in my need to put distance between us. My chest heaved, my breath coming in urgent little pants, my lungs burning, demanding more oxygen.

You're an idiot, Catriona.

He took a step in my direction. My hand shot in the air.

"Don't. Don't touch me. I can't bear it."

He arched a brow, his lips curved in a half-sneer. Compared to me, he appeared calm, in control, completely put together.

"You can't bear it?" His tone oozed sarcasm. "From the way you almost ate my face just then, I beg to differ, *mon petit chaton*."

"Stop calling me that," I yelled. "I am *not* your little kitten. I am nothing to you, and you're nothing to me and never will be. Now please, leave me alone."

I dashed into the house and headed in the direction Lia had taken my grandmother and brother, bumping into her coming out of one of the many doors dotted along the hallway.

"Oh, there you are, Miss Landry." She smiled, but it didn't last. "Are you okay?"

I nodded, swallowing past a thick throat. "I'm fine. Please, would you take me to my room?"

She frowned but didn't question me further. "Of course. This way."

Lia pointed out my grandmother's and Aiden's rooms, which were next to mine, and told me to dial zero on the phone if I needed anything. I quickly unpacked, then checked on them both. They were fast asleep, worn out from the long journey. Reluctant to risk bumping into Garen, and exhausted myself, I took a shower and got changed for bed.

I flicked off the bedside lamp and stared up at the ceiling. I touched my fingers to my lips and called to mind the memory of Garen kissing me. Damn, it'd felt good. So good. His tongue sliding between my lips, the feel of his firm biceps beneath my hands, the smell of him, all man and sandalwood cologne.

Rolling onto my side, I closed my eyes and hugged the pillow toward me, wishing it was him.

19

Catriona

The following morning, I awoke to bright sunshine and the sounds of birds tweeting outside my window. Checking the clock, I couldn't believe I'd slept right through and it was now seven a.m. I squinted, trying to work out what day it was.

Friday. Today was Friday. We'd left Canada on Wednesday afternoon. I'd better get up. Aiden had an appointment at the hospital at eleven this morning for some initial tests before his treatment started in earnest on Monday.

I showered, dressed, then knocked on Aiden's door and entered to find him lying on the bed with his eyes closed.

"I'm awake," he said.

I perched on the end of his bed and brushed his hair out of his eyes, wondering if he'd lose his silky locks or if there was some kind of medication to prevent that happening.

"How did you sleep?"

"Good." He stretched and yawned. "It's so quiet here."

I nodded. "A bit different than the constant traffic noise at home, huh?"

"Yeah."

"Hungry?"

He smiled a little. "I could eat."

"Okay, well, you get dressed, and I'll check on Grams, and then we'll see if we can rustle up some breakfast."

He threw back his covers. "Sounds good."

My grandmother was sitting in a chair by a window that overlooked the lake and the mountains, her trusty knitting in her lap, needles clacking away.

"How long have you been awake?" I pulled up a chair next to hers and leaned over to kiss her soft cheek.

"A while," she said.

"You were fast asleep when I popped in last night."

"Long trip." She narrowed her eyes. "Where did you disappear to?"

My face heated. "Garen showed me the view from the roof terrace. It's so beautiful, Grams."

"What is? Him or the view?"

I inclined my head. "What's that supposed to mean?"

She arched a brow. "Girl, I've lived a long time. I know a spark when I see one. And you and him? Forget a spark. It's more like fireworks."

It was on the tip of my tongue to deny everything, but my grandmother wasn't a woman who was easily fooled. Instead, my shoulders drooped, and I lowered my head.

"One minute I hate him. The next..." I trailed off.

"That's men for you," she said, patting my knee. "When I first met your grandfather back in Ireland, I couldn't stand him. I found him overbearing, obnoxious, arrogant. He constantly riled me and took pleasure in it, too. I used to lie in bed at night and think up ways I could kill him and get away with it." She cackled. "And then I recognized it for what it was. Passion. Lust.

Craving. The kind of attraction me and your grandfather had reminds me of you and Garen. It's rare, girl. Don't throw it away. Embrace it."

"You were the one who told me to be careful," I accused.

She nodded. "That was before I met him. And now I have, that advice still stands. Guard your heart, but don't close it off. If we don't take risks, then what's the point in life?"

I sighed, long and deep. I couldn't deny Garen's attraction to me. It had been right there in the way he'd kissed me on the terrace. But I truly believed I was a dalliance, a brief moment in time, and there was no getting away from the awful things he'd done.

"He's mean to me, Grams. He says and does terrible things."

"And yet here we are." She gestured around the room. "Do you really think he'd do all this for a woman he couldn't stand?"

I pinched the bridge of my nose and shook my head. "I don't know."

"Men are strange creatures, Catriona. Maybe he's like the seven-year-old boy who never grew up and is pulling the pigtails of the girl he likes in the school playground. Or there is some deep-seated psychological issue he's dealing with that makes him a Jekyll and Hyde character. Or he really is a horrible man with narcissistic and Machiavellian tendencies. I don't know the answers to those questions, and neither do you. Only time will reveal the truth. The question you need to answer is whether you care enough to find out."

I turned to stare out the window at the beautiful view of the mountains towering majestically over the lake below. My grandmother was a wise woman, and only an idiot refused to listen to what she had to say. The problem I had was that I didn't know what to do. His mood swings concerned me. I never knew which man would show up. The playful one with a hint of mischief in his eyes or the cruel one who seemed to look for ways to cause the most hurt to whoever he'd set his sights on, and at the moment, that individual was me.

"Come on." I got to my feet. "Let's fetch Aiden and go grab some breakfast. I need to order a cab to take us to the hospital, too." I bit my lip. "Maybe Lia has a number I can call."

Grams set down her knitting and hoisted herself out of the chair. "I'm sure she will have."

As the three of us made our way downstairs, I silently prayed I didn't bump into Garen. After what happened yesterday, I couldn't face him yet. I needed time to work out what that kiss meant to me. I thought I hated him, yet my reaction to his touch had felt very different to hate. Following Grams' perceptive comments, and my own incessant contemplation, I had to face facts: an undeniable attraction to Garen had sprung up out of nowhere, and I couldn't turn it off.

Lia appeared before we'd reached the bottom of the grand staircase wearing a bright-pink apron and an equally bright smile.

"I thought I heard voices," she said, gesturing for us to follow her. "I wasn't sure what you'd like for breakfast so I took the liberty of putting on a whole spread."

My eyes fell on a table groaning under the weight of food. Everything from meats and cheeses, traditional breakfast fare in these parts, to pancakes, bacon, and eggs. Not to mention a variety of cereals, breads, and pastries.

"That's, um, a lot of food," I commented, while Grams, in her inimitable fashion, muttered something about waste. I nudged her, sending her a warning glance. Lia was trying to be nice, that was all.

"Don't worry, whatever doesn't get eaten, the staff will soon devour," she said, correctly reading our dismay.

"How many people work here?" I asked, sliding into a chair and picking up an apple. With Aiden's upcoming appointment, and the way my stomach churned at the thought of it, a piece of fruit was all I could face.

"Seven, including me." She poured coffee into three cups and loaded them onto a tray. "I must admit, it's nice to have someone to fuss over. Mr. Gauthier only comes here about three times a year, and even when he does, he rarely entertains."

"Where is he?" I glanced around as if, by mentioning his name, he'd miraculously appear.

She brought the coffee over and set it on the table. "He's left for the day. He has meetings in the city. I should imagine he'll be back sometime this evening. He did impress upon me that I was to take very good care of you all, and he asked me to let you know the car will be ready outside at ten-fifteen to take you to the hospital."

At that, she cast a sympathetic look at Aiden. Garen must have told her the reason for our visit.

I didn't know whether to feel relieved Garen wasn't here or disappointed. His absence certainly made things a little more comfortable and allowed my shoulders to relax from their new home around my ears.

"Oh, he didn't have to do that," I said, referring to the car. "We could have grabbed a taxi."

Lia sliced her hand through the air. "Nonsense. Mr. Gauthier wouldn't hear of such things."

I felt Grams' eyes on me. I studiously kept my gaze averted, encouraging Aiden to try to eat something before the battery of tests he'd have to undergo today ahead of his first treatment on Monday.

As promised, the car was out front when we emerged into the bright sunshine. A chill wind whipped around my shoulders, despite the clear skies, and I pulled my jacket closer to me, urging first Aiden into the car, and then Grams before I got in last.

The trip to the hospital took about thirty minutes, and as we entered the reception area, the reality of what my brother was about to face surged through me. My heart rate escalated, nearly exploding out of my chest, and my thighs shook. Taking a deep breath, I reminded myself that he was getting the best possible care, and his particular illness had a very high recovery rate.

Positive thinking, Catriona.

Grams and Aiden took a seat while I gave his name to the receptionist. Within minutes, a nurse came to fetch us, and we were taken down a sparklingly clean hallway to the doctor's office.

An hour later we emerged, loaded with information but all of us feeling much more positive about the journey ahead. Dr. Faussman was ebullient about Aiden's treatment plan and his subsequent chances of a full recovery. He explained in minute detail what would happen, and when he said that Aiden could undertake the first two month's treatment as an out-patient, I felt much better. When I returned to Canada next Tuesday, at least Aiden wouldn't be stuck in a hospital room with only Grams for company.

I must talk to Garen about organizing some regular time off, though, so I could fly back to see Aiden and Grams as often as possible. Surely he couldn't deny me that?

Then again, this was Garen Gauthier. Who knew what went on inside his devious mind.

We headed back to Garen's home in the mountains where Aiden promptly disappeared to his room to sleep, and Grams said she felt like a snooze, too. The house was quiet, with no signs of the seven members of staff Lia mentioned this morning. Deciding to explore a bit, I set off for a walk around the extensive and pristine gardens. I'd never seen anything quite like it. The grass looked as though it had been cut with scissors rather than a lawn mower, and the borders teemed with regimented rows of flowers and shrubbery, probably too afraid of the owner to even attempt to grow out of line.

My stomach rumbled, reminding me of the meager apple I'd half-finished a few hours ago. I trundled back to the kitchen and peered inside. No sign of the mountain of food from breakfast. I hoped Lia had called in reinforcements to eat it, rather than let it go to waste.

Driven by hunger, I opened the large stainless-steel fridge and spied a block of cheese. I hunted around for some bread. I worked fast, anxious to get in and out. I wished Lia were here, not because I expected her to make my sandwich, but I wouldn't feel as much of an interloper then.

"Finding everything you need?" a deep, rasping voice asked behind me.

I dropped the knife with a clatter and spun around to find Garen, smartly dressed in a dark-gray suit and looking good enough to eat, standing with his shoulder propped against the wall at the entranceway to the kitchen.

I swallowed, aware of the thump of my heartbeat as I ran my gaze over him. "You scared me. Lia said you weren't due back until this evening."

He shrugged. "My meetings finished earlier than expected." His lips curved into a hint of a smile. "Disappointed, Catriona? Or pleased?"

Do not *answer that.*

I turned my attention back to my sandwich, catching sight of him out of the corner of my eye as he pushed off the wall and walked—or rather stalked—toward me. Passing right by, he leaned down, opened a cabinet, and straightened, holding two white china plates. He set them down beside me, then opened the fridge and removed a bottle of wine. He grabbed two glasses and pointed his chin at my sandwich.

"I'd love one if you wouldn't mind making another. Then perhaps you'd like to join me on the roof terrace for lunch."

I narrowed my eyes, searching his face. For what, I wasn't sure. Maybe I was steeling myself for a cruel taunt or a callous remark. Instead, I found his expression open and interested.

"Sure," I said, hitching one shoulder in what I hoped came across as nonchalant.

I felt his stare heat up the back of my neck as I hastily assembled another cheese sandwich. He sidled up to me until our shoulders touched. I briefly closed my eyes, breathing in the smell of his cologne, his masculine scent, the bodywash he'd used in the shower this morning.

His fingertip touched the nape of my neck, and he traced it slowly down my spine.

"What are you doing?" I whispered, keeping my gaze averted. I didn't trust myself to look at him.

"You have exquisite skin. Soft like silk. And you move with such grace and poise. I could watch you for hours."

My breath hitched. I picked up the knife, cut both sandwiches in half, and put them onto the plates he'd fetched. I picked them up and shifted out of his reach.

"Shall we go?"

Without waiting for a response, I set off up the winding staircase, a fluttery, empty feeling in my stomach.

Just hunger, Catriona. Hunger. Not anticipation and excitement at spending one-on-one time with Garen.

Nope. Not at all.

20

GAREN

This had *never* happened to me before.

I'd left a meeting early, citing a personal issue that needed my immediate attention when I realized I hadn't listened to a single word in more than thirty minutes. Every kilometer that passed during the forty-five-minute trip back here, I'd gotten more and more excited at the thought of seeing Catriona. When she'd run away following our kiss yesterday, I'd left her alone, even though every fiber in my body had urged me to go after her and demand an answer to the burning question: What did this mean?

She'd said she couldn't bear for me to touch her, but that was a lie she told herself to avoid facing up to the reality. She was as attracted to me as I was to her. I felt it in the way her mouth parted, how she clung to my arms, the enthusiasm in how her tongue jousted with mine. Her horrified reaction had been a reflex to the situation she found herself in.

I'd given her some space. Now I was determined to crowd

her, to force her to confront her feelings. I would not allow her to retreat. To run and hide. To continue to lock up the passion I'd sensed coursing through her veins.

I wanted to conquer her, fuck her, watch with fascination as she came undone beneath me, as much as a test for me as for her. Catriona Landry absorbed my every waking moment, and I found myself curious whether that obsession would dissipate as soon as I got her into bed.

It could go either way.

I led her out onto the roof terrace. After a chilly start to the day, normal for this time of year, the warmth of the afternoon sun beat down. I set the wine and the glasses on the coffee table and took a seat on one of two couches set at right angles. Where Catriona chose to sit would give me an idea where her head was at.

When she sat beside me, I held back a triumphant grin. She handed me my sandwich, then rested her plate on her knees and picked hers up. Taking a bite, she chewed slowly while gazing down at the lake. I poured the wine and pushed a glass in front of her.

"It's very peaceful here," she said with a little sigh that perked up my dick. "So beautiful."

"It is," I agreed. "Very beautiful. Made more so by you sitting here beside me."

She turned to me, her expression full of suspicion. "What do you want, Garen?"

I deposited my plate on the table and rested my arm along the back of the couch, close enough to touch her hair. I casually crossed my left ankle over the opposing knee and reached out, clasping a lock that I twirled through my fingers. "I thought I'd made it perfectly clear. I want you, Catriona."

"Why?" she asked, inclining her head in genuine interest. "You're... mean to me."

I chuckled, because it was true. At least sometimes. On

occasion, the urge to say hurtful things to her, to perform heinous acts like making her think she'd have to suck me off to help her brother, overwhelmed me, and I'd give in to my baser, ruthless instincts. Then other times I'd feel a desperate need to protect and support her. To just be with her, and not because I wanted to fuck her, but to hear her laugh, listen to her thoughts, and watch her take pleasure in the simple and unspoiled beauty around her.

The dichotomy was driving me crazy.

"Am I being mean now?" I traced the tip of my finger along the back of her neck, replicating the move I'd made in the kitchen.

She shuddered, and her eyes briefly closed. "No," she whispered. "But in the next breath, you could be."

I cupped her nape and shuffled closer until my thigh pressed up against hers. "How about if I try harder?"

She blinked at me, her green eyes reminding me of Lake Carezza in Italy, so vibrant I wanted to dive right in. I should take her there one day.

Fuck. What the hell am I thinking? There would be no trip to Italy. As soon as I fucked her a few times, I was certain this weird hold she had over me would disappear. First things first—get her into bed. Worry about the rest later.

"I think you're you, Garen. Leopards don't change their spots."

A stabbing inside my chest took me by surprise, and an impulse to prove her wrong engulfed me. Words came cheap. I needed to show her with actions. I'd have to dig deep and demonstrate to her that I had a compassionate side. Hidden very deep, but if I mined for it, it'd come to the surface.

"Come to dinner with me tomorrow night. There's an amazing place not far from here where you can sit out on the veranda and look down at the city and the lake below. It's peaceful, and the food is outstanding."

She bowed her head. "Grams and Aiden might need me."

"Lia will be here," I cajoled. "She'd love to spoil them with a specially cooked meal. And Aiden can watch movies in the cinema room if he'd like. Or play games. Whatever he prefers."

Shielding her eyes from the sun, she said, "You have a cinema room?"

I grinned. "I must get Lia to give you all the guided tour. Come on, Catriona. You know you want to. Aiden'll have a blast, and Lia would love to have some company if your grandmother is willing. I don't come here very often."

"Yeah, Lia mentioned that this morning."

I canted my head, mildly curious about what my housekeeper had shared with our new guests. "She did? What else did she say?"

She nibbled on her lip, drawing my eye. I suppressed a groan. *Patience.*

"She told me to be very careful, that when you do come here, you bring women and then they are never seen again."

My eyebrows shot up, fury zipping through my veins in an instant. I clenched my hands into fists, a reflex to the anger boiling up inside. I'd fucking kill her. Two women I'd brought here. *Two.* And both had been a gigantic mistake.

Catriona burst into a fit of giggles. "You should see your face," she said between gasping for air. "Hilarious."

As I realized I'd been had, I lunged for Catriona. She leaped to her feet and sprinted across the terrace, giggling. I ran after her. She moved fast, but I was faster. I snagged her around the waist and spun her around. She was out of breath, and her hair was all mussed up.

Fuck me, she'd never looked hotter. I hardened instantly.

"Little tip for you," I said, my lips hovering dangerously close to hers. "Giving chase turns me on."

She managed to snatch a single breath before I kissed her. I snaked my arms around her waist and held her against me.

She'd have no doubt how much I wanted her, but just to drive home the strength of my need for her, I slid my hands to her ass, circled my hips, and ground against her like a fucking teenager. The groan she let slip almost made me come in my pants. The scent of her perfume filled my nostrils, sweet and fragrant, and addictive.

I knew the second her mind gained control of her body. She stiffened in my arms, and while our lips were still connected, our tongues still exploring, I'd give it five seconds until she wriggled out of my arms.

I counted to four.

"Garen," she panted, shaking her head at the same time her eyes pleaded with me to carry on, to take it to the next level. "I'm sorry. I just don't trust you not to hurt me, use me, fuck me, and forget me."

I drew my knuckles down her warm cheek. "I could never forget you, Catriona."

A ghost of a smile appeared on her lips. "Interesting that out of the four choices, that was the one you focused on."

Shit. I briefly closed my eyes. "You're reading too much into it."

"Am I?"

"Yes," I insisted. "Look, come to dinner. We can talk. I'm aware we haven't had the most auspicious of starts, but I like you. You don't take my shit, and I respect that. I want a chance to get to know you better, and to have you get to know me, too."

She lifted her chin and stared right into my eyes, her own hauntingly innocent with a steely underlayer. She kept me waiting, a punishment no doubt, and one I'd likely earned ten times over. Eventually, she put me out of my misery with a short nod.

"Okay."

"Great," I said, triumphant in my victory. For a brief

moment, I thought I was losing my touch. "Now, let's finish our lunch and enjoy a glass of wine while taking in the view."

She narrowed her eyes. "You just love getting your own way, don't you?"

I winked. "Who doesn't?"

She emitted an irritated huff, but when I held out my hand and she took it, my heart thrashed about against my ribcage, and my stomach clenched. Somewhere along the line, this had become less about just another conquest, a notch on my overflowing headboard, and while I didn't understand the emotions streaming through me right now, I had enough emotional intelligence to understand they were different, unusual, the kinds of sensations that were fresh and exciting, and that I was eager to explore.

"I still don't trust you." She bit into the second half of her sandwich.

I grinned, picked up my wineglass, and tapped the base against hers. "That's because you're smart."

21

Catriona

I frowned into the mirror and tugged at the sides of my dress. It was a simple wraparound that ended just above my knees. I wasn't all together happy with it, but beggars couldn't be choosers. When I'd packed to come here, it hadn't occurred to me to bring going-out clothes. Why would it have? The original plan had been to stay here until Tuesday morning and then fly back to Canada. Not to mention Garen wasn't supposed to be here at all.

A nibble of anxiety arose within my stomach. I couldn't see Garen eating at the local diner, or chain restaurant, and while I was hardly familiar with smart, exclusive establishments, even I knew I wasn't dressed accordingly. Maybe I should have gone shopping. I could have easily caught a cab into Geneva and purchased a more suitable outfit.

With a resigned sigh, I brushed my nerves aside. If my attire wasn't good enough for Mr. Billionaire, he'd have to suck it up.

He was the one who'd pushed to take me to dinner until I caved.

A tap at my door was followed by Grams hobbling through. She took in my garb with a full head-to-toe eye sweep.

"I know, I know." I threw my hands in the air. "It's more suited to a fast-food joint than a fancy restaurant, but what else can I do?"

Grams arched a brow in query. "Why are you so concerned, Catriona? A couple of days ago, you couldn't stand the man. And now here you are, fussing over a perfectly suitable dress."

I caught the twinkle in her eye and scowled. "Stop teasing me."

She came to stand in front of me, brushing at a piece of fluff that had hitched a ride on the left sleeve. "Remember this, girl. You are his equal. I don't give a flying flick how much money he has in the bank. He still visits the bathroom like the rest of us. Stand tall, shoulders back, and be proud of who you are, which is a damn fine woman he's lucky to have on his arm."

A smile inched across my face at Grams and her curse word stand-ins. "You're a wise woman, Grams."

"Pfft." Her hand sliced through the air. "When you've lived as long as I have, very little surprises you. Now listen to me. I can see how your opinion has shifted over the last couple of days. You thought this man was a monster, an evil, cruel being who took pleasure in taunting you, yet now, you're seeing a different side. As long as you stay true to who you are, you'll be fine. Just don't let him coerce you into anything you're not comfortable with. Remember, you're in control, whatever he might think."

I bent down and kissed her soft, wrinkled cheek. "Love you, Grams."

"Oh, be gone with you, girl," she said, although I could tell my compliment had pleased her.

"Will you and Aiden be all right here by yourselves?"

She raised her eyes to the ceiling. "I don't need a babysitter, thank you very much, and neither does your brother. Now go. Be young for a change. Eat the food, drink the wine, kiss the man."

"Grams!" I scolded.

She shooed me away with a flick of her wrist. "Go, or I'll take your place. I like the idea of a rich, handsome man on my arm for the evening."

I chuckled as I left my room and set off toward the elaborate staircase. Grams was a real character, and my life was richer for having her in it. But her sage words rang in my ear. However much I'd thawed toward Garen, underneath his philanthropy lay a ruthless man who put his own interests before anyone else's. I must remember that he expected payment for funding Aiden's treatment and accommodation. When we returned to Canada next week, I'd no doubt find myself called upon to perform some kind of duties, although the details of those still confused me. To attend dinners and banquets and smile at politicians. No matter which way I cut it, I still thought it a very odd request for a man who could click his fingers and have a bevy of beauties lined up in five minutes flat.

I reached the top of the stairs, and my eyes fell on Garen waiting at the bottom. I hadn't seen him since our impromptu lunch yesterday, and his scorching good looks stole my breath. He'd dressed in a single-breasted suit that probably cost more than I made in a year, and he smiled when he spotted me, sending a shiver of pleasure inching down my spine.

Self-consciously, I picked my way down the stairs, hoping I didn't stumble. Not that I expected to. One thing being a dancer gave me was superb balance. But with Garen's hot gaze traveling over every inch of me as I put one foot in front of the other, it wasn't beyond the realm of possibility to fall over one of them and splat onto my face.

"You look lovely," he said, holding out his arm for me to take. "Shall we go?"

I nodded, ducking my head to hide the dash of pink in my cheeks brought on both by his compliment, and relief my dress mustn't be too out of place after all.

Cocooned in the interior of the car with the smell of leather invading my nostrils, I glanced out of the window as we smoothly drove away to find Grams standing just inside the front door, waving. I waved back.

"Your grandmother is a fearsome woman," Garen said, drawing my attention to him. "And one hell of a character."

I smiled. "I agree, on both counts."

"I'm probably taking my life in my hands by telling you this, but she sought me out earlier to give me a stark warning that if I didn't take good care of you, she'd cut off my balls."

My eyes widened. She never said a thing to me. The sly old woman. Just wait until I saw her next. But despite the hint of annoyance at her interference, the fact it came from her desire to protect me warmed my heart.

"My grandmother did *not* say she'd cut off your man bits."

He snickered. "She didn't use those exact words, no, but her intention was clear."

"Well then, you'd better pay attention. Grams isn't in the business of making idle threats."

He reached for my hand and drew it to his lips where he pressed a soft kiss to my knuckles, his hot gaze on me. "I intend to."

Goose bumps skittered down my arms, and my insides twisted violently. "Can I ask you something?"

He nodded. "Sure."

"Why did you fabricate a job offer when you already had what you wanted the second I signed the sale agreement for my ballet studio?"

He inclined his head, his eyes searching my face. "Who said it's a fabricated job?"

I snorted. "Come on. So far you've had me scan documents into a computer and negotiate with a paper pusher from the council, both of which countless other people could have done equally well."

"I disagree," he said, offering up a lopsided smile. "You had that idiot in the palm of your hand in five seconds. Your approach bore far greater dividends than my idea to throttle the fucker would have done."

"Garen," I said, a warning note to my voice. "Don't do this."

He nonchalantly rubbed his fingertips over his mouth, but the tic in his jaw gave him away. "Okay, I'll level with you. As soon as you agreed to sell the studio, there was no reason for our paths to cross ever again. I didn't want that."

"Why?" I wanted answers that would reveal a little of himself to me. Garen kept his cards very close to his chest, and I wanted to see how much he was willing to share.

"I have no idea," he said. "What I do know is that the impulse to stop you walking out of my life urged me to act." He raised his left shoulder. "This way we both acquired something out of the deal. You got to help your brother, and I... got you."

I couldn't help smiling. "You're a walking contradiction. One minute, cruel and mean, then the next thoughtful and agreeable."

His lips twisted to one side. "I still expect you to work for me, Catriona. Don't be fooled into thinking you've gotten off scot-free. There's a debt to be paid, and you will pay it, one way or another."

I cracked a smile. "And there he is. The asshole is back."

Garen paused for a beat, and then he threw back his head and laughed. "And don't you forget it."

"I wouldn't dream of it."

He slid his tongue along the underside of his top teeth, his eyes roving over my face, then slipping south to linger on my cleavage.

"I should punish you for insolence."

Embers of desire flickered in my abdomen, and I clenched my thighs together to relieve the growing ache in my core. "I wouldn't if I were you. I have my grandmother's fiery spirit."

He edged closer to me until his lips were a mere breath from my own and slid his hand to the nape of my neck. "And that's what turns me on."

He took my mouth in a soft, exploratory, unhurried manner, tasting me and allowing me to taste him. Our tongues touched, and like a firework going off, the tightly contained passion between us exploded. He caressed my breast, and a jolt of electricity fired through me, and when his thumb brushed over my elongated nipple, I let out a moan and arched my back, demanding more.

"I knew your tits would fit my hand perfectly," he murmured, dropping featherlike kisses over my jaw, down my neck, heading toward my cleavage. He separated the two pieces of my dress and tugged down the lace cup of my bra. He drew my nipple between his teeth and I cried out, then clasped a hand over my mouth, remembering where we were. The privacy screen might be activated, but I doubted it was soundproof.

"Make as much noise as you like. It's soundproof," Garen said as if he'd read my mind. "In fact, I insist upon it. By the end of the night, I guarantee you'll scream my name loud enough to shake snow from the tops of the mountains."

"Arrogant men are a turnoff," I retorted, gasping when he pushed my breasts together and sucked on both nipples at the same time. "Fuuuck."

"How easily I expose your lies, Catriona." He nuzzled my skin and burrowed his hand beneath my dress, applying pressure to my inner thighs until I opened them. Easing my panties to the side, he glided one finger inside me. "Christ, you're wet. Look what I do to you, *mon petit chaton*. Do you have any idea how hard that makes me?"

"Garen," I begged, thrusting my pelvis upward, desperate for more.

He pressed his thumb to my clit, moving it in slow, lazy circles, and inserted a second finger into my channel while using his lips and his tongue on my nipples. He grazed his nails along the front wall of my vagina, and I nearly shot through the roof. *I'm close. So close.* But as my body crested, he stopped.

I tilted my pelvis, urging him on. "I'm almost there."

He drew back, licked his fingers, and grinned at me wickedly. "I know."

"Then why have you stopped?"

"I want you on the edge while we eat dinner. I want you right there, desperate for release, but unable to come without me making it happen."

I widened my eyes, stunned at the harsh treatment. "Why would you do that?"

He waggled his eyebrows. "Because it's fun."

"For who?" I cried, frustration making me overreact. I hadn't felt a man's touch in a long time, and to be so close to a much-needed orgasm, and then have it snatched away, had enraged me more than it should.

"If you're good, I'll let you come on the way home."

"If I'm— You know what. Screw you. I can make myself come. I don't need you."

In an act very unlike me—I wasn't remotely the exhibitionist type—I shoved my hand into my panties.

Garen grabbed my wrist, stopping me. "While I am far from averse to watching you masturbate, and I will definitely add it to the list of future enjoyable activities, it's a no."

I expelled a sound that came out remarkably like a growl which only widened his grin.

"If it makes you feel any better, this is as difficult for me as it is for you."

"Doubtful," I groused, pouting.

He took my hand and held it to his groin. Underneath lay a rod of steel, impressive girth, and a length that sent a shudder of anticipation racing through me. My fingers automatically flexed around him, and he groaned.

"Hold that thought, Catriona. Tonight, I'm making you mine."

22

Garen

The scallops tasted like cardboard, the steak like rubber, and the panoramic view might as well not have existed. All I could think about was getting Catriona beneath me, of sliding my dick inside her wet folds, tasting her pussy, shoving my face between her tits and never leaving. It had been a mistake to start things up in the car, although denying her an orgasm was right up there with the most fun I'd had all month. The incensed expression on her face, tinged with a strong desire to kill me, had given me an erection I'd dream about for days to come. Hence, I'd had a semi all night.

"It's really lovely here," Catriona remarked, pulling me from my internal thoughts. "That view is something else. Even though it's dark now, I can still see the lights twinkling on the lake."

I reached for her hand, clasping it in mine. "Next time I'll bring you for lunch so you can get the full experience," I said, brushing my thumb over her knuckles.

"Next time?"

"You sound surprised? Surely you'll want to see Aiden regularly."

"I do," she said. "In fact, I wanted to talk to you about that. I'd like to come see him every two weeks if that's possible."

"You can visit as often as you'd like," I said. "As long as I'm not using the jet, it's at your disposal."

She leaned her elbow on the table and rested her chin on the hand I wasn't holding. "Why are you being so nice?"

I chuckled. "Would you prefer a cruel response? I can oblige if it would make you feel better."

She gave me one of her scolding looks, and my dick perked up, ready for action. *Down, boy. Not yet.*

"What about the things you need me to do for you?"

She licked her lips and lowered her gaze. If the table wasn't in the way, her eyes would be right on my dick.

Fuck me, she's flirting.

I released a soft groan. "We'll work it out," I said, my voice low and husky. Glancing around, I spotted our server and beckoned to him. "Check, please."

"What if I wanted dessert," Catriona stated when he retreated.

We both knew she wasn't talking about key lime pie or Eton mess.

I shifted in my chair, the movement causing my zipper to rub against my dick. "Don't worry," I rasped. "You'll get dessert."

I scrawled my signature on the check and rose to my feet, snatching up Catriona's hand. We weaved through the tables with my dick leading the way, or at least it would be if it wasn't trapped against my stomach by my pants.

My driver had parked right out front, and the second the door closed, encasing us inside the warm cabin, I pushed Catriona onto her back and straddled her. I pulled apart her dress—fuck me, wraparound dresses were the best invention ever—and buried my face between her tits.

"Mmm, the perfect dessert."

She giggled and pushed down on the back of my head while arching her spine. I tugged down both lace cups, bunching them beneath the full, round globes. Flicking my tongue from one nipple to the other drove her crazy if her panting and soft moans were any indication.

I sat back on my heels and glided my hands up her thighs. She gazed up at me, her eyes half closed and drowsy with desire. I hooked my thumbs into her panties and eased them down her legs.

A wicked idea came to me. I grabbed her wrists, wrapped her panties around them, then hooked the makeshift tie through the door handle behind her head. I ran my gaze over her, dress shoved to the side, bra nestled beneath her tits, pussy bared to me, glistening with the evidence of her lust both from now and earlier.

"I think you might be the hottest thing I've ever seen," I ground out, delving my head between her legs. I swirled my tongue in a circle around her clit.

She gasped, her hips writhing, driving forward in the hope of any kind of friction. "Please," she moaned.

"That's it, *petit chaton*. Beg."

"Arrogant bas—ohhhhh."

I lapped inside her, cutting off her response, and floated my fingertips up her sides, reaching for her tits. I kneaded them, then pinched both nipples between my thumbs and forefingers and tugged hard.

"Jesus!"

She exploded onto my tongue, her body jerking and shaking, her hips thrusting upward in a desperate attempt for more contact. The taste of her was better than the finest wine and the most expensive caviar. I could eat her all day, every day.

I caged her with my body and kissed her, licking inside her mouth while rubbing my cock against her. Leaning over, I released her hands and gently rubbed her wrists. She fumbled for the button on my trousers, but I stopped her.

"We're at the house," I said by way of explanation. I drew the two pieces of her dress together, then tucked her panties into my pocket. "No point putting these back on. You won't need them tonight."

"What if Grams sees?" she asked, smoothing her hands over her hair which I'd thoroughly ruffled.

"Unless you're planning to do cartwheels down the hallway, I doubt she'll know you're panty-less," I said, grinning.

She slammed the heel of her palm against my shoulder. "Jerk."

I drew my teeth over her bottom lip. "I think you mean jerk off, which I plan to do all over your tits once I get you to my bedroom."

Shock rolled across her face, and then she laughed. "If your employees could hear you now."

I shrugged. "They've been gossiping about me for years. Nothing new there."

We snuck into the house like a couple of teenagers out past their curfew and sprinted up the stairs. Catriona and her family were staying in the east wing. My suite of rooms was in the west wing, and I turned that way now, striding down the hallway, edging on desperate to get her naked and beneath me as fast as possible.

I opened the door to my bedroom and tugged her inside, then kicked the door closed with my foot. I crashed my mouth down on hers, yanking at the tie that held her dress together. Shoving the material off her shoulders, I allowed the dress to fall to the floor, then leaned into her, giving her no choice but to walk backward. Her knees hit the bed, and she toppled onto the mattress, giggling as she peered up at me from beneath her long eyelashes.

I shrugged out of my jacket and, with my eyes on hers, unbuttoned my shirt. I tossed it on top of the growing pile of clothes, then went for the button on my pants. Removing them also, I stood at the foot of the bed in my boxer shorts, my dick hard and long, the head sticking out over the top of the boxers, a bead of moisture already gathered on the tip. I slid my underwear down my legs then stood there, heat flooding my body as Catriona ate me with her eyes, starting at my feet, lingering on my groin, licking her lips as her gaze moved over my abs, up to my chest, and finally finished on my face.

"You, um, work out then," she stated with another sweep of her tongue over lips that I couldn't wait to have wrapped around my cock.

I climbed on to the bed and straddled her hips. My dick bobbed, and I wrapped a hand around the base and tugged, once. A groan fell from my lips.

"What do you taste like?" she whispered, her green irises sparkling as she focused on the pre-cum oozing from my slit.

I shuffled forward until my knees were level with her shoulders. "Suck," I said, pressing the head of my cock to her lips.

She drew me inside her mouth, and my balls tightened. "Jesus. Oh fuck," I ground out when she hollowed out her cheeks and took me to the back of her throat.

She released me with a pop and shook her head.

"This won't do. I'm at the wrong angle. Let me up, Garen."

She shoved at me until I moved to the side. Grabbing a pillow, she dropped it on the floor beside the bed and knelt. "Come here, to the edge."

I wasn't a man who would normally allow a woman to take the reins in the bedroom, or control what happened outside of the bedroom either, but there was something about the sight of Catriona kneeling in front of me, and the firm tone to her voice, laced with a command I had no intention of ignoring, that had me scrambling to obey.

"Yes, ma'am."

Her smile lit me up from the inside, and not only because I was about to get a blow job which, let's face it, every guy fucking loved. No, something else was going on here, something deeper and more meaningful.

She wrapped her small hand around the base of my dick and licked me from base to tip, right along where a thick vein pumped blood to my shaft. I shuddered, then gasped when she closed her mouth over the crown and sucked.

"Ah, shit."

I fisted the sheets as the head hit the back of her throat before she drew back and repeated the whole thing again.

"Christ, where did you learn how to do this?" I groaned, a pointless question considering her mouth was full, rendering speech impossible. "Actually, forget I asked." I didn't want to know how she'd become so proficient in sucking cock. I feared practice yet hoped for instinct.

I felt her grin and watched with fascination as she sucked me deep, her hand moving up and down my shaft with exactly the right amount of speed and pressure. My balls drew up, and I knew I was about three seconds away from orgasm.

I gripped her hair and lifted her off me, then spurted all over her tits, exactly as I'd promised back in the car.

"Fuck," I bit out, pumping my shaft, my dick jerking, my balls emptying of my seed. My head lolled back, and my eyes closed as I absorbed the pleasure shuddering through my body. When I opened them, I found Catriona still kneeling at my feet, white blobs of cum dripping between her breasts and onto the soft swell of her stomach. A weird feeling, a kind of pressure settled on my chest, and, on examination, I recognized it as pride. I was *proud* I'd marked her, that she was sitting there with *my* cum all over her.

She smiled up at me. "You look hot when you orgasm."

I laughed and stood. "Stay there. I'll get a cloth."

Turning on the faucet, I waited for the water to heat up, then reached for the stack of face towels and ran one underneath the warm water. After wringing it out, I returned to the bedroom and cleaned her up. I held out my hand and helped her to her feet, then reached into the nightstand and removed a box of condoms.

"Get on the bed, Catriona. It's my turn to be in control. Prepare yourself. You're in for a long night."

23

Catriona

I shuffled up the bed, my eyes greedily skirting over Garen's taut frame, watching with a growing sense of need as his muscles bunched and flexed with every movement. Despite having only just climaxed, his cock was already semi-hard. I reached for him only to find my wrists clamped together, held solidly in one of his.

He canted his head. "Uh-uh, kitty cat. I already told you I'm in charge."

A shiver traveled the full length of my body, and I bit my lip, anticipating Garen's next move. Keeping my hands imprisoned, he reached beside the bed and returned holding his discarded shirt. "Now, if we were at my home in Canada, I'd have more… weapons in my armory. As it is, this will have to do."

He swiftly tied each sleeve to my wrist then looped the two parts of the shirt around the headboard, leaving me securely bound and unable to move my arms. My stomach fluttered like the wings of a bird bashing against its confines, and I struggled to control my breathing.

"What do you mean, weapons?"

He grinned lasciviously. "When we return home, you'll find out."

The soft tissue of my heart beat against my ribcage, and blood roared through my ears. Garen sat back on his heels and studied me, the tips of his lean fingers stroking his chin, considering. His gaze flicked over me, settling on the thatch of hair between my legs. A blush crept over my skin at his open appraisal of my most private area which, *come on, Catriona*, was ridiculous considering that not long ago, he'd had his mouth and his tongue in that exact place. The time for embarrassment had long since passed.

He climbed off the bed. "Don't move."

"A pointless request since you have me tied to your bed."

He laughed, then crossed the room and disappeared through a door. I caught a glimpse of rows of suits and pants. Must be his closet. He reappeared, and clutched in his hands was a red tie. He stalked toward me, threading it through his fingers, his cock now fully erect and bobbing between his hips.

"What's that for?" I asked, even though I could guess, and the very idea had a flush of wetness surging to the apex of my thighs. I'd had sex before, but never anything more than your common or garden variety. Missionary mainly. A few instances of oral sex, bad oral sex usually, but nothing remotely adventurous. When Garen had bound my hands with my panties in the car, the inability to move my arms, to touch him, had excited me far more than I would have ever thought possible, and now I had an urge to experiment. Looked like I'd found the right guy for that.

"I'm going to blindfold you."

Straddling me once more, he fastened it around my head, covering my eyes. I should be scared, or at the very least wary. A few days earlier I hated this man with every part of my being, yet now here I was, lying naked in his bed and allowing him to tie me up, to blindfold me.

To fuck me.

Yet I wasn't fearful. I was turned on.

I'd study how I'd shifted my opinion so considerably another day. Today was not that day.

Light seeped in from above and below the makeshift eye mask, but as far as seeing anything other than the occasional shadow I was, for all intents and purposes, completely cut off from any visuals.

Music filled the room, soft notes, and then a woman's haunting voice echoed, the incredible sound covering my skin in goose bumps. Classical music. My favorite. Reminded me of ballet.

"Comfortable?"

Garen's rasping voice sounded off to my right. At least I think that was where it came from. The general consensus was that when one or two senses were cut off, all the rest heightened to make up for the loss. Mine hadn't gotten the memo because when his voice came at me again, it was in my left ear.

"Cat got your tongue, *chaton?*"

I swallowed past a boulder lodged in my throat. "I'm good."

His lips brushed against mine. I lifted my head to maintain contact, but he moved away, chuckling. I growled, drawing a louder snigger from him.

"My little kitty has claws, I see." His teeth grazed my earlobe. "Good thing I restrained you then."

I bit down on my lip and squirmed my legs, desperate for any kind of friction. Garen's hands clamped on my inner thighs, and he pushed my legs apart, leaning on me so I couldn't move.

"I could stare at your glistening pussy all day," he said, blowing on my folds.

I gasped, then groaned when he did it again. "More," I begged.

"More what, Catriona?"

"More you."

"Do you want my tongue, my hands, or my cock here?" He grazed a fingertip from my clit to my ass, then back up again, then inserted two fingers into my channel.

I tried to arch my back but couldn't with my arms secured behind my head and Garen holding down my legs.

"All of it," I begged.

"Greedy girl," he murmured, crooking his fingers to graze my inner front wall.

Just as I was relishing the fullness, he withdrew, and then his fingers touched my lips.

"Suck."

The repetition of the word he'd used when he'd pressed his cock to my mouth pulled a long groan from me, one that came from deep within my belly. I lapped at him, tasting my own arousal, licking every drop he gave me.

He fingered me again, then withdrew. I parted my lips, waiting for a repeat. Instead, he said, "Mmm. I could get addicted to the taste of you, Catriona."

I writhed, heat flooding my core. He clamped a large hand down on each of my thighs. "You're a wriggler," he said. "I'd tie your ankles, too, but then I wouldn't have the enjoyment of your legs around my neck when I fuck you."

"Jesus," I muttered, images flooding my mind, made more vivid by the inability to see. Garen, jaw tight, forehead creased, concentration warring on his features as he thrust into me over and over. Watching the way he squeezed his eyes closed and chewed down on his lip when he came. The way his face smoothed at the end of his climax in pure bliss at the height of pleasure.

He licked my clit slowly, then traveled up my body,

leaving a trail of kisses and little flicks with his tongue in his wake. When he reached my breasts, I held my breath. *Please.* My nipples ached for his attention, and while I couldn't see them, I knew they were elongated, waiting for his mouth, the areola pebbled and drawn inward. I thrust my chest upward, toward what I hoped was his mouth. I could feel his warm breath, and I imagined him hovering over me, reveling in my torture.

"You're killing me."

"I know." A soft puff of air blew over my right nipple. "Should I pay attention to this one first?" Another wisp over my left nipple. "Or this one? Or maybe both together."

My intended reply died on my lips the second his large hands clasped my breasts. He pushed them together and then sucked on them simultaneously. An explosion of raw need turned my insides out, and I thrashed my legs, searching for something to give me a little friction. I found his cock, long, thick, hard as a rod of steel. I ground against him, my clit finally getting the contact it needed.

"God, yes," I moaned, craving him everywhere at once.

He reared back, and then I heard the distinctive sound of a foil wrapper being ripped. As he settled between my legs again, I wrapped my ankles around his hips, dug my heels into his ass, and drove him into me in one swift move.

"Fuck," Garen expelled. "Jesus Christ."

A sense of accomplishment hurtled through me. He thought he was in control, but he wasn't. Even bound and blindfolded, I was running the show.

"You're a bad girl, Catriona Landry," Garen whispered in my ear, his stroke sure and even, although his voice had a hitch to it that gave him away. He wasn't nearly as disciplined as he liked to make out. "Wrap your legs around my neck."

I did as he asked, grateful for the supreme flexibility gifted to me by dancing. From this angle, he drove deeper, filling me completely. The head of his cock bumped the neck of my womb, or at least that's what it felt like, and I grunted.

"Okay?" he ground out, and I imagined him spilling the words between clenched teeth, the hard planes of his jaw flexing as he fought for control.

"Yes. Don't stop."

He pounded into me, his balls slapping against my ass, helped by the angle of my lower body. Heat spread through my belly, and my legs quivered as a growing pressure built up, hurling me toward an inevitable climax. Just a little more friction.

As if he read my mind, he rubbed my clit, and I fell, tumbling over and over into a blissful state I never wanted to leave. I cried out his name, my calf muscles twitching against his ears.

"Fuck, Catriona," he murmured. He thrust twice more, then stilled, his breathing sharp and short in my ear.

I lowered my legs to his waist and hugged him to me, and we lay like that for at least a minute, our breaths slowly leveling out.

Garen pushed the tie over the top of my head, and I blinked, squinting as light flooded my retinas. He swiftly untied my wrists, then rolled to the side. His arm came around me, and he tucked my head into his chest. I snuggled into him, feeling more relaxed than I had in a very long time.

"Are you an only child?" I asked, the desire to find out about his background coming over me.

He raised his head a bit and caught my eye. "Why? Are you hoping for a more attractive brother?"

I raised my eyes to the ceiling. "No. I'm just curious. I don't know anything about you."

He flopped back onto the pillow. "Yes, I'm an only child. I bet you're thinking that explains why I'm such an asshole.

Spoiled as a kid." He chuckled. "You'd be right. I have wonderful parents."

A rush of envy sent tears to the backs of my eyes. I blinked them away. "My parents died when I was twelve."

He shifted onto his side and caressed my cheek. "I know. I'm sorry. I can't imagine how rough that must have been."

"It was. For me. Aiden doesn't even remember them. He was only two." I sighed. "I hope you tell your parents that you love them all the time. None of us know what's around the corner."

An odd expression crossed his face. "They live in Montreal. I don't get to see them very often, but I call once a week."

"Good." I pulled my lips to one side as a thought occurred to me. "How did you know about my parents?"

He grinned. "I know everything, Miss Landry. Remember that."

He began to tickle me, and I squealed and shoved at him, but he was an immovable wall. Our laughter filled the air, and then, in the next breath, he stopped, a frown drawing his eyebrows inward.

"What's the matter?" I asked, my chest tingling. I didn't like that expression. He appeared confused at best, regretful at worst.

He shook his head. "I don't know who I am with you. I'm not me."

I moved onto my side, trying not to let his words upset me. I tucked my palms underneath the pillow. "What does that mean?"

He expelled a long breath through his nose, and *still* he wouldn't look at me. I started to regret allowing him to use the blindfold. If he'd let me see him while he fucked me, I might have been able to read his mood easier. We'd gone from light flirting to solemnity in a couple of minutes. The problem was, we didn't really know each other. We'd met through adversity, discovered a mutual attraction, and now our relationship had shifted into unknown territory for both of us.

I placed a hand on his chest. "Do you want me to go?"

He gave me his eyes then, his head swiveling so fast he must have cricked his neck. "No," he stated firmly. "I don't want you to go."

"Then what do you want?"

He shifted onto his side, and my hand fell away. He clasped my wrist and placed my hand on his chest again, this time right over his heart.

"I'm no good for you. You know that, right? I will hurt you. It's in my nature."

My throat tightened, and my chest felt as though someone was sitting on it, the pressure forcing air from my lungs. His words and his actions were diametrically opposed.

"You already hurt me when you bought my studio," I said, hiding how even saying that out loud wounded me. "I survived."

He blinked slowly, running the tips of his fingers over my knuckles where my hand still rested on his chest, his heart beating steadily beneath my palm.

"I'm twenty-nine years old, and the most dates I've ever been on with any woman is four. And believe me, there have been a lot of women. And that fourth date? I'd only show up because I'd had a shitty day and I knew that a fuck would release some of the tension riding me. That's the kind of man I am. The man who ruthlessly blackmailed you into selling your ballet studio, the one who forced you to your knees and told you to blow me if you wanted to save your brother's life." He grimaced. "The man who takes pleasure in causing you pain and upset, like I did that day at the building site. I enjoyed your tears, your agony. I fed on it. That's what I do, Catriona. That's where I get my joy. I don't know why. I haven't a clue what it is about you, specifically, that makes me want to hurt you one minute and kiss you the next, but it's there, and I can't control it." He blew out a steadying breath. "There's something about you that brings out the very worst in me, and it's fucking with my head."

Oh, Garen. My heart squeezed tight. I flexed my fingers beneath his, and he let me go, but those eyes, he kept them right on me.

"Want to know what I think?"

He shrugged. "Probably not."

A faint smile touched my lips. "Y'know, a week ago, I hated your guts. Or at least I thought I did. And yes, you've hurt me with the relentless pursuit of your own agenda. And that is who you are, at least when it comes to business. Single-minded, merciless, heartless even. But then there're these moments when you're kind and thoughtful, and it's that man I'm attracted to, not the one you describe. You might not be any good for me, Garen, and yes, if I stick around, I might get hurt, but I'm willing to take the risk."

His gaze flickered over my face, searching for the truth in my words, and then he rolled onto his back and pulled me on top of him. "You might live to regret it."

"I might," I agreed. "But at least I'll have lived."

24

Catriona

The warmth of the sun peeking through the blinds drew me out of my slumber. I stretched my arms overhead, my fingers brushing the headboard. Memories of last night when Garen tied me up with his shirt came flooding back, and I squirmed, pressing my thighs together to stem an ache that instantly appeared.

I shifted onto my left side. Garen lay on his back, the sheet around his waist revealing taut, tanned abs and a light dusting of hair that started at his navel and arrowed downward. He had one arm flung overhead, the other resting on his stomach.

I reached out to touch him, then withdrew. He looked different in sleep, peaceful, and the often-present harsh tilt to his lips was absent.

My bladder felt fit to burst, and I folded back the sheet and slipped out of bed, padding over to the door where Garen had fetched the cloth to wipe his cum off of me last night. My face heated at the memory, and I snuck inside quickly in case Garen woke and asked why I was blushing. Not a conversation I particularly wanted to have. Doing the deed was all well and good, but talking about it afterward... nope. I'd rather not.

Garen's bathroom was the height of luxury. Underfloor heating warmed the soles of my feet, and a large, freestanding tub sat in the center of the room, while twin sinks were affixed to one wall. A huge walk-in shower was at the far end with a view down to the lake and over at the mountains on the opposite shoreline.

What a view.

I used the toilet, then padded over to the sinks. My gaze fell on Garen's toothbrush, and I even went to use it, then changed my mind. I could borrow his shirt and make a dash for my own room, but knowing my luck, Grams would materialize and demand answers I wasn't ready to give.

Instead, I spread toothpaste on my finger and scrubbed my teeth as best I could, then swilled with alcohol-free mouthwash. Smoothing my bird's-nest mop of hair as best I could—see, *this* was why I put it up at night—I washed my face with cool water, then ventured back into the bedroom to find Garen lying on his side, his head propped up by his right arm. He gave me a full head-to-toe appraisal and licked his lips.

"Ah, now there's a sight I don't mind waking up to."

It took a lot of effort to leave myself uncovered. After what we'd done together in the last twelve hours, it would be stupid to act coy now. Praying I didn't blush, I muttered, "Oh, you're awake," then dashed over to the bed and slipped beneath the covers. I pulled them up and over my breasts.

Garen gripped the edge and yanked downward, then to the side, exposing me to his heated gaze. "Don't hide."

He bent his head and grazed his teeth over my nipple, drawing a gasp from me. His tongue formed a point, and he circled the erect nub, then suckled. My core clenched, and somehow my hand found its way between my legs.

Garen stopped, lifted his head, then grinned. "Oh, that's right." He sat up, knitted his hands together, then folded them behind his head. "We discussed this last night when I denied you an orgasm. You promised you could make yourself come." He jerked his chin. "Let's see it."

I blushed to the tips of my ears and quickly removed my hand. Saying what I had in the heat of sexual frustration and anger at his merciless denial was one thing. To actually masturbate in front of him? Quite another.

"I was mad at you," I mumbled.

"Oh, I know. Which is why I spent the entire meal with a sizeable erection rubbing against my zipper." He circled my wrist and pushed my hand back between my legs. "Go on, Catriona. I want to watch. I might pick up some tips."

"You don't need any tips."

His eyes glittered, and a cocky smirk touched his lips. "We can all learn something if we're willing to pay attention."

I stared at him, beseeching. "Don't ask me to do this. I can't."

He shifted to the bottom of the bed and gripped my ankles, then planted my feet flat on the mattress and pushed them toward my ass. He applied pressure to the insides of my knees, and they parted, exposing me fully.

"Touch yourself," he demanded. "And I'll do the same."

He wrapped a hand around the base of his cock and pumped once, twice, a third time. "See, it's easy. Come on, *mon petit chaton*. Don't you want to please me?"

"Oh God," I moaned, my hand automatically moving between my legs.

"Watch me," Garen said softly.

I lowered my gaze to his groin. Already his cock seemed impossibly hard, the head swollen and angry-looking, his slit seeping with pre-cum.

A deep groan released from low in my chest, and I rubbed

my middle finger over the bunch of nerves at the top of my sex, my movements slow at first but accelerating in time with Garen's increasing speed. I drew in a ragged, shuddering breath, clenching my inner muscles to stem the tide, but all that did was send me hurtling to the shore. A swell began in my abdomen, peaked, and then I was coming, crying out in ecstasy, any embarrassment chased away by the force of my climax.

"Fuck me, that's hot," Garen uttered, and then cum spurted from his cock, all over my pussy where it mingled with evidence of my own arousal. "Jesus, Catriona. You are a goddamn revelation."

As he'd done last night, he fetched a cloth from the bathroom and cleaned us both up, then dropped it unceremoniously beside the bed and flopped down beside me, kicking at the sheets until they, too, fell to the floor.

Transferring his weight to his right side, he caressed the swell of my stomach, then trailed a fingertip through the soft curls at the juncture of my thighs. "Have you ever removed this?"

My eyes widened at his out-of-the-blue question. "What?" I asked, even though his question was perfectly clear.

"Or had it waxed, maybe?"

I flinched at the very idea. Having my legs waxed was bad enough. To wax my pussy... it would hurt like fuck.

"No."

"Hmm." He licked along the underside of his top teeth. "I'd like to. Let's add it to the list."

I shifted my elbow into his side, giving him a sharp nudge. "Okay. Let's add it to the same list where I wax your balls."

He pressed his head back into the pillow and laughed. "Yeah, no."

"Then you waxing my bits is off the table, too."

"How about shaving? Would you let me do that?"

"Let you loose with a sharp blade? Try again, mister."

He tugged his bottom lip between his thumb and forefinger. A sharp stab of desire punched at my stomach. Those lips, that tongue, his cock. I now knew what he could do with all of them, and I wanted more. So much more. I wanted to steal every part of him.

Slow down. You're going too fast.

Ah, screw it. I was having far too much fun. I needed this release to ground me, given everything else going on in my life. I could handle my emotions, keep a lid on them. Recognize this for what it was—a couple of singletons having a good time. No future. No problem.

"What about if you did it and I watched?"

I rolled my eyes. "You are a hell of a kinky bastard, you know that?"

A chuckle left his mouth. "Oh, *mon petit chaton*, you have no idea. But as soon as we return to Canada next week, you will."

The fine hairs on the backs of my arms stood to attention, goose bumps propping them up. "Oh yeah. When you show me your 'weapons'?" I accentuated my point with air quotes.

He arched a brow, leaning up onto one elbow, his head resting in the flat of his palm. "Are you mocking me, kitty cat?"

I clasped a hand to my chest. "Would I?"

In an instant, I found myself beneath him, caged by his broad shoulders, lean hips, and strong thighs. He reached for a condom, slipped it on with practiced ease, and nudged the head of his cock at my entrance. "I guess this weapon will have to do for now."

25

Garen

I hovered at the end of the hallway as Catriona slipped inside her room with a grin and a wave. She'd worried that her grandmother would catch her sneaking back wearing the same clothes as she had last night, and had demanded I act as a human shield, a part I'd reluctantly played. Getting into a confrontation with the fearsome Mrs. Kelly was an experience even I'd prefer to avoid.

Catriona needn't have worried, though; the house lay silent with only the sound of the birds chirping outside disturbing the peace.

I virtually skipped downstairs, a lightness to my shoulders that hadn't been there in some time, and while I battled with the coffee machine—Sunday was Lia's day off—I thought back to the confession I'd made to Catriona last night, the one I'd fully expected would have her sprinting back to her own room and wishing me dead. Except she hadn't. She'd stayed and given me several of the best orgasms I'd had in my entire life. If not *the* best.

But nagging at the back of my mind was the truth I'd uttered.

I didn't do relationships.

I got bored once I'd been on one or two dates.

For me, the fun was all in the chase. Once caught, women lost their luster in seconds.

Last night counted as one date. Catriona and I would probably have two more, maybe three at an absolute push, before I treated her with disdain, bored with the monotony of fucking the same woman over and over.

And when that happened... well, she couldn't say I didn't warn her.

"Good morning, Mr. Gauthier."

I spun around to find Catriona's grandmother entering my kitchen. She peered at me with suspicion, and I wondered whether she knew that I'd spent most of last night and a good portion of this morning screwing her granddaughter.

"Call me Garen," I said, gesturing to a seat at the large glass-topped table that overlooked the gardens at the front of the house. "Would you like a coffee, or a tea, maybe? And something to eat?"

She stiffly dropped her slight frame into a chair. "Coffee sounds good."

"With cream and sugar?"

"Just cream, please."

I managed to coax another cup out of the machine after a lot of spluttering and spurts of steam. I set it down and took one of the chairs across from her, then sipped my own drink and waited for the inquisition to begin.

"Did you take good care of my granddaughter last night?"

Oh yes, I did. Very good care.

"We had a nice time," I said, nodding and thanking good

fortune that reading minds was only possible in fantasy books. "The restaurant has a lovely view, although it was a little dark to appreciate it fully."

She knitted her fingers together and lay them in her lap. "May I offer you some advice?"

She framed it as a question, but a steely tone to her voice told me I didn't have a choice other than to listen. "Of course." I swept my hand out to the side as a sign for her to go for it.

"My granddaughter is a good girl, a thoughtful girl. A *trusting* girl. She's fiery and headstrong, but she cares very deeply about those who mean a lot to her. She appears tough on the outside, but she has a heart that can break very easily." She set those emerald-green eyes on me, so reminiscent of Catriona's. "Please take that into account."

I locked gazes with her and nodded. "Mrs. Kelly, I like Catriona very much, but I will be as honest with you as I have been with her. I am not a man who has a history of long-term relationships, and right now, I don't expect this liaison to be any different. Catriona is aware of my shortcomings, and she accepts them and our involvement for what it is. Two grown adults who have a mutual attraction, enjoying each other's company."

Her lips, thinned with age, curved in a faint smile. "I appreciate your honesty. My granddaughter means everything to me. If, as you say, she's comfortable with the temporary nature of your... entanglement, then that is her prerogative. But if you don't treat her with respect, you shall have me to deal with."

A chuckle spilled from my lips. "You are magnificent, Mrs. Kelly. Has anyone ever told you that?"

Her lips twitched again. "My late husband may have, on occasion."

I opened my mouth to continue the conversation when a shuffling in the hallway alerted me to someone else's presence. Catriona appeared with Aiden in tow, her newly washed hair teased into waves, a light dusting of makeup gracing her smooth skin, and a pair of tight jeans clinging to her pert ass and narrow hips. A tingle shot up my spine. Fuck, the woman was sex on a stick, one I wanted to lick over and over.

"Morning, Grams." She flicked her gaze in my direction, then cut away sharply and kissed the top of her grandmother's head. "Sleep well?"

Something in the way her grandmother twisted her upper body which brought us both into her line of sight made me sit up and take notice.

"Better than you, I should imagine," Catriona's grandmother replied sarcastically.

I laughed, then tried to stifle it so it came out as a half-snort instead. Catriona shot me a glare. "I had a good night's sleep as it happens, Grams."

A sip of coffee, a tightening of the eyes, and an arch of a brow was followed by, "Hmm, well, I guess you young ones manage very well on a couple of hours."

This time I couldn't help it. I burst out laughing, draped my arm around Catriona's shoulder, and squeezed. "She knows."

Aiden's gaze bounced between the three of us as Catriona's gaze snapped to mine, dismay swirling in the depths of her eyes.

"How?" she mouthed.

I didn't get to answer because Aiden cried, "Oh my God. Are you two doing it?"

"Aiden!" Mrs. Kelly barked while Catriona turned beet red, bowed out of my hold, and mumbled something about making breakfast.

"You are so busted, Catriona," Aiden continued.

His giggles stiffened Catriona's shoulders, and her knuckles turned white as she gripped the countertop. I searched for a way to divert his attention away from mine and Catriona's sex life. Not for my benefit. I didn't give two shits if her teenage brother found it highly amusing that me and his sister were fucking. But Catriona's body language told me she was horrified at the direction of the morning's conversation, and that bothered me. An unusual reaction, but I'd go with it for now and examine my reasoning later.

"How are you feeling today, Aiden?" I asked, an idea coming to me. "If you're not too tired, would you like to go sailing with me and Catriona? You're very welcome to come along, too, Mrs. Kelly."

My diversionary tactics worked when Aiden exclaimed, "Sailing? Like on a real boat?"

I nodded, catching Catriona's eye across the kitchen. I winked. "A real boat, yes. How about it? You game?"

"Hell, yeah," he gushed.

"Aiden!" his grandmother scolded again. "Language, young man. And thank you, Mr. Gauthier, but I think I'll leave bobbing about on the water to you young ones. I plan to sit in your garden with my knitting and enjoy the sunshine."

"Of course," I murmured, secretly relieved she'd decided not to take me up on my invitation. Mrs. Kelly saw far too much and wasn't afraid to share her thoughts. This way, once we'd set off, I'd ask the skipper to show Aiden how to sail and I'd get Catriona all to myself. "If you'll excuse me, I have a few work things to attend to first. Please help yourself to breakfast, snacks, anything you like. Shall we meet here at eleven-thirty?"

Aiden beamed. "Excellent."

I smiled back, unable to stop myself. He was a nice kid, unusual for most teenagers I'd come across, most of whom I'd stick in the 'fucking brat' box. Maybe the serious illness he faced made him different than other kids, but whatever the reason, I had a surge of pride that I was able to help him. Sure, my original intentions had been immoral rather than philanthropic, but even now I'd achieved my primary aim of bedding his sister, it made me want to help this family *more* rather than *less*.

I withdrew to my office to work, setting an alarm on my phone, a necessary step given my ability to forget the outside world existed once I became engrossed in ROGUES business. Before I knew it, the reminder buzzed. I sent a final email, locked my laptop, and went to meet Catriona and Aiden at the prearranged location.

I found them sitting in the kitchen nibbling on cookies and chatting, or rather teasing, the banter between them the kind that came from a deep love. Growing up as an only child, I found the idea of having a sibling was a foreign one, but when I examined it, I guessed the relationship I had with the other ROGUES guys was similar. In some ways, better, because we *chose* to spend time with each other.

"Ready?" I asked, seizing Catriona's half-finished cookie from between her fingers and taking a bite.

She snatched it back. "Hey."

Aiden leaped to his feet. "I'm so excited. I've never been on a sailboat."

I held out my hand toward Catriona, pleased when she took it. "Then let's go."

My driver dropped us off at the quayside, and I led the way to the mooring. Catriona gasped when she saw the sleek, white yacht floating on the crystal-clear waters, its red sails fastened to the mast.

"Whoa..." Aiden declared.

"This is your boat?" Catriona asked.

"One of them, yes."

"You have more than one?"

I grinned. "I like sailing, so I keep one wherever I have a home." I pointed to the side of the hull which proudly sported the boat's name. "They're all named after my mom. This is the first one I bought, hence *Giselle I*."

Catriona's eyes softened as she looked up at me, while Aiden tore up the gangplank where the skipper, Laurin, waited to greet us. Once the introductions were complete, I gave them a guided tour of the boat including the private areas below deck which included a lounge, galley kitchen, two bedrooms and a shower room.

"Somehow I imagined you with one of those super yachts with about seven decks, and are like two thousand feet long or something," Catriona said as we emerged from below deck back into the sunshine. "Although this is luxurious, it's quaint, too."

"Confession time," I said. "I do have a mega yacht. It's moored in Monaco."

Shielding her eyes from the sun, she tipped back her head and squinted at me. "You have a lot of money. I should have demanded double for my studio."

Aiden had his back to us, so I bent my head and stole a kiss. "And if you had, I would have paid it," I whispered. "Your negotiation skills suck."

"Is that so?" she hissed, folding her arms over her chest, but I could tell she wasn't at all mad. "Let's see if you still think that the next time you try to get me into bed."

I gave a fake shudder. "I can't wait."

She slammed the heel of her palm into my shoulder. "Jackass."

Grinning, I called over to Laurin, "Ready to take her out, skipper?"

"Yep." Laurin set off toward the wheel located at the stern. "Want to help me, Aiden?"

"Do I ever." Aiden jogged after him.

I draped an arm around Catriona's shoulder, and together, we walked to the bow. I gestured for her to take a seat on the long leather bench on the port side.

"Did you tell Grams about last night?" she asked as soon as we'd sat down.

"No," I said. "I didn't have to. Your grandmother is a very astute woman."

"Tell me about it," Catriona muttered.

"I got my second warning in as many days, though." I laughed.

Catriona's mouth popped open, and her eyes went saucer-round. "You're kidding."

I pulled in my lips to suppress the laugh that threatened at her horrified expression. "She has this uncanny ability to make her point by saying very little."

Catriona flattened her lips, and her jaw flexed, causing a nerve to beat in her cheek. "I shall have words with her as soon as we get back."

I reached for her hand, curling my fingers around hers. "No need. She loves you very much."

"What did you say to her?"

"I told her the truth. That I like you, but I'm not looking for any kind of a commitment, and that's something you're aware of. That we're two adults having fun, nothing more."

I caught a flash of some kind of emotion crossing Catriona's face, but then she schooled her expression and nodded. "Good. Next time, you have my permission to tell her to mind her own business."

I chuckled. "I value my life far too much to take such a risk."

The boat eased out into open water, and Catriona tucked up her feet and nestled into my side, a soft sigh leaving her lips. As for me, a heavy weight settled on my chest, squashing my lungs and filling my veins with unease.

26

Catriona

The excitement of the sailing trip sapped every ounce of Aiden's energy, and by the time Garen's car drew to a halt in front of his mountain retreat, he'd fallen asleep, his head on my shoulder, his breathing soft and steady.

I twisted my head and found Garen's hooded gaze on me.

"Thank you for today."

He nodded. "It was my pleasure, but maybe a little too much for Aiden. I should have known he'd get tired and insist we return early."

"I'm glad you didn't. Once his treatment starts tomorrow, he won't feel like doing much of anything for a while. The doctors warned us that extreme fatigue is a known side effect. At least he'll have a nice memory to call on in the coming weeks and months."

Fear for what my brother had to face—alone—caused pain to twist in my gut. Sure, he'd have Grams by his side, and I'd come visit as often as I could, but as much as I wished to swap places with Aiden, this was a battle he'd have to tackle on his own.

"He'll be okay, you know."

Garen's smooth, deep baritone pulled me from the dark thoughts swirling in my mind. I offered up a faint smile, but it fell away almost as soon as it touched my lips. "I hope so."

He grazed his knuckles over my cheekbone. "I'm learning that the Landrys and the Kellys are made of stern stuff. He *will* make a full recovery, Catriona."

"Yeah," I said, unwilling to commit one hundred percent to a future filled with uncertainty.

"I know we're due to fly back to Canada on Tuesday, but I can rearrange my schedule if you'd prefer to stay with him?"

Shock widened my eyes, the unexpectedness of Garen's gesture coming at me from left field. "You'd do that? Allow me to stay?"

"Only if I'm allowed to stay, too." He captured my hand and pressed a soft kiss to the inside of my wrist. "I don't want to return without you."

I froze in place, my mind struggling to make sense of Garen's words. The push and pull was confusing to say the least. "What's going on?"

His lips twisted to one side in a wry grin. "I don't know. Suffice to say I'm as confused as you are, but for now, I'm going with it."

"But last night you said—"

"I know what I said, and I meant it. I don't do relationships, and at any moment, I might realize I'm bored and have no further interest in you. Sorry if that sounds blunt, but it's the truth." He pinched the bridge of his nose between his thumb and forefinger. "I've done a lot of thinking today, and the only thing I'm certain of is that where you go, I go. If you want to stay here to see your brother through his first set of treatments, or all of his treatments, I'll make it work. I'll have to return to Canada on occasion and make a trip to New York once a month for the ROGUES board meeting, but if you want to stay here, then I will relocate for the foreseeable future."

My throat tightened up, and when I tried to swallow, I found it impossible. "Garen, I-I don't know what to say."

"Say yes."

I wanted to. God, I wanted to. How the hell had this happened? To go from despising a man so much I would have happily watched him burn in the street without lifting a finger, to this avalanche of relief that not only was he allowing me to stay by my brother's side during the fight of his life, he also wanted to be right there with me.

"What if, after a day, a week, a month, that boredom you mentioned becomes a reality?"

"Then I'll return to Canada."

I suppressed a wince at how quickly he'd responded without a flicker of hesitancy. I guessed that meant he expected exactly that to happen, that he'd grow bored and drop me.

"And what would that mean for me, for Aiden?"

"You can remain here. My side of our deal will stand, Catriona. I will fund your brother's treatment for as long as needed. The only difference is that I'll release you from your end of the bargain."

I cut my gaze to Aiden, sleeping peacefully, his dark eyelashes gracing his smooth cheeks, unaware of the bomb Garen had dropped right in my lap, one that had shredded me completely. Allowing him into my body last night had also granted him access to my heart. This wasn't love. It was far too soon for that. Besides, I had serious doubts whether Garen was a man remotely capable of falling in love. But for me, the shift was that I realized I *could* love him. In time, I could.

"I want to stay." I swung my focus from Aiden to Garen. Brother to lover.

He gave me a lopsided smile, and an ache bloomed in my core, and a swarm of butterflies took flight in my abdomen.

"Then we stay."

∽

I sat with Aiden until he fell back to sleep, then set off to search for Grams. I found her in the living room gossiping with Lia. Considering the two women barely knew each other, they were nattering away as if they were lifelong friends. Five minutes later, I realized my presence was not required and excused myself.

Wandering from room to room feeling like a spare part, I happened upon the cinema room Garen had mentioned. I snuck inside and settled into one of several comfortable leather recliners. I fiddled with a few buttons and managed to get the thing to come on. The screen displayed several movies, and as I scrolled down, I found hundreds more. Wow, talk about spoiled for choice. I selected a rom-com and curled my feet up beside me to watch. All the fresh air must have made me tired because the next thing I remember was Garen shaking me awake.

I rubbed my eyes, peering up at him. "What time is it?" I asked, covering a wide yawn with my palm.

"Nine-thirty. I've been searching everywhere for you."

I squinted at the screen where the credits were rolling. "I missed the movie," I said with a pout.

"That's not such a bad thing." He arched a dark brow. "*Maid in Manhattan*? Really?"

"Hey, rom-coms are fun."

"If you say so," he retorted, reaching to pick up the remote control to turn everything off.

"If you don't like rom-coms, then why do you have several in your library?"

"Lia lives here all year round. I expect she downloaded them."

"Oh, yeah." I grinned. "Nicely dodged, by the way."

He raised his eyes upward, which had me giggling.

"Let's go to bed. Unless you're hungry?"

I shook my head, still full from the enormous late lunch we'd had on the boat. "I should say goodnight to Grams and Aiden first."

"You do that, and I'll get naked."

Sensing a chance to tease him, I yawned again, this time a fake one. "Actually, I'm pretty tired. I might sleep in my room tonight."

He gave me a blank stare. "Fine, although when I make you scream my name right before you orgasm, your grandmother is likely to hear. The walls in that part of the house aren't all that thick. If you're comfortable with that, then so am I."

I gaped at him. "No, I mean… no."

"Excellent." He captured my hand and headed for the door. "My room it is then."

A growl rumbled through my chest at him besting me. He responded with a low chuckle.

"Five points for effort, *mon petit chaton*."

I'd originally hated that nickname, but now, every time he used it, a shiver of delight shot down my spine. There was something intimate about the way he said it, and it didn't hurt that it was in French, either. The language of love, wasn't that what people said?

Don't, Catriona. Just don't.

I shoved the hope from my chest, loath to walk that path or even set a single foot on it. I had to remember Garen's history with women. He'd been completely honest with me, and for my own sanity and the protection of my heart, I must keep that in the forefront of my mind.

He didn't do relationships.

On any level.

And no matter how much kindness he showed to me and my family, I wouldn't be the exception.

I checked on Grams and Aiden to say goodnight while he waited at the top of the stairs. When we reached his suite of rooms, he released my hand and crossed over to the window to draw the drapes. I toed the carpet, a wave of uncertainty holding my feet to the floor. Garen kicked off his shoes and crooked his finger, beckoning me to him. I willed my legs to move, edging toward him on muscles that might as well have atrophied for all the use they were. *What the hell is wrong with me?*

"You look nervous," Garen said, inclining his head to one side. "Are you having second thoughts about our conversation earlier today?"

"No. I want to stay here with Aiden, and I'm glad you're staying, too."

"Just as well." He twisted a lock of my hair and fed it through his fingers. "Because I'm going nowhere. I haven't had my fill of you yet, and until I do, you're stuck with me."

A twinge of disappointment pinched my gut, which was why I blurted, "But you will, one day, have your fill of me. Yes?"

Silence filled the room while I waited for his reply. My heart thrashed against my ribcage, and I watched his eyes flick over my face, his jaw flexing as he bit down on his molars.

"I haven't lied to you, Catriona, and I don't intend to start now with false promises history would show I'm certain to break. All I can say is that I enjoy your company enormously. I like the way you challenge me, sometimes quietly, sometimes right in my face. Very few people are that brave, and the fact that you are excites me." He tucked a lock of hair behind my ear. "Plus, I like fucking you."

When I remained quiet, processing what he'd said, he responded by sighing softly.

"It's all I can offer right now, Catriona. Can you live with that?"

Could I? Or was I falling headlong into a heartbreak I might not ever recover from?

I forced a smile, but it felt strange on my lips. "Of course. We're both adults enjoying each other. It lasts until it doesn't."

Relief swamped his face, which caused an even deeper depression to take root in the depths of my stomach.

"Great."

He lifted me over his shoulder, fireman style. I squealed loudly, thankful we weren't in my room. Grams would have a heart attack thinking he was torturing me. He tossed me on the bed then went for his shirt buttons.

"It's just as well you had a snooze in the cinema room," he said, raking his gaze over me where my skirt had ridden up, showing a good few inches of thigh. "It's the last rest you'll get for a while."

27

Garen

"Bullshit," Upton said with a grin. "Come on, Garen. What's the real reason you're staying in Switzerland for the foreseeable future? You don't really expect us to buy this unexpected business opportunity cover story, do you?"

His openly skeptical stare was matched by the other four ROGUES board members attending an impromptu meeting arranged by me so I could update them on my temporary change of location.

"Yeah," Sebastian piped up. "If it *is* true, then I'd like to know what the fuck you think you're doing pissing on my territory. Europe is *my* patch. Canada not big enough for you or something?"

I inwardly groaned. I should have known it wouldn't be this easy, and Sebastian had a fair point. Europe was his baby. I needed to head this off by being my usual belligerent self.

"For fuck's sake, you bunch of egotistical jackasses. I thought I made myself perfectly clear, but for those hard of hearing, I'll try again. There *is* a potential business opportunity, and it might take a couple of weeks to work through it. All I'm asking for is a little time to do some due diligence, and if it's got legs, then I'll hand it over to you, Seb, okay?"

I expected to stay here longer than two weeks, but I needed to buy myself some time. It all depended on how long it took me to get Catriona out of my system. Given how my dick perked up at the mere thought of her, and the hours I'd spent fucking her last night, two weeks wouldn't cut it. I refused to acknowledge how many dates that length of time would induce, but it'd be more than four.

A new record.

It didn't mean anything, though.

She was a good fuck. That was all. And spunky and fun. And challenging.

And frustrating.

And intelligent and beautiful

It didn't mean anything.

"Tell us more about this opportunity." Ryker rubbed his chin thoughtfully. "I'm intrigued. How did it land in your lap?"

Bastard man was far too astute for his own good. I locked him with a hard stare. "It's early days. Might come to nothing. There's no point going into details until I have more information."

"Hmm," Ryker said, leaning forward so his face appeared larger on the screen. "And while you're doing... whatever it is you're doing in Switzerland, who's keeping an eye on the hotel construction?"

Fuck. I'd barely thought of the hotel since we'd landed in Switzerland last Thursday. The ground would have been flattened by now, and I winced at the thought of Catriona's beloved studio no longer sitting proudly in the middle of the row of businesses, and all because I wanted that location for my own venture.

"I have an excellent project manager and a very capable team who are reporting to me on a regular basis. If you're that worried about me managing this project remotely then maybe Upton can get off his fat ass and fly up to Vancouver to check on things. It's only a hop and a skip from L.A."

I shot Upton a hard stare. Serve the bastard right for spotlighting my weak-as-piss excuse for staying in Switzerland for an extended period of time.

Upton responded to my venomous glare with a wide grin. "I have a delicious ass. Nothing fat about my pert derriere, thanks very much. You can cop a feel if you like, next time we meet."

I rolled my eyes. "Oh, I'm sorry, I thought I'd dialed into a grown-up discussion. Seems my call was diverted to the kindergarten."

Elliot barked a laugh, but it was Oliver's expression that worried me the most. He knew me almost as well as I knew myself, and the way his eyes narrowed and he brought his arms over his chest told me I could expect a separate conversation before too long. If he called today, I wouldn't answer. I needed time to figure out a response that wouldn't have him drilling until he got to the truth.

Even I didn't know the truth. All I did know was that leaving Catriona behind wasn't an option. I craved her pussy and her company far too much for that. Once I got her out of my system, then I'd return to Canada. Until that happened, I planned to spend every night buried inside her.

"Okay, Garen," Ryker said. "Keep us informed. Upton, fly to Vancouver tomorrow and make sure the plans for the hotel are on track, then report back to Garen."

"Yeah, no worries," Upton said, shooting a sinful grin into the camera. "I'll get everything back on track."

I grimaced, my jaw clenched. "It's *already* on track," I bit out. "I only left there five fucking days ago."

"A lot can happen in five days," Upton said, clearly enjoying his moment, one I'd make him pay for the next time our paths crossed in person.

"Fuck off," I shot at him.

He laughed. "You're so easy to wind up, Garen. Always have been."

"Whatever," I muttered childishly which, given my earlier comment, wasn't exactly wise, especially when Upton's grin widened so far, I expected his face to split. "Are we done?"

Ryker nodded. "Let's catch up on Friday at the usual time. We can talk more then."

The screen went blank.

I pinched the bridge of my nose, my eyes closing, and let out a deep sigh.

Can't fucking wait.

∽

Like a caged tiger, I paced, waiting for Catriona to return from the hospital. She, her grandmother, and Aiden had been there all day for his first treatment, and while I hadn't expected her to call or text, the fact she hadn't made me antsy. I didn't like being kept in the dark, even when it was none of my business. I'd found myself praying to a fucking god I didn't believe in that it had gone well, although given what Catriona had told me Saturday over dinner, we wouldn't know the success or failure of the experimental treatment for several weeks or even months yet.

A beam of yellow light swung across the front of the house, signaling their return. I strode to the front door and opened it wide, then stood on the step waiting for them to appear.

Her grandmother got out of the car first, and I moved to offer her my arm, which she waved away with a flick of her wrist. Stubborn female. Aiden followed, his face pale and wan, his eyes drooping, but I didn't miss the determined set to his jaw. I patted his shoulder.

"How'd it go? How are you feeling?"

He glanced up at me. "Tired."

I nodded, catching Catriona's eye over the top of his head. "You all must be. Lia has cooked dinner if you're hungry."

Aiden shook his head. "I'm gonna go to bed if that's okay."

"Of course it is," I said. "It'll keep."

"I'll take him up," Mrs. Kelly said. "Then I'll turn in myself. I'm dead on my feet."

The two of them went inside, leaving me and Catriona standing beside the car. I waited, wanting to take my lead from her, but when her face crumpled, I pulled her into my arms and pressed her head to my shoulder.

"I've got you," I said with more gentleness than I ever thought myself capable of. "I'm here."

"God, Garen, it was awful. I mean, the doctors and nurses were lovely, but just watching Aiden lying in that bed having drugs pumped through a tube into his arm. He seemed so *small,* so *fragile.* I know it's stupid, but I've never thought of him that way. Until these last few weeks, he's always been my rambunctious little brother, and seeing him today has brought home just how sick he is."

"Come on, let's get you inside," I said, conscious of a chill in the air. "Do you want some food?" As if feeding her could make it all better, but something in me urged me to try to get a meal inside her.

"I'm really not hungry. We had sandwiches at the hospital."

"At least you've eaten something. How about a bath then? And a cup of tea?"

She tilted her head back and gazed up at me, emerald eyes glistening in the buttery-yellow light of my entranceway. "That sounds like heaven."

"You go on up. I'll fetch that tea."

I tugged on my lip and watched as she used the handrail to virtually haul herself upstairs. She turned left, toward her own room rather than my suite, and I almost called out to stop her, then suppressed the impulse. If she needed space tonight, then I'd give it to her. I didn't like it, but even I recognized demanding she spend the night in my bed was a dick move.

Walking into the kitchen, I found Lia kneading dough. She loved us to wake up to freshly baked bread in the morning, so this was her final routine before she went to bed. She glanced over her shoulder as I entered.

"Tough day for them all," she said in her usual sage manner. "I'll cover this food and leave it in the fridge in case any of them get hungry during the night."

"Thanks," I said, flicking on the electric kettle. "Catriona wants tea."

"I'll make it." She rinsed her flour-covered hands under the faucet and dried them on a towel, then bustled about the kitchen. Within five minutes, she set two perfectly brewed mugs of tea on the table for me to take upstairs. "Let me know if you need anything else, okay."

I shook my head. "Turn in, Lia. I'll see you in the morning."

Sounds of water running came from Catriona's bathroom as I nudged the door open with my hip. Switching the two cups of tea into one hand, I tapped a knuckle on the bathroom door.

"Come in," she called out.

The bath was almost full, bubbles rising above the rim. Catriona was sitting on the toilet seat, her expression weary. I handed her one of the cups.

"Here you go."

"Thanks." She took a sip and sighed. "I needed that."

I shuffled my feet, uncertain whether she wanted me to stay or go. Indecision wasn't a normal go-to emotion for me, and I didn't like it.

"I'll leave you to it," I said, half turning away.

"No, Garen, stay. Please." She scrubbed her face. "I could use the company."

She slipped off the robe she'd changed into and let it fall to the floor. I caught a flash of side-boob and the curve of one cheek of her ass before she slipped into the water. My dick jerked in appreciation, a desire to shuck my clothes and climb in the other end then have her ride me to orgasm strengthening by the second.

Wrong move, asshole.

She leaned her head back, staring at the ceiling for a moment. Her eyes fell closed. "I ache all over," she murmured. "Weird, considering I've done nothing but sit down all day."

"That'll be why." I moved behind her. "Lean forward."

"Why?"

"I'll massage your shoulders."

She twisted to look behind her to where I'd already sunk to my knees. "You're going to give me a massage?"

I gave her a lopsided grin. "Yeah."

She lifted her brows. "Who are you? Where has the mean asshole gone?"

"Oh, he's never far away," I drawled. "Just that all the orgasms have pushed him into a brief retreat."

She chuckled but obeyed my order. I dug my thumbs into the knots at the back of her neck, and she groaned. "Christ, that feels good."

I must have massaged her for a good fifteen minutes, which surprised the hell out of me. I wasn't the kind of man who really cared that much about another's pleasure, yet with Catriona, it felt different. And I hadn't even slipped my hands over her shoulders to squeeze her tits either.

Catriona emitted this deeply contented sigh. "You're a good man, Garen Gauthier. Whatever face you show the world, I've seen the real you these past few days."

An uncomfortable sensation stirred in my chest, an alien

feeling that caused a ball of anxiety to take root in my stomach and prickles to coat my skin.

What's happening to me?

A sudden impulse to get the hell out of there sent me staggering to my feet. It wasn't only Catriona who needed space tonight. I needed time alone to work through where the hell the ruthless, fierce, arrogant jackass who only cared about his own agenda had fucked off to. He wasn't in this fucking room, that was for sure.

"I'll leave you to it," I said, drying my hands on a nearby towel. "I have work to do."

I didn't stick around for her to question me, although the surprised expression on her face left me in no doubt my reaction hadn't been the one she'd expected to such a compliment.

Too bad. I needed out.

28

Catriona

"Are you busy this evening?"

I glanced up from where I'd settled down with a book in the garden room where light flooded in through the glass roof and amplified the warmth from the weak fall sun. I'd discovered this space yesterday after a fitful night's sleep caused by what happened with me and Garen Monday night on our return from the hospital. I still couldn't figure out what had gone wrong. One minute he was giving me a massage worthy of a professional masseuse, his talented hands eradicating the tension that had burrowed into my muscles. The next he'd scurried off, and I hadn't seen him since.

Until now.

Lifting my brows, I gave him a cold stare. If he thought he could wander in here and act like nothing had happened, he had another think coming. "Yes," I said in a curt tone.

A hint of surprise graced his face, and then his jaw flexed.

"Well, whatever plans you have, cancel them. There's a work thing I need to go to, and you're coming with me."

I closed the book and set it down on the coffee table next to my half-finished glass of juice. "What work thing?"

"Does it matter?" he snapped. "We might be in Switzerland rather than Canada, but our deal stands. I told you there would be occasions I need you to attend functions. This is one of those times. It's black tie, so dress appropriately."

His snippy attitude stiffened my spine, and I sent him a venomous glare. "I don't have appropriate clothing for an event like that. I wasn't planning on staying long, if you remember."

"I'll have the driver take you into the city this morning. I have accounts at several suitable establishments in town. I'll leave the list of venues with him. Meet me in the entranceway at seven o'clock."

He spun on his heel and strode off before I could impart a suitably sarcastic retort.

"Asshole," I muttered. I'd mistakenly assumed that Switzerland Garen was a lot nicer than Canada Garen. How wrong I was. Well, fine. If that was the way he wanted to play it, I'd meet him blow for blow.

I asked Grams and Aiden if either of them wanted to come dress shopping with me. Aiden's exhaustion from Monday had receded quickly, as the doctors had promised us it would. Just as well, considering his next session was tomorrow. Both of them hurriedly declined, Grams citing the desire to finish the latest sweater attached to her knitting needles and Aiden pretending he'd had a sudden relapse. Couldn't blame them, really. Shopping for clothes wasn't something anyone in my family did very often, and as such, it wasn't what we considered a fun activity.

As it turned out, though, I *did* have fun. The establishments Garen mentioned were the kinds of stores where the members of staff treated their customers like royalty, and they had a real flair for dressing women. It was at the third place I visited that I found the perfect gown. The deep-purple coloring went perfectly with my green eyes. The off-the-shoulder design and cinched waist gave me the illusion of an hour-glass figure, even though my dancing roots had left me a little lacking in that department. Paired with three-inch heels, necessary given the length of the gown, I reckoned I'd almost be as tall as Garen.

The driver dropped me back off at the house, and after a late lunch with Grams and Aiden—with Garen nowhere to be seen—I headed off to my room to get ready for the evening.

As soon as I entered, I spotted a square box sitting on the edge of my bed and a folded piece of paper on top. With a frown, I padded over and picked it up.

I'm sorry for my bad mood. Peace-offering?

I picked up the box and opened it, a gasp falling from my lips. Inside, nestled amongst swathes of wine-red satin, lay a sparkling three-tiered diamond choker and a pair of drop earrings. With trembling fingers, I removed the necklace and examined it in the dim light. These gems couldn't be real. Could they? No, surely not. They had to be cubic zirconia. If these were real diamonds, it must have cost… shit, an unbelievable amount of money. More than I'd probably earn in a lifetime.

I returned my focus to the note, my heart softening. Whatever the reason for Garen's dark mood since Monday night, he appeared to have shaken it off. At least I hoped so. I'd find out for sure in a few hours.

At five before seven, I stood in front of the full-length freestanding mirror in the corner of my bedroom, shocked at the image staring back at me. Grams had offered to put my hair up, and it had been the right call. The style elongated my neck and brought attention to the choker and earrings. Paired with this beautiful dress and light makeup, I scarcely recognized myself.

I carefully picked my way downstairs, holding my dress up

to make sure I didn't snag a heel in the hem. As I reached the bottom, I glanced around, searching for Garen. The entranceway was empty, an eerie silence gracing the wide space. Frowning, I set off toward the kitchen. I poked my head inside. That, too, lay empty, the countertops cleaned down for the day, the surfaces gleaming where Lia had polished them religiously.

If Garen had done this as a form of punishment, I'd... I'd...

I whirled around, ready to hunt him down and give him a sizeable piece of my mind, and then gasped. He stood with his shoulder propped against the door, his elegant fingers stroking his chin.

"Wow," he murmured. "Aren't you a sight for sore eyes?"

I clasped a hand to my neck, my fingers touching the cool diamonds at my throat, reminding me of his extravagant gift.

"Hi."

I dipped my chin, peeking up at him through a pair of unfamiliar fake eyelashes that one of the women at the store had convinced me to buy. Damn, he looked fine, his tuxedo fitting him like a second skin, the crisp, white shirt offsetting his darker coloring to perfection.

He crossed the space between us and captured my hand, bringing it to his lips. "You got my gift and my apology then?"

I touched the necklace again, then my fingers fluttered to the earrings where I lightly tugged. "Are they real?" I whispered.

He traced his thumb over my knuckles. "As real as you, but not nearly as beautiful."

I dipped my chin, shaking my head. "It's too much, Garen. I'm happy to wear it tonight, but then you must take it back."

"No," he said bluntly, then stood back to study me. "That dress is gorgeous on you. I'll enjoy removing it later."

I drew in a shaky breath as my pulse leaped at his compliment. Had Switzerland Garen made a return? I hoped so. The other one made me want to bring my knee up and aim right for his groin.

"What's going on in that head of yours?" he mused.

I almost laughed aloud. *You don't want to know.*

"Nothing. Shall we go?"

He inclined his head, then stuck out his arm. "I'll have to keep a very close eye on you this evening."

I frowned up at him. "Why?"

"Because every man in that room, single or otherwise, is going to try to steal you away, and the first one who makes an attempt will live to regret it."

My heart skipped a beat, and a lightness settled over my chest at his possessiveness. He walked me to the front door. Out of the corner of my eye, I caught Grams and Aiden standing at the top of the stairs peering down at me. Aiden stuck up both his thumbs, a broad grin almost splitting his face in two while Grams gave me a brief nod, her approval in that slight movement of her head. I wasn't sure how Garen had managed to win over my grandmother, but it appeared as though he'd achieved the impossible.

"What is this event, anyway?" I asked as the car pulled onto the main highway into Geneva. "You didn't say."

"The Federal Chancellor heard I was in the city and invited me to attend an event in aid of a local charity he's supporting," he explained. "No doubt he'll tap me for a sizeable donation before the evening ends."

I wrinkled my nose. No idea who this man was, although his title made him sound important. "Who's the Federal Chancellor?"

"A senior member of the Swiss government," Garen said.

I widened my eyes. "The government? Wow. Do you often mix with foreign governments?"

He smiled. "All the time. Unfortunately. These gatherings are usually decidedly dull." His eyes darkened as he lowered his gaze, settling on my cleavage. "I think tonight might be an exception."

My breath caught in my throat, and I swallowed. "Why's that?" I whispered.

A chuckle left his mouth. "Fishing for compliments, Catriona? You, *mon petit chaton*. You are the difference." He lifted his gaze to my mouth. "I hope you have a spare lipstick in your purse."

His palm skimmed along my jaw, and then he pulled me to him, his lips gently roving over mine in a kiss filled with unspoken promise. Goose bumps pebbled my bare arms, and I sank back against the buttery leather seat. Garen removed his seat belt, shuffled closer, and deepened the kiss.

Long before I'd had my fill of him, he broke away. He touched his fingertips to his mouth, rubbing back and forth. "Take off your panties."

A flush of heat rushed through me, and I ducked my head as I realized what I'd have to admit given his question. "I'm not wearing any."

A groan rumbled through his chest, and his eyes briefly closed. "Fuck, you're perfect."

"They ruined the line of the dress," I hurriedly explained. I didn't want him thinking I was some kind of hussy who regularly went around panty-less. Nor did I want him thinking I'd done it for him. Or maybe I did. Shit, my thoughts were all over the place.

"If we weren't almost there, I'd hoist up that dress and fuck you in the backseat of this car. As we're only about five minutes away, my plans will have to wait until the return journey." He gave me a wicked grin. "Or maybe I'll spirit you off into a dark corner somewhere when no one is paying attention."

A shudder of pleasure rippled down my spine. One he noticed if his roguish grin was any indication.

The car eased to a stop, and I peered out of the window at

an imposing mansion set amongst lawned gardens adorned with mature trees and shrubbery. Several smartly dressed men and women milled around the entrance, and a line of luxurious cars were ahead of us, winding their way back down the driveway. My palms dampened, and a fluttering in my belly made me feel slightly nauseated. *Nerves. Just nerves, Catriona.* It was to be expected. I'd never mingled with dignitaries before. What if I said something stupid and embarrassed Garen and he turned back into the Canadian version I didn't like?

"Relax," Garen said, his thumb rhythmically stroking my inner wrist. "You'll be fine."

I nodded, dampened my lips with what little moisture I had in my mouth, and stepped onto the paved driveway. Garen was by my side in a second, and he captured my hand, his warmth a comfort I desperately needed.

I smoothed my free hand over my hip and ignored the chill breeze blowing across my bare shoulders. We'd be inside shortly. I could manage a short period of discomfort while we waited to be admitted.

"Walther," Garen said, releasing me to shake hands with a man in his forties with thinning blond hair and crinkles around his eyes. "Allow me to introduce Catriona Landry. Catriona, this is Walther Meyer, the Federal Chancellor."

The omission of any additional introduction such as *girlfriend* didn't escape my notice. Then again, I wasn't his girlfriend, so why would he introduce me as such? He'd made it perfectly clear we were a casual item enjoying each other until we weren't. At least he didn't saddle me with something like *associate* or, worse, *secretary.*

"Miss Landry, welcome."

Walther smiled and thrust out his hand for me to shake. He had a firm grip, but not overly so. In my opinion, men who almost crushed bones when they shook hands were usually jerks trying to make a stupid point.

"Nice to meet you," I murmured.

"Come on in. Mingle. Have fun. There's champagne right inside. I'll come find you later, Garen."

He winked, then turned away to greet the next set of guests.

"Told you," Garen whispered in my ear. He swiped two glasses off a loaded tray held with impressive steadiness by a waiter in a smart suit. Handing one to me, he clinked his glass against mine. "Cheers."

We wandered around, Garen stopping to speak to various people about things that went over my head. I took the opportunity to scan the room. People-watching was one of my favorite activities, and this room provided excellent fodder. As Garen expected, Walther cornered him and secured a sizeable donation to the beneficiary of tonight's event, the amount Garen cheerfully donated making my eyes water. Yet he waved it off as if it were nothing more than a dollar.

"Let's go outside," Garen whispered when Walther moved on to his next target, his lips brushing against my ear and sending a delicious shudder through my body. "I've had enough of sharing you."

"I didn't bring a wrap," I said. "It's chilly out."

He swept his tongue over his plump bottom lip, drawing my eye. "Don't worry, *chaton*. I'll keep you warm."

We wandered out onto the enormous decked area at the rear of the house. I needn't have worried about the chill. Several heaters were dotted around, making it feel as warm as a spring morning. A few other people wandered about, but apart from nodding to one or two of them, Garen didn't engage. Soft music played from speakers I couldn't see as he steered me to a quiet corner, maneuvering me until I found myself flush against the wall of the house.

"Every man in that room wanted you tonight," he said, dropping little kisses along my jawline.

His hand gripped my ass and he ground his erection into me. I closed my eyes, savoring the sensation.

"But they can't have you, Catriona. No one can have you except me. And I will. Repeatedly."

He drew back, his eyes burning with a possession that scared as well as thrilled me.

"You're mine, and only mine."

I inhaled a sharp breath, his words playing on a loop inside my head. Was this a declaration of something more? If we discounted the lunch on the roof terrace the first day we arrived in Switzerland, then tonight was our third date. Dinner in the mountains the night we slept together, the sailing trip, and now tonight. Although maybe this didn't count as a date. Oh, who the hell knew? I had to stop trying to second-guess Garen's intentions. The man was unreadable at the best of times. Seeking to figure out what went on in his head was a futile exercise.

He shuffled back a step or two, and a weird expression crossed his face, darkening his features. Shaking his head as though he had water in his ears, he muttered something under his breath that sounded remarkably like "No fucking way."

"Garen?"

He met my query with narrowed eyes and shoved a hand through his hair. "I've had enough. Let's go."

29

Garen

Silence hung heavy in the air as my driver negotiated the winding driveway that led back onto the highway. I sensed Catriona's confusion in the way she fiddled with the strap on her purse and the amount of times her hand touched the diamond choker I'd gifted her, almost as if she wanted to rip it off and ram it down my throat.

I didn't blame her.

One minute I'd declared she belonged to me, and in the very next breath, I backed off as if I'd spotted a grizzly bearing down on me, threatening my very existence.

When I'd uttered those words, I'd meant them with every fiber of my being, the strength of my pronouncement coming as a hell of a shock. A few weeks ago, I hadn't even known this woman existed, and now I struggled to acknowledge a life without her in it.

The same mantra started up in my head.

I didn't do relationships.

I grew bored with female company after a couple of dates and a few meaningless fucks.

Yet with her, every kiss, every touch, every conversation we shared drew me to her *more*. My attraction toward her had spiraled out of control, and with that came a fear that both rooted me to the ground and screamed at me to flee at the same time.

Unfortunately they were mutually exclusive.

It was fight *or* flight.

Which one would I choose?

I didn't have a clue. The only certainty right now was that I wasn't ready to let her go. Not by a long shot.

I felt for her hand in the muted light coming from the streetlights as we sped down the highway. She didn't pull away, thankfully, but her fingers were stiff beneath my own. I slowly caressed my thumb across her knuckles, and gradually, she relented.

"What was that?" she asked. "What happened back there, Garen?"

I turned my head to find her staring at me with a furrowed brow and a droop to her shoulders that tightened my chest. I'd hurt her feelings, and it bothered me, and I hated that it did. I didn't give two shits about other's feelings, so why did I care about Catriona's obvious distress at my actions?

"I don't know," I replied honestly and with an accompanying shrug. I hadn't sorted through it all yet, so there was little hope of explaining my reaction to Catriona.

She fixed her gaze out the window but left her hand in mine. I took that as a positive sign.

"You're confused. I get it. If it helps, so am I. A week ago, I would have happily watched you burn in the street. Hell, I'd have lit the match that set you on fire, yet now here I am, sharing my bed with you, enjoying your company. It's as strange for me as it is for you."

I lifted her hand to my face and placed her palm over my cheek. "Give me time," I said. "I'm a man who thinks things through. Carefully, meticulously. I'm a planner, not a reactor."

Yet my response to her in Walther's backyard hadn't been planned or thought-out. I'd spoken from a heart I didn't think I possessed. I'd allowed my emotions to rule my head, but emotions were fickle beasts. Listen to them at your peril.

"I haven't demanded anything, Garen. The only one applying pressure here is you."

I nodded, smiling grimly. "I hear you."

We traveled the rest of the way home in a more comfortable silence, but as we stepped inside and meandered upstairs, I hesitated at the top. I hadn't fucked her in days, and my dick was definitely up for a round of sinking into her wet heat and powering to a much-needed orgasm. But at the same time, there'd been a shift tonight, one that had me pausing to wait for her reaction.

She blinked up at me, or rather over at me, given her heels had added a good few inches to her height. "Well, Mr. Full-of-Promises. I'm panty-less and waiting."

A smile broke across my face, and I reached down, lifting her into my arms. She squealed as I strode down the hallway to my bedroom.

"And soon, you'll be dress-less."

~

I opened my laptop and clicked on the meeting app. Three windows opened. Ryker, Oliver, and Elliot in New York, Sebastian in London, and Upton in Los Angeles. I held up a hand in greeting.

"Sorry I'm late. Lost track of time."

"Sounds like you," Oliver said, grinning.

I responded by flipping him off, which expanded his smile.

"Okay, children," Ryker cut in. "We've a packed agenda, so I suggest we get started."

The ROGUES board took it in turns to chair our regular weekly and monthly meetings. This month, Ryker was on rotation. I actually preferred it when he chaired. We usually ran on time then, and I had a very good reason for wanting this meeting over with as soon as possible. I'd decided to surprise Catriona with a trip to Oeschinen Lake, about three hours east of us by car. Fortunately for me, I owned a helicopter and planned to fly us there this evening, then stay overnight and see the sights tomorrow morning. The hiking around the lake allowed for outstanding views, and at this time of year it should be fairly quiet, meaning I'd get to spend time with her alone. I'd even arranged to have warm clothes, a thick coat, and hiking boots and socks delivered, which should arrive any time soon.

I gave an update on progress with the hotel. Upton had made a flying visit, and I'd had a long conference call with the foreman. Things were moving along nicely, and ninety percent of the build should be complete in three to four months, which was no mean feat, given the scale of the property. Then again, my builds often ran ahead of time. I pushed my workers hard, and they usually delivered.

And if they didn't... I saw to it that work became a little harder to come by.

Sebastian wanted to know whether I'd made any progress on my bogus business venture. I brushed him off with a few platitudes which he seemed far too eager to accept—and that made me suspicious.

"Okay, that's the agenda covered," Ryker said, glancing at his watch. "Ten minutes ahead of schedule, too. Let's go to any other business and then we'll close out."

One by one, Ryker went around the table, first in New York, then to Upton, me, and finally Sebastian.

"I do have something I'd like to raise actually," he said with an impish grin. He poked his finger at the screen which, given the nature of video conferences, could be aimed at anyone, until he went on to say, "With you, Garen."

Here it comes.

"Is it true that you attended Walther Meyer's charity bash on Wednesday night?"

Something in the tone of his voice set my radar off. I remained slouched in my chair, giving off a relaxed air.

"I did. He heard I was in town and invited me. Problem?"

"Oh, no problem," Sebastian said, his grin widening. "Only that rumor has it you had a pretty little thing on your arm and, by all accounts, you were acting rather smitten."

I schooled my expression, painting an almost bored look on my face. "I took a date. So what? It's hardly front-page news. And let me set the record straight. I'm far from smitten."

"That's not what I heard," Sebastian said, getting into his stride and dragging the rest of the board along with him, their postures showing they were much more interested now than thirty seconds ago. "My spies tell me you couldn't keep your hands off her."

"I don't give a flying fuck what your spies told you," I bit out.

"Ohhh," Sebastian said, outright laughing now. "He's getting all defensive. That must mean he likes her. Aww, Garen's in luurve."

Elliot snorted a laugh.

"Fuck off," I snapped. "I am not in love. I barely know the girl. We've had a couple of dates, and that's it. And if you must know, I'm already getting bored. Give it another week and she'll be gone, just like all the rest."

"And there's the man we know and love," Upton said. "You had me worried for a second there, buddy. What with Ryker and Oliver giving up their bachelorhood, I thought you'd fallen for the feminine wiles, too."

"As if," I scoffed. "I prefer to eat at a buffet. I just need to find a way to let her down gently."

"Gently?" Sebastian scoffed. "You don't let them down gently. You rip the Band-Aid off and enjoy watching them bleed."

My gaze fell to Oliver, the one person who knew me better than all the rest. He hadn't said a single word while the others ripped into me. He'd just stared pensively into the camera, his fingertips stroking a couple of days' stubble, but I saw it right there in his face.

Suspicion.

I heaved a sigh. That grilling I'd expected would arrive soon.

"Yeah, well, her brother's ill. That's what she's doing in Switzerland. He's at a hospital here. Once I work out the right thing to say without crushing her, then it'll be sayonara, sweetheart. I'm not a complete heartless bastard."

"Yeah, you are," Elliot chimed in. "There's a concrete slab where your heart should be."

I flipped him off. "Whatever."

Elliot was wrong. And the reason I knew was that the very heart he accused me of missing constricted so much, I thought I was having a heart attack. I hadn't meant one word I'd uttered, yet for some reason, Sebastian's ribbing had hit a nerve, forcing me to put him off the scent by lying about my feelings. Far from getting bored with Catriona, I craved more, but this was a very new experience for me, and I didn't want my growing attraction toward her examined in minute detail. These five men might be my best friends, but that didn't mean I desired to bare my soul to them. Catriona was my secret to keep, and until I understood what was going on between us, she'd remain that way.

"And on that note, if you're all done ribbing me, I have work to do. Speak next week."

I cut the call and leaned forward. With my elbows propped

up on my desk, I covered my face with my hands. For some unfathomable reason, I felt as if I'd betrayed Catriona, when in reality, I just wasn't ready to share yet. First, I needed to figure out what was going on. Then I'd be ready and willing to have the conversation.

And that conversation would be with her, not ROGUES.

30

Catriona

A few minutes earlier...

Balancing a sandwich in one hand and two bottles of beer in the other, I strolled to Garen's office. I hadn't planned to interrupt him while he was working, but Lia had let it slip that he hadn't eaten since breakfast, and it was already past four. He must be starving. I also might have an ulterior motive.

I missed him.

Something had changed on Wednesday night at the chancellor's event. I felt it. He felt it, although the difference between us was that Garen was clearly struggling and fighting against our growing attraction. But like he said, give him time, and I intended to do just that.

As I approached his office door, voices reached me. Several of them. He must be talking to the other ROGUES members. I hovered, wondering what to do with his late lunch. Maybe I should just leave it outside the door. But then he wouldn't know it was there, and it'd go stale.

No, I'd wait until he finished the call and then interrupt him.

I guessed I'd caught the tail end of the meeting when one of them called for any other business. Seconds later, I heard something that pricked up my ears.

"Rumor has it you had a pretty little thing on your arm and, by all accounts, you were acting rather smitten."

A grin inched across my face, tightening the skin over my cheekbones. I held my breath, waiting to hear Garen's reply.

When it came, I'd never wished for a time-turner more in my entire life. The old saying 'eavesdroppers never hear anything good about themselves' couldn't have held more poignance than when Garen denounced our relationship so viciously, his cold tone splintering my heart into a million pieces. I'd never know how I managed to stagger away from there without dropping his lunch and alerting him to my presence, but somehow, I did.

Shutting myself in my room, I allowed my trembling legs to collapse beneath me. With my back to the door, silent tears tracked down my face, the betrayal too much.

But was it a betrayal? Garen hadn't made any promises. In fact, he'd been honest with me from the very start of our... whatever this was. He'd never had a long-term relationship, and he wasn't going to break that habit with me. What happened on Wednesday had been a lie, although I didn't understand his motives for such a deception. He'd made me think he was changing, but...

Leopards and spots, Catriona.

I pulled myself together, washed the saltiness from my face, and steeled my spine. Placing my hands on either side of the sink, I stared into the mirror.

"You're in control. You. Do *not* let him see he's broken your heart. Stay strong. Own the outcome. Like Grams would say: stand tall."

And that was the moment I knew exactly what I had to do.

I made sure there wasn't a trace of evidence I'd been crying, then returned downstairs. This time when I approached Garen's office, I couldn't hear a sound. I tapped on the door. He called out for me to enter.

"I brought you a sandwich and a beer," I said, brandishing both when what I really wanted to was smash them over his duplicitous head.

He greeted me with a smile that showed just what a great actor he was. I had no idea what his game was, but he could play it alone. I was done with him.

He patted his lap. "Come here."

I remained where I was, inching forward to put the food and drink on the edge of his desk. He frowned, his eyebrows arrowing inward.

"What's the matter?"

"I need to talk to you."

He swiveled his chair around to face me, his frown switching to a concerned head tilt. "Is everything okay? Is it Aiden?"

I sucked in a deep breath and went for it. "Yes and no. I came to Switzerland to support my brother in a fight for his life, and yet it feels as though I've spent more time with you than him."

It wasn't true. Sure, my nights were spent locked in Garen's arms, or most of them anyway, and we'd gone to dinner and to that charity thing on Wednesday, but the vast majority of the day I spent with Aiden. I'd been with him all day at the hospital on Monday and again yesterday, and in-between, when he wasn't too tired, we played chess, watched movies, or strolled around the grounds talking about our hopes and dreams for the future.

Garen crossed his arms over his chest. "I see."

No. You don't. Not yet, anyway.

"And so I've been thinking," I plowed on. "This. Us. It won't work. I appreciate everything you've done for me and my family, and I always will, but Aiden is my priority. I've taken my eye off the ball because I've been having too much fun with you. But that's all it is, Garen. Fun. And I'm calling time."

His jaw slackened, and his brows shot up toward his hairline. "Wait a second. You're breaking up with me?"

I poked my tongue into my cheek. "I wouldn't use those words exactly. I don't think we know each other well enough to attach a term like 'break up' to whatever this was. And like you said, you don't do relationships. As it turns out, neither do I. Not right now when my brother needs me more."

Inside, my heart cracked open wide, so wide I doubted angels sent from Heaven could stitch it back together. But this was the only way I could escape with my honor intact. I'd always known Garen was ruthless and cruel, yet I'd dared to believe there was something about Switzerland that changed him. Turned out it was just a facade, one that had crumbled when he'd shared his true feelings with his friends.

His eyes darkened, eliminating his soft gray irises until they resembled two lumps of charcoal. Cold and hard. A violent tremor shook my entire body, almost as if someone had walked over my grave, and an icy lump settled in the pit of my stomach.

"Good. I was getting bored with you anyway."

I gasped, his comment a dagger to my chest. "That's not true."

Except it was. I'd heard it for myself all too clearly. Something deep inside, though, had hoped I'd misheard. I longed to be wrong about him, prayed he'd stand up and fight for me. For us. That he'd fall to his knees and beg me to reconsider.

I was a fool. A stupid, gullible fool who'd fallen for a man who didn't deserve me. Yet that little voice I couldn't ignore kept whispering that it wasn't all fake. The things he'd said on Wednesday, that I was his. He'd sounded so genuine. He wasn't that good of an actor.

A spark of hope lit within me. Maybe he had a good reason to say those cruel things to his friends. I couldn't come up with what those reasons might be, but I didn't believe he'd feigned his feelings for me either.

"You said I was yours," I whispered, more to myself than to him.

He snorted. "Yeah, and the blow job you gave me that night that was worth the lie. Gotta give it to you, sweetheart. You've a very talented mouth."

Air shot out of my lungs on a whoosh. My lungs flattened, and I struggled to take a full breath. A trembling in my legs had me blindly reaching out to steady myself. My palm connected with the cool drywall.

"No... I..." My tongue felt too large for my mouth, and I couldn't form a proper sentence. My original thoughts about this man were right on. He was a monster, a cruel, heartless beast who used and abused people, then tossed them aside like trash once they'd fulfilled their usefulness.

"And if you recall," he continued, ignoring my attempts to speak, "I also said I wanted you to give me some space to figure things out. What I actually meant was space to work on an easy way to break things off." He barked a laugh. "Y'know, I feel sorry for you. You're desperate and clingy and capitulate far too easily for me to find you interesting beyond what's between your legs. I got what I wanted—your studio and your pussy—and now I've lost interest." He looked me up and down, his gaze disparaging, then got to his feet, turned his back, shoved one hand in his pocket, and stared out the window.

A sob climbed into my throat. I swallowed it down. I wouldn't give him the satisfaction of knowing how much his vicious words had hurt me.

"We'll be out of here first thing in the morning."

"Don't bother. I'm heading back to Canada tomorrow." He pivoted slowly, his expression unreadable. "I told you I'd keep my end of the bargain once I grew tired of you. I'm a man of my word. I will continue to fund Aiden's treatment, as per our original agreement. None of this is his fault, and I want him to recover."

Relief flushed through me. I'd taken a prideful stance, one he'd thankfully thrown back in my face for reasons unknown. Aiden's treatment had only just begun, and although I had the money from the sale of the studio, it would only cover the fee for a couple of months, whereas Aiden would need far more to complete the full treatment program his doctors had designed.

"Thank you," I whispered.

Ice poured from his eyes as he held my gaze. I waited for more, but it never came. He just stood there, loathing seeping from every pore. Silence weighed down on me like a blanket with lead stitched into the lining.

"Get out, Catriona. We're done."

Swallowing my emotions, I made it as far as the entranceway before my legs gave out. I gripped the handrail of the impressive staircase, my fast reactions the only thing preventing me from tumbling to the floor, my breathing staccato as I tried to gulp in air. I hated conflict. Detested it. And going up against Garen Gauthier, a man who excelled in divergent situations had made me feel sick.

You've done the right thing.

I'd need that to become my mantra over the coming days and weeks while I rebuilt my fractured heart.

31

Garen

I jammed a finger against the intercom and barked, "James, get in here."

Within seconds, my executive assistant strode into my office, trusty iPad in hand, and a quirk to his eyebrow that signaled an upcoming query.

"What?" I snapped.

He set the iPad on my desk and—uninvited—took a seat across from me. I gave him a flat stare but allowed the transgression to pass without comment.

"Ever since you returned from Switzerland on Monday, you've been like a grizzly with a hangover. It's not my place to interfere, but—"

"No, it's not," I interrupted. "And I arrived back from Switzerland on Saturday."

"Fine, Saturday then," he parroted with a sigh. "Clearly that detail is important to you."

I canted my head to one side. "Careful, James."

He threw his hands in the air. "Okay, I'm sorry. That was uncalled for. But, Garen, something is very wrong. All I'm saying is that if you want to talk, I'm happy to listen."

"I don't," I bit out, tossing a printed-out email across the desk. "Have you seen this?"

He gave it a cursory glance, then nodded, his lips pursed in that way he did when I'd hurt his feelings. "That's why it's in your 'for action' folder."

I lifted my eyebrows. "Sarcasm reduces the value of your annual bonus." The comment was my way of apologizing, my tone holding a teasing note. James' lips didn't even twitch.

"I'd give up every cent if you'd talk to me."

I let out a deep sigh and pinched the bridge of my nose. "I'm fine."

I'm not fine.

In fact, I doubted fine was a word that I could ever use to describe my feelings again.

I missed Catriona, desperately.

Her lopsided smile, those emerald-green eyes that saw the good in me when I doubted its existence, the tinkling of her laugh, the way she rubbed the space between her eyebrows when deep in thought. How she nibbled her lip as she sat with her feet up in my garden room, reading. I missed the feel of her walls closing around me when I pushed inside her, the softness of her tongue as she licked up and down my shaft.

I just fucking missed her.

James expelled a frustrated huff. "Have it your way. I'm going nowhere."

"Don't bank on it," I muttered.

He laughed. "Darling, you couldn't cope without me, and you know it." He pointed his chin at the email. "Want me to deal with that?"

I shook my head. "I've got it."

"Okay." He rose from the chair and picked up his tablet.

"And please call Oliver. He called again yesterday and twice the day before."

I rubbed my forehead, knowing I couldn't put off my best friend for much longer. He had a sixth sense when it came to me, and ever since I'd spouted all those lies about Catriona at last week's video conference, he'd constantly called as I'd expected. So far, I'd managed to avoid him.

"Garen?"

I lifted my head and gave a curt nod. "Will do."

He left me alone. I glanced up at the clock on the wall. Two p.m. That meant it was five p.m. in New York. I stroked my chin. Too early for a scotch?

Nope.

Striding over to the corner of my office where I kept a small array of drinks, I poured two fingers into a cut-crystal glass and went over to the couch. Instead of sitting, I stood by the window and stared at the city landscape. Gray clouds rolled in, and a few spots of rain splattered the windowpane. On the street below, umbrellas appeared, pedestrians upping their pace to escape the oncoming downpour.

Five days had passed since I'd flown back from Switzerland. Six days since I'd last seen Catriona and said those awful things to her. I hadn't meant one word. Not a single one. Yet she'd swallowed each and every malicious syllable.

At the back of my mind, a gnawing feeling that I was missing something wouldn't let up. Why had she gone from putty in my hands to breaking things off in only two days? On the journey home from Walther's charity bash on Wednesday, she'd melted every time I laid a hand on her or looked at her with hungry eyes. Then two days later, she's breaking it off, citing Aiden as an excuse. Which was bullshit. The whole time we were in Switzerland, she spent the majority of it with Aiden and her grandmother. We'd kept our meet-ups to the evening, which had allowed me to work during the day, and that suited me fine.

The answer hit me like an arrow through the heart.

No.

She couldn't have.

It wasn't possible.

But if it were possible, that would explain everything.

I snatched up my phone and called Lia. Despite the late hour in Switzerland, she answered within a few seconds.

"Lia, sorry to call so late. I need a favor."

"What is it?" she answered. "Do you need me to get Catriona?"

As if I'd been punched in the stomach, I curved in on myself. The mere mention of her name was like a hot knife to the gut.

"No. But I do need two of you for this. Can you wake Raphael and get him to come up to the house? I need both of you to go to my office."

Raphael was my gardener and, like Lia, he lived on-site in a small house in the grounds.

"Of course."

The sound of bedsheets rustling reached me.

"I'll call you back in ten minutes," I said. She'd need that long to get in touch with Raphael and have him make the short walk up to the main house.

I paced while I waited. If my experiment proved what I feared, that would explain Catriona's strange turnaround, so out of character and diametrically opposed to her actions. Once I'd waited the allotted amount of time, I pressed redial.

"Okay, we're in your office. I have Raphael with me."

"Great," I said. "Lia, I want you to stand outside and close the door. Ask Raphael to talk, and you let me know if you can hear him."

"What do you want him to say?" she asked.

I rolled my eyes. "Anything. He can read from a book on the shelves. It doesn't matter." I managed to keep the frustration out of my voice. I'd woken the woman up and asked her to do something that probably sounded strange. Couldn't blame her for asking questions.

"Hold on."

The sound of her giving him instructions came over the line, and then I heard a definite click which must be Lia leaving my office.

"I'm standing outside," she said.

"Great. Now tell me if you can hear him by simply standing there or whether you have to press your ear against the door."

"No need for an ear," she said, giggling. "I can hear him loud and clear."

My heart plunged to my feet.

Fuck.

Catriona must have heard every lying word spilling from my lips.

Fucking Sebastian and his inane delving into my goddamn private life. If he'd kept his mouth shut, none of this would have happened. Next time I saw him, I'd ram my fist into his throat.

It isn't Sebastian's fault, dickhead. It's yours.

"Thanks, Lia," I said despondently. "Tell Raphael thanks, too. Go to bed. Oh, and don't mention any of this to Catriona, please."

"As you wish," she said.

I hung up and sank into the plush cream leather sofa, my head in my hands.

It didn't matter how Catriona had heard what I'd told the ROGUES board. The fact remained she'd never believe it was all a lie, a way of saving face because I was a fucking idiot who needed to grow the hell up and admit to my friends that I'd met someone that I actually liked being around. Instead, when Sebastian had teased me over my *smitten state*, rather than smile and agree, I'd acted like a stupid teenager denying his first crush in front of his school friends.

For the first time in my life, I couldn't figure a way out of the dreadful mess I'd created.

So I did the only thing I could think of.

I called Oliver.

He answered like a man who'd been expecting my call. Fast.

"Fuck me, he lives."

"You saw me last Friday," I said.

"Oh yeah. So I did." His voice held a heavy dose of sarcasm. "And since then, I've called you several fucking times, and you've either let my call go to voicemail or you've blackmailed James into doing your dirty work. What I want to know is why?"

"I haven't blackmailed James," I said. "He's paid to protect me."

"Yeah, and his talents are usually put to use placating your latest conquest with an arm around the shoulder and a gift from Tiffany's after you've gotten bored with her, not finding excuses for why you're ignoring calls from me."

"I've been busy," I muttered. "How's Harlow and Annie?"

Asking about his girlfriend and eight-year-old daughter, the absolute apple of his eye, usually turned him to mush and allowed me to control the conversation. Not this time.

"They're fine, and you're a liar."

"Fucking charming," I bit out. "And what is it you think I've lied about?"

"I *know* you lied about this girl you were seen in Switzerland with. I get why you clammed up when Sebastian behaved like a dick, but I know you, Garen. I saw it in your eyes. There's something different about this girl, and the fact you've avoided speaking to me since proves it." He took a breath. "Do you like her?"

"It doesn't matter whether I do or I don't. It's irrelevant."

"Why?"

"Because she dumped me."

I winced and grabbed a fistful of my shirt as if that would stop the cramping in my chest. Air whistled through Oliver's teeth, and silence hung between us.

"Why?" he eventually asked. "What did you do?"

"How come you think I did anything?" I responded like an innocent man when I was anything but.

"Garen, I love you like a brother, but when it comes to relationships, you suck. It's a matter of deduction that I'd lay odds on any breakup being caused by you."

"She heard me," I said, scratching my cheek and blowing out a deep sigh. "She heard the bullshit lies I told you all last Friday. And to make matters worse, when she broke it off, I said some pretty nasty things that guaranteed she'll never speak to me again."

"Oh, buddy..."

"Don't," I said, despondency weighing heavily on my shoulders and curving my spine. "What should I do?"

"When you say nasty, how nasty?"

I closed my eyes, the vitriol I'd spewed seeping into the forefront of my mind. "Brutal."

"Shit. Okay..." A pause, then, "Here's what I would do. Send her a letter—it's more personal than an email—along with a bouquet of flowers and apologize. Just that. Don't ask her to take you back, don't say you want to see her. Offer up a simple apology and make sure it's from the heart."

"And then?"

"And then you wait."

"For what?"

"For her reply."

I swirled the glass of scotch, then took a sip, the burn warming my chilled insides. "And what if that never comes?"

Oliver's resigned sigh filled me with despair. "Then there's your answer."

I knocked back the rest of the liquor. "That's it? You wouldn't fight for her?"

"I didn't say that. You'd have an uphill battle on your hands, that's all. It's up to you whether you want to scale that mountain only to have her push you off when you reach the summit and watch with glee as you plunge to your death."

"Nice analogy," I muttered, rubbing the ache in the back of my neck.

"Thanks. I thought so."

I smiled despite my dark mood. "I'll give it a try." What else could I do other than sit here bemoaning what might have been?

"Good luck. For what it's worth, I really hope it works out for you, man."

"You and me both," I stated.

As soon as I cut the call, I stepped over to my desk. Writing letters wasn't a regular activity, but on occasion, I sent one to my mother. She was an old-fashioned kind who liked to keep written correspondence in a tattered cardboard box that she'd had ever since I could remember. She kept all kinds of shit in there, from my first school picture to my first tooth, to the cap I'd worn when I graduated college.

I retrieved a sheet of thick, cream paper from the small stack in the second drawer of my desk, and a matching envelope. Addressing it to Catriona at my Swiss home, I stared at the blank page for a good few minutes while I tried to rearrange the jumble of words in my head into something that would make sense and demonstrate not only my heartfelt sorrow at what I'd done, but how much I missed her and sought her forgiveness.

Eventually, I picked up my pen and began to write. By the time I'd finished, I'd used two more sheets of paper, and as I reread what I'd written, I thought it clearly showed how much I regretted my behavior.

Feeling a lightness I hadn't in days, I dropped the letter on James' desk and instructed him to send it to Switzerland along with an enormous bouquet of burgundy roses and white tulips. I researched the flowers. Burgundy roses represented unconscious beauty which fitted Catriona perfectly, and white tulips, in some quarters, symbolized an apology.

A week passed by without a word from Catriona. I tried not to lose hope, but when James entered my office holding a large box that, when I opened it was filled with dead petals off the roses and tulips, their once vibrant soft leaves a crumpled mess, and my letter torn in two, I had my answer.

There would be no forgiveness, no belief in my admittance that what she'd overheard was a lie. No retraction of the bitter and merciless things I'd said.

It had taken me twenty-nine years, but I'd finally found a woman I wanted.

And I'd ruined it.

32

CATRIONA

"Aiden is responding beautifully to the treatment," Dr. Faussman said, the edges of his hands resting on his desk as he leaned forward to discuss my brother's progress.

Almost three months had passed since we'd arrived in Switzerland, and Garen had kept his word, the payments for Aiden's treatment arriving regular as clockwork. Since his pitiful attempt at an apology arrived ten days after I'd broken things off and I'd responded with a clear "Screw. You", I hadn't heard from him, and I didn't expect to. I hadn't even read the damned letter. I had no interest in anything the man had to say after the way he'd behaved.

These days, at least I didn't think about him every hour. Sometimes I went an entire day without his handsome face creeping into my mind and making me long for him so badly, I could barely stand from the pain in my chest.

Grams had drilled into me with her constant questioning, trying to understand what had happened, but when I remained tight-lipped and said nothing more than we'd decided to call it a day, she'd relented and had switched to mother hen mode instead, cooking up a storm and trying to force-feed me the myriad baked goods that appeared each afternoon. How Lia put up with Grams taking over her kitchen was a mystery to me. Then again, the two of them had become fast friends despite the eighteen-year age gap.

"We should be able to move on to the next phase of our plan."

I jerked back to the present from the dark corners of my mind and mustered a bright smile. "That's really great news, Doctor. I can't thank you enough for everything you've done for Aiden and continue to do."

"It's our pleasure," he said. "He's a joy to be around, always so positive in his outlook. It's one of the criteria for success, you know. Positivity. That's why he's only had to stay in for three weeks for this portion of this treatment. For most patients it is at least four weeks. He's a trooper."

I smiled at his compliment. "That he is. When do you think he'll be able to return home to Canada and continue his treatment remotely?"

I wasn't in a rush to be in the same city as Garen, but equally, living in his home in Switzerland had grown torturous, especially as in every corner there seemed to be a memory I wanted to expunge. I couldn't bear to go up onto the roof terrace where Garen and I shared our first kiss, and I was grateful that his suite of rooms were at the opposite end of the house and I could avoid them. Every part of me ached for him. Day and night. There was no respite from the agony of being apart, especially knowing we'd never be together again.

Dr. Faussman twisted his lips to one side, considering. "Hmm. Maybe in another three to four weeks. I want to keep an eye on his transition back to a twice-weekly treatment program and continue to run regular tests until I'm sure the oral medication is enough to eradicate the last vestiges of the disease and push him into remission."

"I understand." I rose from the chair and leaned forward to shake his hand. "Thank you once again."

"You're welcome. I'll see you on Thursday as normal."

I left his office and returned to Aiden's room to take him back to Garen's place. I couldn't call it home. It wasn't my home. It was *his*. And I couldn't wait to leave.

Grams was sitting beside Aiden's bed, clacking her knitting needles as usual while Aiden sat on the edge, anxious to leave the confines of the hospital where he'd resided for the last twenty-two days. The first couple of months they'd treated him as an out-patient, but the past three weeks, they'd intensified the therapy which meant he'd had to stay as an in-patient where the nurses and doctors could keep a close eye on his progress.

"Ready to go, kiddo?" I asked.

He jumped off the bed, a huge smile almost cracking his face in half. "Am I ever."

I slung an arm around his shoulder and ruffled his hair. "Dr. Faussman is really happy with how you're doing. He's hoping that after a few more weeks of treatment, you might be able to go home."

"To Canada?" Aiden asked excitedly, while Grams lifted her head and gave me a questioning look.

"Yep. To Canada. It means we'll have to stay here for Christmas, but hopefully early in January, we can head home."

"Awesome." His grin widened. "Christ, I've missed my friends."

"Wash out your mouth," Grams said, waggling a finger in warning.

I caught his eye and winked. "Let's go. I don't know about you two, but I'm starved."

We walked down the hallway toward the exit. As I pressed

one hand on the door to open it, someone called my name. I turned around to see the administrator, Mrs. Schmid, gesturing to me.

"Miss Landry. I hoped I'd catch you. Do you have a moment?"

"Sure," I said congenially. I turned back to Grams and Aiden. "You two grab a drink, and I'll see what she wants."

I headed back the way we'd come and followed Mrs. Schmid to her office. Taking a seat across from her desk, I smiled. "Dr. Faussman thinks we might be able to return to Canada in a few weeks."

"That's wonderful news," Mrs. Schmid said. "We'll miss seeing you around here, especially Aiden, but it's better he's at home where he has familiar things around him. It can't have been easy for you these past few months."

My eyes glazed over. At first, I'd had the best time of my life. With *him*. And then I heard what couldn't be unheard, and that was that. Shit city from there on in. At least at home with my own possessions and comforts around me, I wouldn't see Garen wherever I went.

Lies, lies, lies.

Of course I would. The man had burrowed into my head and my heart. There was no escape. I only had to close my eyes to see him, feel him. Want him desperately.

Conscious Mrs. Schmid was still waiting for an answer, I pasted on a fake smile and hoped she couldn't tell it lacked sincerity. "We've loved living in Switzerland. I'll miss the place terribly, but I am looking forward to going home, and I know Aiden is. He can't wait to see all his friends."

She nodded sagely. "Not an easy thing for a young boy to go through, but he's handled it with aplomb."

"He's tough."

She knitted her hands together and leaned forward. "I have something a little... delicate to discuss." A trace of pink stained her cheeks. "I have left it as long as I can, but unfortunately, I have no option other than to raise it with you."

I mirrored her posture, my gut swirling. She seemed uncomfortable and embarrassed. What the hell was going on? I bounced my legs up and down. "What is it?"

Her teeth nipped at her bottom lip, apprehension coming off her in waves. "Aiden's last payment... well, it didn't arrive."

My pulse raced, and a numbness spread to my fingertips. Garen wouldn't. Would he? No, he'd promised, *promised* to keep paying Aiden's fees. And he had. The last two payments had gone through fine. Why would he suddenly renege on his pledge?

"There must be a mistake," I said. "Can you check again?"

"There's no mistake," Mrs. Schmid replied, her face crimson now. Clearly the woman wasn't used to conflict situations. This was a hospital where only the rich attended. A missed payment must be a rare thing indeed. "I called the bank in case there was a holdup at their end, but they assured me there wasn't. The money has simply not been transferred by the other side."

I almost questioned the bank and then remembered... Swiss banks don't make mistakes.

"I'll get right on it."

A great ball of nausea put down roots in my stomach at the thought of having to call Garen and discuss this issue with him.

"I'd appreciate that," she said. "I can give you a couple of days but..."

She trailed off, but she didn't need to finish the sentence. This was a private facility, a for-profit organization. Services had to be paid for, or they wouldn't be delivered.

"I understand, Mrs. Schmid. Please don't worry. I will get the money to you."

If Garen had gone back on his pledge to continue to fund Aiden's treatment here, then I'd have no choice other than to use the money he'd paid me for the studio. The majority of which I'd locked into a long-term savings account to increase the amount of interest earned. If I removed it now, I'd have to pay an exit fee, and that wouldn't be cheap.

Goddamn you, Garen. You absolute bastard.

If he'd woken up one day pissed at some shitty business deal gone wrong and decided to pay me back for the way I rejected his pitiful apology by using my brother's illness, I would take a scalpel to his fucking balls.

I said goodbye to Mrs. Schmid and returned to the waiting area where Grams and Aiden were drinking steaming mugs of cocoa. Grams gave me a look in the form of a raised eyebrow, but I shook my head slightly. *Not right now. Later.*

Aiden filled the silence on the way home, his excited chatter and vows to call all of his friends this evening somehow forcing my lips to smile when inside my anger built, a bubbling inferno ready to spew ash and lava the second I got Garen on the phone.

Hang on, Catriona. Wait and see what he says first.

Yeah, that's what I'd do. I'd calmly tell him that the payment hadn't arrived and wait for his response.

And if he'd withheld the payment on purpose, then I'd boil him alive.

Aiden shot straight upstairs the second we got back. As soon as he was out of sight, Grams folded her arms across her chest. "What did the administrator want?"

I blinked slowly and blew out a breath through pursed lips. "Garen didn't send the last payment."

Grams widened her eyes, then shook her head. "There has to be some mistake. He wouldn't. Would he? There has to be a reason."

I heaved a sigh. "Well, I'm about to find out."

I trudged upstairs, entered my room, and took a seat by the window, I rummaged in my purse, eventually locating my phone where it had fallen from the slot where I normally kept it.

Five times I went to press the call button that would connect me to Garen. And five times I backed out. Just the thought of speaking to him sent me into a tizzy. Pulling the petals off that enormous bouquet of flowers and tearing up his letter—the one I never read—had been cathartic, but now I worried that if I heard his voice, I'd relent, and some of the anger I'd cultivated would wither and die.

I opened my mind and allowed the memory to form. The memory of that day weeks earlier when I'd stood outside his office and heard him denounce me to his friends. And then I replayed every single cruel word he'd uttered, from his admission that he'd lied when he'd told me I was his, to the offensive comment about the blow job I'd given him that night, and then how he'd further insulted me by saying he felt sorry for me.

I didn't want his pity.

But I did need his generosity.

And that killed me. If it were my treatment he'd offered to pay for, I'd tell him where to shove it. But I couldn't do that to Aiden.

Then again, I did have the money to pay for it now, especially if, as Dr. Faussman had alluded to, we only had another few weeks of hospital treatment. I could just suck up the penalty by withdrawing cash from the locked-in account and pay for it myself. It'd make a hell of a dent in money I'd hoped to retain to pay for any further therapy Aiden might need, now or in the future, but at least I'd keep my pride intact.

Yep, decision made.

But not before I'd called to tell him exactly what I thought of him.

I jabbed a finger at the screen, and a second later, the ringing tone sounded in my ear. I could barely breathe as I waited for him to answer. I heard a click, and then his voicemail message.

You've reached Garen Gauthier. Leave a message.

I almost hung up. Almost. Especially when I realized it was the middle of the night in Vancouver, and the late hour was the probable cause for my call going to voicemail.

Screw it.

The man deserved to feel my rage, my anger, my betrayal. He deserved it to flay his skin and sear his heart—not that he had one. No, where his heart should be lay a black hole.

"It's me. Catriona. I just wanted to call and say thanks. Thanks for dropping the payments on Aiden's treatment without having the courtesy to tell me. Then again, why would you? This is you we're talking about. You probably got bored. A bit like you did with me. Making three payments. Yeah, you managed that, but the fourth? Nope. Impossible. If payments were dates, right?" I snorted a laugh. "Well, don't worry about it, okay. It's all in hand. But you should know that I think you're a vindictive asshole. I hope revenge tastes sweet. I hope it's so sweet, all your teeth fall out. Have a nice life."

Shaking, I hung up. I had no idea how much time passed as I sat there staring at my phone, half hoping, half dreading a call back.

None came. Not that hour, or later in the day when even the winter sun would have kissed the horizon on the west coast of Canada.

I hadn't expected anything else. Not really.

Despite that, the pang in my heart wouldn't go away.

Sometimes, being right sucked.

33

Garen

A shrill ringing jerked me awake from a deep sleep. I tried to open my eyes, but they refused to budge. I rubbed them, blinked rapidly, then squinted at the clock.

Three forty-seven a.m.

What the fuck?

The ringing stopped only to begin again immediately. I felt around for my phone. My chest tightened when, through blurred vision, I spotted the caller ID and the missed calls from my mother.

"Mom," I rasped, my voice heavy with sleep. I struggled to sit up. "What's the matter?"

"Oh, Garen." The worry in her tone pushed away the last remnants of drowsiness. "We're at the Santa Ana hospital. It's your father. They think he's had a heart attack." A sob broke from her throat. "His lips were blue."

A tightness gripped my chest, my heart pounding painfully against my ribcage. My father was healthy as an ox. For Christ's sake, he was only fifty-eight. Fit, a regular runner, not overweight.

"Is he alive?" I managed to croak.

Please say yes. Please say yes. I wasn't ready to lose my old man. I loved the fucking bones of him.

"Yes," she said, and a wave of relief left me lightheaded. "But they're saying it was severe, Garen. They told me the next several hours are critical."

"Hold tight, Mom. I'm on my way."

I hung up the phone and dived out of bed. Grabbing a leather duffel bag, I began opening drawers and stuffing in the first items to hand. Boxers, socks, shirts, and pants. In the bathroom, I packed a toiletry bag and my electric razor, then threw it in the duffel bag alongside everything else.

I sped down the stairs, taking them two at a time. Within ten minutes I was on my way to the private airfield. I phoned Simon, my pilot, told him where we were headed, and he promised to have my plane fueled and ready to fly by the time I got there.

True to his word, as I slewed the car to a stop, he already had the steps of the plane down. I strode over, my face grim with worry.

"Thanks for this. Sorry about the early hour."

"It's not a problem. I've filed our flight plan and I have a take-off window for twenty minutes' time."

I jogged up the steps, Simon right behind me.

"I'm sorry about your dad," he said with a sympathetic twist of his lips. "I'll get you there fast as I can."

"I know you will."

My head spun as the plane taxied to our takeoff position, and as we soared into the air, I quickly composed an email to the ROGUES board telling them what had happened. Due to the time difference, everyone except Upton replied almost immediately telling—no, ordering—me to forget work and concentrate on being there for Dad and supporting Mom. They knew me too well, my workaholic reputation earned over many years, and evidenced by a follow-up email to Upton asking him to take care of some elements of the hotel build. We were at a crucial stage and on track to beat my original four-month target for the vast majority of the hotel to be complete. We were already taking bookings, our opening night planned for New Year's Eve, a little over two weeks' time. My final message went to James with a list of instructions of which meetings to cancel and which I wanted to go ahead, albeit over the phone or videocall rather than in person.

I dozed, sleeping only fitfully, and when we landed almost five hours later, I felt almost hungover, my legs wobbly, and a tremor in my hands wouldn't let up. A car waited at the bottom of the steps ready to whisk me straight to the hospital. I called Mom, but it went to voicemail, so I left a brief message assuring her I'd be there soon. I saw I'd had a few other voicemails, but they'd have to wait. My primary concern right now was getting to Dad and being there to support Mom.

By the time I arrived at the main entrance to Santa Ana, more than six and a half hours had passed since Mom's call. Striding through the reception area, I sent up a silent prayer that Dad was still alive. God, if he'd passed while I was in the air, it'd crush me. Fuck only knew what it'd do to Mom. My parents shared that one-of-a-kind connection that was rarer than a blue steak. I believed my wandering eye and unwillingness to consider a long-term relationship was due to the fact I didn't believe lightning struck twice in the same family. The chances of finding someone who loved me and I loved in return so completely, like my parents did, was slim to none.

And like in the rest of my life, I refused to settle for second best.

My mind went to Catriona, but I slammed the door shut. That ship had sailed. And it wasn't even a ship. More a dinghy, or a raft built with rotten wood that sank on the first wave that hit.

I gave my name and Dad's to the nurse sitting behind the desk. She smiled kindly, tapped on a keyboard, then met my gaze.

"Room four twenty-two. On the fourth floor. The elevators are over there, right behind you."

"Thank you." I went to ask her if she knew his status, but it was unlikely. This was a large hospital. She wouldn't know the condition of every patient here.

On Dad's floor, another nurse sitting behind an identical, although smaller, desk, greeted me. I repeated my name, and she nodded and stood.

"I'll take you to him. Your mom told us to expect you."

"How is he?" I asked, then held my breath as I waited for her answer.

"He's had a restful night. He's not out of the woods yet, but his doctor is hopeful that, in time, he'll make a full recovery."

Air whooshed from my lungs, and I put out a hand to steady myself against the wall. "Oh, thank god."

She opened the door to Dad's hospital room. I'd barely gotten one foot inside before Mom leaped to her feet and threw herself into my arms.

"You're here," she said, hugging me tighter than her slight frame would indicate her capable of.

I kissed the top of her head, my gaze going to Dad. A pile of pillows was propped behind his head, and he had a tube in his arm and wires attached to his chest. His eyes were shut. If it weren't for the medical paraphernalia, I'd assume he was completely healthy.

"How you holding up, Mom?"

She leaned back, her neck craned to look up at me. I got my height from my father. The top of Mom's head barely reached my shoulder. "I'm better now that you're here."

A fist wrapped around my heart and squeezed, making it difficult to take a proper breath. I tried to see my parents as often as I could, but running a multi-national company with interests all over the globe, and living over five hours away by aircraft, made dropping by for a cup of tea an impossibility. It was a miracle if I got to Montreal three times a year.

No more.

After this, I'd make the effort to visit them far more regularly.

Funny, wasn't it, how it took the near-death of someone you adored for you to realize what was important.

Family.

Love.

Catriona.

No!

She'd made her feelings clear, and I couldn't blame her. What I did, the lies I told, the things I said to her were unforgiveable. A bunch of flowers and a letter written from the heart weren't enough. I'd destroyed the one thing in my life that hadn't deserved it, and I'd have to live with the consequences.

I pulled up a chair and sat next to Mom. She held Dad's hand, and I held hers. We discussed mundane things, but it was better than the crisp silence, interrupted on occasion by a gust of wind whistling through the windows. A couple of hours later, his little finger twitched, and then his eyes flickered open. He closed them again almost immediately, but there was no doubt he was coming around.

"Rayan." Mom rose from her chair and loomed over him. "Rayan, it's me, darling. Garen's here. Can you open your eyes for us?"

"I'll get the doctor," I said, making for the door.

"No."

Dad's first word since I got here might have sounded little more than a croak, but regardless, he'd spoken. I peered over

Mom's shoulder. Dad's gray eyes, so like my own, stared back at me, a clarity to them that sent a shot of hope ricocheting through me.

"Hey, old man." I hit him with a grin. "Y'know, you could have just asked me to visit. No need to fake a heart attack to get me here."

"Less of the old," he rasped. "And fake my ass."

And that was when I knew Dad was going to make it. I closed my eyes briefly as Mom pressed a kiss to Dad's forehead.

"I thought I'd lost you. Oh, Rayan."

A sob broke from her throat, and a lump crawled into mine. I swallowed it down. If I gave in to the emotions swirling within me, I wouldn't be able to stop, and Mom needed my strength to bolster hers.

Dad lifted his arm and patted Mom's shoulder. "Giselle, don't make a fuss now."

"Let me get the doctor," I said, stepping toward the door for the second time. "They'll want to check you over."

I left the medical staff with Dad and went to grab a couple of coffees for Mom and me. On the way there, I pulled out my phone to listen to the voicemails I'd ignored earlier.

The most recent was from Upton, telling me not to worry about a goddamn thing and he'd take care of everything. I smiled as I listened to the command in his voice. The ROGUES guys had my back, always.

The second was from James confirming he'd carried out my instructions and to call him when I got a minute, and to give his best to my dad.

The third caused my heart to leap into my mouth, but as I listened to more and more of Catriona's vitriolic tirade, my heart turned to a slab of granite, and fury sent a burning fire of rage careering through me.

Finding a quiet corner from which to vent, I stabbed at the

screen and waited for the call to connect. She answered on the third ring.

"Hello, Ga—"

"Who the fuck do you think you are?" I barked before she'd even finished her greeting.

"I beg your pardon?"

"You fucking should beg my goddamn pardon. Let me make one thing clear. I keep my promises, got it? I have no idea what's happened to the transfer for Aiden's medical treatment, but when I said I'd fund it, I fucking meant it. My guess? It's a simple admin error, but that's right, Catriona, you go ahead and assume I spend all my time thinking up ways to make your life miserable."

The sound of her taking a deep breath came over the line, while my chest pumped furiously. I flexed my fingers while waiting for her to respond.

"Can you blame me for thinking the worst? Especially given how we left things between us."

"There is no *us,* as you've made perfectly clear. And if I'd had revenge on my mind, why do you think I'd have paid the last two payments and not this latest one? Did you think I'd woken up one day and just thought 'fuck it' and decided to play fast and loose with the health of a fifteen-year-old boy who's done nothing to deserve my wrath?"

She gasped, air whistling through her teeth, but I'd gotten into my stride now.

"Do you want to know where I am right this second? Do you?"

"Okay," she said, her voice small and quiet.

"I'm at the Santa Ana hospital in Montreal. My father had a heart attack. I've only just gotten your message, you know, because I was too fucking busy flying to be by his bedside while he lay at death's fucking door."

A passing nurse shot me a glare. I turned my back on her.

"God, Garen, I'm so sorry. How is he? Will he be all right?"

"What the fuck do you care, Catriona?"

The line fell silent, but I knew she was still there. I could hear her breathing. I kept the call open. As angry as I was, just being on the phone with her made my heart weep with joy. Fuck, I missed her worse than an absent limb. I wanted to climb down the phone line and crawl into her arms and tell her how much she meant to me, but I'd seen red, and all I wanted to do was hit out at her especially.

"I do care," she whispered, a hitch to her voice that sounded like she was holding back tears.

I squeezed my eyes closed. I couldn't do this right now. Maybe never. But definitely not with my father lying close by in a hospital bed. I had more pressing things that needed my attention.

"I've got to go. I'll get James onto the missing payment."

Stabbing the end call button before she responded, I rested my forehead against the wall.

I wanted her, but I didn't know how to win her back. I had no experience to call upon. I twisted my lips to the side in a wry smile. Yelling at her following months of silence probably wasn't the right strategy. I pinched the bridge of my nose and bowed my shoulders as exhaustion swept through me.

Come on, jackass. Focus on Dad's recovery and supporting Mom and then work to win back Catriona.

34

Garen

I wandered from room to room at my parents' house, eventually stopping outside my childhood bedroom. A grin inched across my face. Every time I visited I told Mom to redecorate, but she stubbornly refused. I stepped over the threshold, and a sense of belonging came over me. I'd left home at the age of eighteen when I moved to America to attend college, only visiting at the end of each semester, and while I'd assumed I'd come back here to live after I graduated, the unexpected launch of ROGUES and the subsequent need for the six of us to mobilize the company and ride the sudden wave of success had sent me to Vancouver instead.

But each time I returned, the fact Mom had kept my bedroom exactly the same, from the posters of ice hockey players on the walls, to the soccer and swimming trophies I'd collected during my sporty days in high school, and even the colorful bedspread she'd painstakingly sewn square by square, told me how loved I was. Me being an only child—despite Mom and Dad both wanting more kids—had meant they'd spoiled me.

My thoughts turned to Catriona and how much she'd missed out on by losing her parents at such a young age and how privileged I'd been. I closed my eyes.

Fuck, I miss you.

"Penny for your thoughts."

I twisted around to find Mom standing behind me. I pushed away the darkness that threatened to pull me under and smiled at her. "You're stealthy."

She cocked her head. "Dinner's ready."

I nodded and followed her to the kitchen. Sitting down to one of Mom's home-cooked meals was a rarity I relished, and the sight of her specialty—grilled salmon with maple glaze and a side of wild rice—flooded my mouth with saliva.

"That looks amazing," I said, taking a seat at the kitchen table. "Dad'll curse when he finds out you made his favorite and he wasn't here to enjoy it."

"I'll make it again when he comes home in a couple of days."

I dug in, savoring the sweet, sticky fish and rice Mom had flavored with dill. "I really must visit more often, if only for your cooking."

She grinned. "Whatever means I get to see my boy more often, I'll take it."

We ate and I cleared the table, then Mom and I ventured into the living room to relax in front of the TV. Spending all day in the hospital mightn't sound tiring, but surprisingly, it was. Or maybe it had something to do with the relief that my father was making a speedy recovery and would be home soon, in time for Christmas.

I stared blankly at the TV show Mom had picked, not really paying attention. With time to think, my mind turned, once again, to Catriona. I knew she was still in Switzerland; Lia gave me regular updates, and right now she was probably curled up in bed, fast asleep, with thoughts of me far from her mind. She hadn't called me back after I berated her so viciously. I wasn't the least bit surprised, but still, disappointment nibbled away at my insides. I still hadn't come up with a strategy for winning her back, and even if I did, there was no guarantee of success.

I didn't like those odds.

"Garen, what's the matter?"

My brow furrowed as I moved my gaze from the TV to my mother. "Nothing, why?"

She inclined her head to the left. "You seem sad. Depressed even. And that makes me unhappy."

I patted her arm and forced a smile that wavered, then fell. "I'm fine, Mom."

"Is it a woman?" she asked. "You can talk to me, you know. I remember all too well what it was like to be young. All those raging hormones giving me grief."

A chuckle left my mouth, and I went to allay her fears with empty platitudes. But then I changed my mind. Talking to her could help. She might have the answer to my conundrum. It couldn't hurt to bring her up to date with the last few months.

"Yeah, it's a woman. A beautiful, amazing woman who I do not deserve."

"I'm sure that's not true."

"Hold that thought," I said with a grin.

I told her everything. Well, almost everything. Admittedly, I left out one or two encounters. My mother did not need to know the full extent of my immorality. She listened in complete silence. Not a single interruption, just the occasional murmur or head nod while I spilled my guts. It felt so damned good to just get it all out there, the cathartic baring of my soul reaffirming how much Catriona meant to me.

"You love her," my mother stated with a knowing bob of her

head. "You're in love with this woman, and you've messed up and don't know how to fix things."

A denial was on the tip of my tongue, but it died there, slain by the truth of my mother's shrewd proclamation.

I hung my head. "Yes."

"Have you told her you love her?"

I snorted. "I don't think she'd be interested in declarations of love after I yelled at her."

"From what you told me, she gives as good as she gets."

A smile formed on my lips. "Very true. She does."

"Do you have a picture?" Mom asked.

Leaning forward, I picked my phone up from the coffee table and opened the photos app, flicking through until I found the one I was looking for. I didn't have many pictures of Catriona, but from the few I had taken during our short time in Switzerland, this one was my favorite. Taken on our yacht trip in Geneva, Catriona was smiling, her face flushed by the keen wind, sunglasses on top of her head and her hair blowing about wildly. I handed the phone to my mother.

"That's Catriona."

Even I could hear the tenderness and wonder in my voice, along with a sizeable dose of pride.

Mom stared at the picture for a few seconds, her brow furrowed. "She's beautiful. Have I met her before?"

I shook my head. "Definitely not. Why?"

"She reminds me of someone." She rubbed the space between her eyebrows. "It'll come to me in a minute." A few more seconds passed, and then she touched her fingertips to her forehead. "Got it. She reminds me of Rosie Moreau."

I frowned. "Who?"

"You remember," Mom said in that way parents always did when you'd just stated you hadn't a clue what they were going on about. "Rosie. She was in your class at elementary school.

Third grade. You took a liking to her, and one day on the way to school, you picked her a bunch of wildflowers and plucked up the courage to give them to her. A group of older boys saw you, and they laughed at you and called you pathetic. I remember you came home from school bawling your eyes out. You were a sensitive boy in those days. After that incident, the bullying started, and Rosie, wanting to fit in, sided with the mean kids and refused to talk to you. That's when you developed a stammer."

Fuck. Me. I must have blocked the memory of Rosie *and* the speech impediment I'd had in my early years. Christ, yes, it was coming back to me now. I'd visited a speech therapist for two years, and it eventually disappeared.

"Jesus." I rubbed my forehead. "I haven't thought about her in years. I remember she really hurt my feelings, though, when she refused to have anything to do with me. Looking back, I guess, like all kids, she just wanted to fit in. Wonder what happened to her?"

Mom shook her head. "No idea. Her parents left the area later that school year."

A sudden notion occurred to me, one I contemplated keeping to myself. Catriona *did* resemble Rosie Moreau. It was faint but there all the same. The eyes. That's where the similarity was. And her smile. But mostly the eyes.

I decided to voice my thoughts to Mom. "Do you think the vague similarity between Catriona and Rosie is part of the reason why I took such pleasure every time I landed a low blow and hurt Catriona? That in some way I was trying to assert myself as the powerful one because I'd been bullied at school, and somewhere in my subconscious, I'd attributed the bullying with being nice to Rosie?"

Mom twisted her lips and shrugged. "Could be."

"Fuck," I muttered as another thought occurred to me.

When Seb teased me about Catriona, I'd rushed to deny I felt anything for her, almost as if I was still that little kid scared my buddies would tease me over a girl.

Mom squeezed my hand. "Sweetheart, even if that is why, you were completely unaware of it, and so I don't think you should be too hard on yourself. The subconscious is a funny thing, as is memory. Both can play tricks on us."

"Yeah, I guess."

"As for what you should do," Mom continued, oblivious to how much I was reeling from her astute observation. "Wait for her to return to Canada and then go to see her. Stay calm and explain everything. Including Rosie and the bullying you suffered as a child, if you feel it's important enough, but most of all, tell her how you feel."

"And what if she says she doesn't feel the same?"

Mom's mouth turned down at the edges. "That's life, sweetheart."

I scrubbed a hand over my face, then palmed the back of my neck. "I don't think I can accept that outcome."

Mom smiled, my answer clearly the one she'd been hoping for. "Then fight for her. Show her she's worth it. Unearth a grand gesture that demonstrates your love."

"A grand gesture," I mused, my heart racing, drumming in my chest as I realized I had the perfect way to show Catriona what she meant to me. One I'd put into motion long ago, a long time before I realized she was the love of my life. Back then, I hadn't understood why I'd done it, especially as it had been fucking expensive. Now, of course, it all became clear. Maybe even then I'd realized our futures were intertwined, that we were meant to be together. Perhaps my subconscious had known the truth all along and patiently waited for my heart to catch up. I couldn't show her until she returned to Canada, but it was fucking perfect. She'd have to realize how much she meant to me as soon as she saw it.

I leaned over and kissed Mom on the cheek. "You, Mother dearest, are a genius."

She grazed her knuckles over my cheek. "And you, my darling boy, are my proudest achievement. Now go get the girl."

35

Catriona

The airplane wheels touched down with a hard bump, and I gripped the sides of the seat, my fingers brushing Aiden's who grinned over at me and mouthed "Lightweight."

I stuck out my tongue, and as the captain throttled back, I was thrown forward in my seat. I cursed under my breath but still caught a fierce glare from Grams. The woman never missed a thing.

"Glad to be back?" I asked Aiden, although I knew the answer. He hadn't stopped going on about the first things he was going to do as soon as we arrived back in Vancouver. Number one on the list was meeting up with his friends and going bowling. His energy levels had returned in spades over the last few weeks which, according to Dr. Faussman, was due to the drugs pushing back on the disease. In a few months, he might be in remission, and his life could get back to normal. Every day I hoped and prayed for that outcome.

Garen, as good as his word, had sent the missing payment

as well as a lump sum to cover future drugs that Aiden would need. His generosity in the face of my awful behavior humbled me. Most, if not all, other men would have stopped all financial assistance, especially after I'd left that terrible message the day his father became ill. I hadn't known that, of course, but it didn't stop me from feeling absolutely awful every time I thought about it. The things I'd said, the terrible blame I'd heaped on his shoulders when he was dealing with the possible loss of his father. He hadn't spoken of them much, but enough for me to know how much he loved them.

"Yes!" Aiden said, beaming. "Can I go see my friends as soon as we get home?"

I opened my mouth, but Grams beat me to it. "No. You've had a long trip. Rest up today and you can visit with them tomorrow."

I expected an argument, but he simply nodded and grumbled, "Okay."

I guessed that meant he was feeling more tired than he wanted to let on. Then again, I felt just as exhausted after a seventeen-hour journey from Geneva to Vancouver, and sitting in a cramped economy seat without room to stretch your legs was a far cry from Garen's luxury jet with its plush leather reclining chairs and couches that converted to a double bed.

An ache bloomed in my chest, and breathing became a little trickier, as if my windpipe closed over and each breath took far more effort than it should. I'd busied myself for the last few months, and while I thought about him every day, I usually found something to distract me and keep the agony at bay. But now, returning to Canada, to the city we both lived in, I had a feeling I'd find it harder to divert my attention.

I'd searched online to see if I could find anything out about his father's condition, but there hadn't been a single mention of it. Not even in the gossip columns that flooded the internet. For all I knew he was still in Montreal, thousands of miles away from Vancouver.

I pressed a fist to my sternum and briefly closed my eyes.

The pilot switched off the 'fasten seat belt' sign. Aiden leaped to his feet. I urged him to sit back down. "We can't go anywhere until they open the doors. No point rushing."

Aiden helped me haul the bags off the luggage carousel, and we lined up for a cab. The biting January wind coiled around my ankles, sending a shiver down my spine. Nearby, energetic children jumped into puddles left behind by the winter rains.

I slipped my arm around Grams' shoulder and rubbed up and down.

"Stop fussing, girl," she groused but then leaned closer to me.

I grinned at her and continued stroking her. "Grouch."

The cab drew up outside our house, and a longing swept through me. Over four months had passed since we'd left here, and the weeds in our little front yard had taken full advantage of our absence, their dull green shoots sprouting up despite Mother Nature's best efforts to suppress them.

"Funny how they continue to grow while everything else dies during the winter months," I mused as I handed over the fare to the driver along with a healthy tip. He got out and helped us carry our suitcases to the front door, then left with a smile and a wave.

The inside of the house was like an icebox, and I cursed to myself. I should have asked our neighbor to pop in and put the heating on. After four months away at this time of year, it'd take an age to warm up.

I righted the wrong immediately and turned the thermostat to high in the vain hope that would encourage the heat to come through faster. In the meantime, I lit the gas fire in the living room. At least we'd have one room warm and cozy while the rest of the house caught up.

Aiden rushed upstairs muttering something about Xbox and an online gaming challenge while Grams settled herself in her chair, shuffled it closer to the fire, and riffled in her shoulder bag for her knitting.

Back to normal.

I ate a light dinner and headed off to bed to read, but my attention span lasted about three seconds. I owed Garen an apology and my heartfelt thanks for all he'd done for me and Aiden. What happened between us, and the atrocious things he'd said didn't negate his generosity in helping my brother to, hopefully, recover from a disease that could have killed him. Garen's reasons for such altruism were his own, especially after the original form of payment—for him to summon me to do his bidding whenever he felt like it—had fallen by the wayside. Regardless, the man deserved to know how grateful I was and how I'd never forget him or how much he'd helped my family.

My heart hurt as I sat at the small desk in the corner of my room and began writing. I tore up several letters before I settled on one that I thought communicated my gratitude while not completely letting him off the hook for the mean and cruel things he'd said in Switzerland. I sealed it in an envelope and stared at it for several minutes.

God, I miss you. I ache for you. I love you.

I've lost you.

I awoke at four a.m., the time difference between here and Switzerland messing with my body clock. I tossed and turned for an hour, then huffed and climbed out of bed, shivering as I stuffed my feet into my slippers and tugged a thick robe around my shoulders. I'd never experienced jet lag before—hell, until the trip to Switzerland, I'd never even left the country. I presumed it would take me a few days to adjust back to my normal sleep pattern, and in the meantime, I'd better get used to waking hours before the weak winter sun touched the horizon.

At least the early hour gave me a chance to sneak over to Garen's house and post my attempt at an apology without the risk of bumping into him. And that way, if I didn't hear anything, I'd know where I stood. I hadn't visited his home before, but thanks to Google and his position as a man of substance in this city, I easily found his address. Unsurprisingly, he lived over in Shaughnessy Heights, one of Vancouver's most eminent neighborhoods and a far cry from where I lived.

I showered, dressed in a warm sweater, jeans, and boots and, as it was too early for public transport, I called an Uber. Five minutes later, my phone pinged with a text letting me know the driver was outside. Peering through the drapes, I spotted him idling by the curb. I slid my arms inside my quilted jacket and opened the front door as quietly as I could. The lock clicked into place, and I jogged down the path and dove into the back of the cab.

We had to take a detour due to a road closure which, unfortunately, took me right past where my studio used to be, and where an eight-story hotel now towered above the street.

Garen's hotel.

My gut twisted in mourning for all the good times I'd had before selling out to a man who wouldn't take no for an answer and who, despite my initial hatred, was someone who'd never leave me. Not now that he'd burrowed his way so deeply into my heart.

I missed the kids and the parents, and the way my chest puffed with pride when one of my little charges mastered a particularly difficult move.

But most of all, I missed Garen.

Why did I have to fall in love with *him?* There was something like three or four billion men on the planet, yet my stupid heart set its sights on the one person who seemed to take pleasure in hurting me. I shouldn't care about the man after the way he'd treated me, but someone who gave so charitably to my little brother would always have a special place in my life.

As we drew up outside Garen's impressive property, my heart plummeted. Of course he'd live behind secure gates meant to keep the crazies out. I could hardly stick my letter to the railings now, could I? With fresh rain already falling, it'd turn to pulp in seconds.

Hang on. The postman must have a way to drop off his mail. I scanned along the impressive frontage, and that's when I spotted a small mailbox attached to the wall.

"Can you hang on a sec?" I asked the driver.

I stepped onto the sidewalk, taking care not to slip on the damp ground. I made my way over to the black box and lifted the flap, but I didn't get to post the letter. Instead, a voice I'd both dreaded and longed to hear called my name.

"Catriona?"

36

GAREN

I couldn't believe my eyes. Maybe I was hallucinating after a ten-mile run in cold, damp conditions. Catriona was here, outside my house, her tall, slim frame bundled up in a thick winter jacket and leather gloves. Rain dampened her hair, a few drips trickling down her temple. My chest tightened, my heart pounding, and not from the exercise, but from seeing her again. I'd dreamed of this moment for weeks, yet now it was here, the things I wanted to say stuck in my throat.

"Catriona?" I rasped.

She spun around, shock gracing her face, her green eyes appearing almost black in the dim streetlights. She nibbled her lip, then held an envelope toward me.

"Here," she said. "You're up early."

I stared at the envelope without making a move to take it. "Couldn't sleep."

"Me either." She shrugged. "Jet lag."

"When did you get back?" I asked, my eyes raking over her

face, a swell of yearning growing in my abdomen. Christ, I'd forgotten how beautiful she was. I wanted to wrap her in my arms and never let her go. "Why didn't you tell me you were coming home? I'd have sent my plane for you."

"We got back yesterday." She made another attempt to give me the letter. "Here. You can tear it up if you want."

I still didn't take it.

The cabbie poked his head out the window. "Miss, do you still need me?"

"Yes."

"No."

"Yes," Catriona reiterated, glaring at me.

I fished my wallet out of a zipped pocket in the back of my sweats and handed over a wad of cash, then tapped the roof of the car, and it drove away.

"Hey!" She folded her arms over her chest. "Now I'll have to call another Uber."

I inclined my head. "Come inside? Just for a few minutes."

She narrowed her eyes suspiciously. "Why?"

I offered up a lopsided grin. "Because it's cold out here, and the sweat is drying on my skin, and I desperately want a hot shower." *With you.* "But most of all, I don't want you to go."

"Why?"

I locked my gaze on her, a strand of hope growing in my chest and the words I desperately needed to say finally spilling out of me. "I think we have a lot to say to each other, things that should have been said a long time ago, but I'm an idiot, and a stubborn fool who let you walk away. I won't do that again."

"You didn't let me walk away, Garen. I chose to walk away."

Because of me.

I suppressed a wince at a sharp pain that arrowed through me and nodded, my gaze somber. "Come inside, Catriona." I extended my hand toward her. "Please."

I gauged the chances of her accepting my invitation as fifty-

fifty, so when she slipped her gloved hand inside mine, relief shot through my abdomen. I pressed the remote that opened the gates, then strode up to the house.

"Can I take your jacket?" I asked.

She hesitated, then raised her right shoulder. "I guess."

Tugging down the zipper, she removed her coat. I hung it over the banister, then toed off my sneakers.

"I really need a shower. The kitchen is through there," I said, pointing down the hallway. "I put on a pot of coffee before I left. Help yourself."

I sprinted upstairs, showered in record time, and returned to the kitchen. Catriona was sitting at my kitchen table sipping a cup of coffee. She'd removed her boots, which I probably shouldn't read too much into, but I did anyway. That meant she wasn't planning on a fast escape.

I grabbed a mug and poured myself a cup, then sat across from her.

"I wasn't sure whether you were still in Montreal," she said, meeting my gaze over the top of her cup as if it was a shield of sorts. "How's your dad?"

"Recovering well," I said. "Thank you for asking."

"That's good," she murmured, then blew across the hot liquid and sipped.

"I got back a couple of weeks ago," I said. "I stayed on through Christmas and New Years to help Mom when Dad came out of the hospital."

"They must have liked having you there."

"They did, yes."

Fuck. Where was all this formal shit coming from? This wasn't the conversation we needed to have at all. I pinched the bridge of my nose, then rubbed my eyes.

"We have to talk."

She nodded then pointed her chin at the letter. "I jotted down some things. I thought you weren't here, you see."

"I did the same in the letter I sent you."

Her lips twisted to one side. "I never read it."

My brow furrowed. If she hadn't even read it, then she still thought that what I said to the guys was true. Damn, when she'd sent it back, the envelope seal must have still been in place. Why the *fuck* hadn't I noticed that?

I touched my mouth, then tugged on my bottom lip. "So you still think that what you overheard was the truth?"

"You knew then? That I'd overheard you?"

"Not immediately, no. I figured it out later."

She nodded, pulling at a thread on her sweater.

"It wasn't true, Catriona."

Her head came up. "Wasn't it?"

"No," I expelled, raking a hand through my damp hair. "Jesus, I can't believe you still think that all these months later. No wonder you were so angry when Aiden's payment didn't go through, and why you thought it was me being cruel for the sake of it." I got up from my chair and kneeled beside hers, gazing up at her and hoping she could see the love I had for her in my eyes.

I took her hand, and she let me. "What you heard was me being a fucking idiot. A childish, stupid asshole who didn't know how to handle teasing from my friends about a woman who, at the time, I was feeling things for that I didn't know what to do with." I pressed my palms to her cheeks. "A woman I've since realized I'm in love with."

Her eyes went wide, the vibrant green of her irises disappearing as her pupils dilated. "You... sorry, what? You love me?"

I nodded, a smile inching across my face. This was so much easier than I thought it would be. Telling her I loved her had set me free. The one thing I'd avoided my entire life—putting myself out there and risking rejection—hadn't killed me. Even if she didn't feel the same way, she would. In time. What we had together in Switzerland wasn't a lie. I hadn't killed it with my stupidity, just put it in intensive care for a while.

A tear beaded on her eyelashes, and when she blinked, it trickled down her cheek. I wiped it away with my thumb.

"I broke up with you to save face."

I brushed her lips with mine. "I know. That's why I wrote you the letter and sent the flowers. I worked it out. I even had Lia and Raphael test how soundproof the door was." I grinned. "Yeah, turns out not so much."

Her lips curved upward, and in that moment, I knew it was going to be okay.

"And then you didn't even read it. If I'd known you hadn't... Christ, *mon petit chaton*." I shook my head and dropped my gaze to the floor.

Catriona's forefinger tilted up my chin. "I love you so damn much," she said, a sob bursting from her throat. "I thought I'd lost you forever. You broke my heart, and I'm going to make you spend the rest of your life piecing it back together."

Dizzy with happiness, I stood, pulling her upright with me. I covered her mouth with mine, the kiss meant as an apology that quickly escalated into one of hot, raw need. My tongue tangled with hers, and my hands went to her hips, tugging her closer. I burrowed underneath her sweater and dipped a hand inside the cup of her bra.

"Fuck."

I yanked the sweater over her head, tossing it to one side, then eased down the lace cup and sucked her erect nipple into my mouth. She gasped and buried her fingers into my hair, urging me on.

I lifted her into my arms. "I'm taking you to bed and I'm going to fuck you for hours, so if there's somewhere you need to be, you're not going to make it."

37

CATRIONA

I zipped up my jacket and laced up my boots. "Where are we going?"

Garen gave me one of his looks that told me I wouldn't get a single word out of him. The arched brow, the slight head tilt, the mischievous glint in his eye. I could bombard him with a million questions and get nowhere. He wasn't a man who submitted to pressure.

He captured my hand and walked me over to his garage. Inside, three cars were lined up side by side, his usual form of transport—the limousine—absent.

"Where's the limo?" I asked.

"Darryl takes it home. I don't have a use for it unless Darryl is driving."

He pressed down on a black fob, and the turn signals of a large, black SUV flashed. He opened the passenger door and guided me inside, then walked around the hood.

I rubbed my hands together and blew on them. Despite

wearing gloves, the cold morning still got through the thick, insulated leather. Garen started the engine and jacked the temperature up.

"It should warm up in a couple of minutes."

Thirty minutes later, Garen pulled onto a road I knew all too well. My heart plummeted, and melancholy for what I'd lost swept through me. I'd already seen this view this morning out of the cab window. I didn't need a second viewing.

"Can we take a different route to wherever we're going?" I asked.

"Bit difficult," Garen said as he nosed the car into the underground car park of the hotel.

I shifted in my seat to face him and shook my head. "No, Garen. I'm sorry. I know things are different between us, but no matter how much I love you, I don't want to see the hotel. It's just rubbing salt in the wounds."

He ignored me, pulling forward into a space marked 'Reserved'. Cutting the engine, he twisted in his seat.

"Trust me?" He caressed his knuckles down my cheek. "It's not what you think. I don't want to hurt you or bring back sad memories of what I took from you. But there is something inside that I really want you to see."

I grimaced and rubbed at the back of my neck. "Okay," I said reluctantly, my vow to never set foot in the place falling by the wayside in the face of his earnest expression.

He led me through an entrance marked 'Staff Only'. We passed by a storage area with boxes piled high, through an industrial kitchen, sparkling with new appliances and cookers, the steel countertops gleaming.

Plush carpeting underfoot and bright-colored artwork adorning the walls told me we'd left the staff areas behind and were now in the public parts of the hotel. I spied the lobby, but instead of walking in that direction, Garen veered left. I followed, my curiosity growing with every step.

He stopped outside a double set of oak-paneled doors with shiny chrome handles. There was a sign affixed to the wall, but before I could read it, Garen moved, obscuring my view. He gestured to the door.

"Go on in."

I pushed down on both handles, and the doors gave way, opening inward. I gasped.

No, it couldn't be. How had he... what... wait... *That's impossible.*

Spinning on my heel, I pressed both palms to my face, my mouth falling open in shock. "How did you do this?"

He smiled and strolled inside to join me. Bending his head, he brushed his mouth over mine in a barely there kiss that sent tingles to my toes.

"I guess, right from the start, something deep within me believed you were different. I didn't expect to fall in love with you, but I knew I couldn't rip apart your life without some kind of compensation. I wanted us both to win." He drew his knuckles over my cheek. "And this was the answer."

I stared around the familiar-looking space, dazed and more than a little overwhelmed. Garen had somehow preserved every single piece of my old studio, from the mirrors on the walls to the scratched bar where my students would balance to practice their steps, and even down to the flooring. The walls were painted exactly the same color—a soft pink—and a replica of my old office sat in the corner. The only thing missing was the stacks of paperwork that I never seemed to find time to address.

"Are you happy?"

I pivoted and ran into his arms, wrapping my legs around his waist. Planting a quick kiss on his mouth, I drew back. "Happier than I ever thought possible."

"It's built on the exact same footprint as the old studio."

"No?"

"Yep. The architect wasn't happy as it meant he had to change a lot of other things to accommodate it, but tough shit. My dollar, my hotel. My girl." He kissed me this time. "I took the liberty of putting up a sign, but if you don't like it, we can get another one made."

"Is that what you were hiding before, outside?"

He nodded. "I'd completely forgotten about it. If you'd spotted your name, it'd have totally ruined the surprise."

I darted outside to take a look. A shining silver plaque read 'Catriona Landry's School of Ballet'. I blinked, tears threatening to fall. If I let them, I wouldn't be able to stop.

"Hang on," I said, walking back inside as a thought occurred to me. "We broke up and you still went ahead with this."

He pulled his lips to one side. "I put this in motion when you still hated me. Before the bulldozers moved in, I had each piece painstakingly removed. The builders had to take so many photographs to make sure they could replicate it exactly." He grinned. "They think I'm some kind of weird eccentric."

"I-I don't know what to say."

"Tell me you love me."

I curved my hands around the back of his neck and stood on tiptoes to kiss him. "I love you. I love you so much, Garen Gauthier."

He gave me a crooked smile, one that fell quickly as his eyes locked on a spot over my right shoulder. "That was where I made you get on your knees thinking you had to suck my cock before I'd fund Aiden's medical treatment."

My jaw flexed involuntarily at the memory. He'd humiliated me for no other purpose than to test my limits.

"I despised you that day."

"One of many days you must have hated me for the things I did." He rubbed a hand over his chin, dark with day-old stubble. "I couldn't figure out why I loved tormenting you so much.

I've always enjoyed getting one over on my opponents, but with you, it felt... more personal somehow. When you hurt, I felt a sense of gratification. It was only after I returned home following Dad's heart attack that Mom put it all together."

I canted my head and narrowed my eyes. "There's an actual *reason?*"

Raking a hand through his hair, he nodded. "I was telling Mom about you, how I'd fucked everything up. She asked to see a picture. I showed her one that I took on the boat on Lake Geneva, and she pointed out that you resemble a girl I went to elementary school with. Rosie Moreau. I had a bit of a crush on Rosie and one day I picked her some flowers, intending to declare my undying love." I chuckled. "You know, like you do at eight years old. Anyway, a group of older boys witnessed my first foray into wooing the opposite sex, and they teased me terribly, and then the bullying started. It got pretty bad, and Rosie, probably fearful of being targeted by the bullies herself, refused to have anything to do with me. After that, I developed a stammer. I'd forgotten all about her until Mom brought it up, and then the memories came rushing back. You have similar eyes, same color, same shape. And your smile strikes a chord, too, except yours is much more beautiful." He shrugged. "I think somewhere deep in my subconscious I was trying to assert myself, as if by being mean to you now, I could somehow rewrite history. And when Seb mocked me about liking you, my first thought was to rebuff the idea that you meant anything to me. In that moment, the little boy who had put himself out there and ended up being miserable for an entire school year had the upper hand. And so I denied how I felt about you."

"Wow." I caressed his cheek. "I wish I'd known your dad was sick. I wouldn't have dreamt of leaving that message if I'd had any idea. You must have hated me that day."

He tucked a lock of hair behind my ear. "You couldn't have

known what had happened. And I could never hate you. Never."

"You were so mad."

He fiddled with his watch, slipping a finger beneath the strap as if he found the metal irritating. "I was pining for you so much by then that when I heard your voice, I thought you were calling to tell me you'd forgiven me. By the time I listened to the whole message, and on the back of my worry over Dad, I kind of lost it. Afterward, shit, I felt bad."

"I deserved it. I should have known you wouldn't go back on your word, no matter what."

He captured both my hands in his, staring down at them linked together. "We've both fucked up. Let's not do that anymore." He lifted them to his lips and kissed my knuckles.

"You had a stammer? I wouldn't ever have believed it."

He brought his gaze up to me and made a face. "Yeah. Once a week for two fucking years, I visited a speech therapist. Eventually, it went away."

"How awful for you. Some kids can be so cruel for no reason."

"Don't feel sorry for me. It was a long time ago." A broad grin inched across his face, and he winked. "Luckily, it didn't have any impact on my confidence."

I laughed. "Yeah, I can vouch for that."

He slung an arm around my shoulder. "Let's go home, *chaton*."

38

CATRIONA

Six months later.

Dublin, Ireland.

Hand in hand, Garen and I wandered down Grafton Street, the area bursting with tourists enjoying the warm summer sunshine in Dublin's premier shopping district. Baskets teeming with pink and yellow summer flowers hung outside shop entrances, and the sidewalks boasted a multitude of coffee shops, restaurants, and unique one-of-a-kind stores.

 I stepped into a gift shop and bought a bottle-green hoodie daubed with 'Dublin Ireland' right across the front, as well as a teabag holder in the shape of a teapot that I knew Grams would adore. It even had an Irish blessing painted in greens and blues and reds. We were meeting Grams and Aiden later. Grams' old legs wouldn't stand up to hours of walking—her words not mine—and Aiden and his friend Joe were off doing whatever it was sixteen-year-old boys got up to. I dreaded to think about it.

Aiden had formally gone into remission, with no trace of the leukemia in his blood. To celebrate, Garen had suggested we take a vacation to Dublin. Aiden and I had never visited our historic roots, and Grams had jumped at the chance to revisit her home, especially as she hadn't been back since she and Gramps emigrated to Canada in their thirties.

We left the shopping area behind and took the short walk to Trinity College. The sun beat down as we walked up the main pathway toward an impressive archway that led into a large courtyard.

"This is the oldest university in Ireland," Garen said. "Founded in fifteen ninety-two by Queen Elizabeth I."

I shielded my eyes from the sun and peered up at him. "How do you know all that?"

He tapped his temple. "Photographic memory. I scanned the tourist guide before we left the hotel." He slipped an arm around my waist. "Here's a few more facts for you. Bram Stoker, Oscar Wilde, and Samuel Becket went to college here, and Trinity is also renowned for owning several priceless artifacts, including an ancient Irish harp."

"Y'know," I said, licking my lips and giving him a full head-to-toe eye sweep as I sensed an opportunity to tease him. "That kind of geeky talk turns a girl on."

For a split second, he appeared startled. And then he read the mischievous glint in my eye. He bent his knees, and the next thing I knew, I found myself hoisted over his shoulder in a proper fireman's lift.

I squealed and smacked his backside, earning a swat against my own ass in revenge.

"Put me down," I demanded, but as I was laughing so much, it came out garbled.

He marched across the grass, completely oblivious—or rather he didn't care—about the open-mouthed stares from the tourists milling about.

He finally set me back on my feet beside a large oak tree that cast dappled shadows on the closely cut lawn. Walking me backward until my spine connected with the thick bark, he captured both my hands in one of his and held them over my head, then used his free hand to cup my jaw and angle my head for his kiss.

His tongue swept along the seam of my lips, and then he tugged on my chin and closed his mouth over mine. My lower belly tightened, my core flooding with warmth, as it always did with this man. I couldn't get enough of him. His touch set me on fire. His kiss melted my insides. His laugh brought me so much happiness, I could burst.

We broke apart, panting from having gone from zero to one hundred in five seconds. It was always this way with us. The passion, the lust, the desire. I caught sight of a guy gaping at us while his girlfriend or wife steered their child in the opposite direction, her face red with annoyance, muttering something about inappropriate behavior in a public place.

Garen chuckled, unfazed by their displeasure, while I tried to paint on a contrite expression, holding up a hand to the guy in apology.

"You're a bad man," I said, poking him in the chest.

He caught my finger, lifting it to his lips where he nibbled the tip then sucked it into his mouth. My abdomen clenched, my body completely on board with carrying on where we left off, despite my brain urging me to behave with more decorum.

We finished off the rest of our sightseeing without upsetting any more locals or visitors and returned to the hotel to pick up Grams and Aiden for dinner. They were waiting for us in the lobby as arranged. Garen dropped off our purchases in our room, and then we set off to the restaurant.

Stuffed after an enormous dinner, I relaxed back in my chair with a sigh. "Damn, the Irish know how to cook," I said, groaning under the weight of food in my belly. "I'm going to leave here seven pounds heavier at this rate."

Garen's eyes lingered on my chest as if to say, "Yep, and if those seven pounds end up on your tits, I'll be very happy indeed."

I glared at him. He grinned at me.

"Do you mind if we take a detour on the way home?" Grams asked. "There's somewhere I'd like to visit."

"Of course not," Garen said. "Do you need me to arrange a cab?"

Grams shook her head. "It's only five minutes or so from here. Maybe ten on these old legs."

I raised my eyes to the ceiling. "Grams, stop already. You'll outlive us all."

She absentmindedly patted my hand. "You're a good girl. Your mother would be proud."

She had this faraway expression that worried me a little bit, but there was no cajoling Grams into talking if she didn't want to. Whatever was wrong, I'd find out when she wanted me to, and not a second before.

With Grams leading the way, using her frame for support, we wound our way through the streets, the evening time as busy as during the day, maybe even busier. One of the great things I'd discovered about Dublin during the last couple of days was how compact it was. Everything was within walking distance. I definitely wanted to come back here again someday.

We arrived at a beautiful church, its spire towering above us. In front of the church, colorful borders and mature trees were set amongst pristine gardens.

"Wow, this is beautiful," I said.

"St. Patrick's Cathedral," Grams said, pushing her walker straight past the entrance.

I frowned. "Don't you want to go inside, Grams?"

"No." She continued, clearly with a destination in mind.

"Is this where you and Gramps married?" Aiden asked.

Grams cackled. "Goodness me, no. We didn't have money for a fancy church service. Not that we needed the trimmings. We had each other."

My heart squeezed, and I glanced up at Garen. "I understand," I said, meaning it. If Garen lost every cent he had, I'd still love him fiercely.

At the back of the church, in a little alcove that was set back from the rest of the building, Grams stopped. She reached out and touched the stonework, and I could tell she'd gone inside her mind to memories that clearly meant a huge amount to her.

"Your grandpa kissed me for the very first time, right here," she said. "He used tongue, too."

I burst out laughing, as did Garen. Aiden's face twisted as if the idea of Grams and Gramps kissing was akin to eating slugs, while his friend, Joe, turned beet red at the unexpected turn in the conversation.

"Grams!" I expelled. "On sacred ground? And a good Catholic girl like you, too."

Grams waggled her eyebrows. "I was young once, you know. You kids don't have the cornerstone on bad behavior."

I slipped my arm around her shoulders and kissed her cheek. "Love you, Grams. You naughty girl."

She cackled again. "I won't tell you what happened the next time we came back here."

I stared at her in mock horror and clutched a hand to my chest. "No, please don't."

Aiden turned a little green. "I second that," he said.

Garen's phone rang, and he excused himself to answer it, strolling a short distance away.

"So this was the reason for coming here," I said. "You wanted to reminisce about Gramps?"

Grams nodded, her eyes misting over. "He drove me mad at times, but I adored the old fool. I miss him."

I hugged her tightly. "Me, too."

Garen's voice wafted over, rising in volume. He barked out, "When?" and then turned around, seeking me out, his face ashen.

Oh no, not his father.

I walked over to him and touched his upper arm to show my support as he spoke with whoever was on the phone. I held my impatience for information in check. No point me asking questions while he was trying to listen to whoever was on the other end of the line.

"Okay. Yep. Right. Got it. I'll head for the airport now."

I held my stomach, chills rushing through me despite the mild evening and light winds.

"Garen, what is it? What's wrong? Is it your dad?"

He shook his head, dragging a trembling hand through his hair. "It's Upton," he said, referring to his friend and a member of the ROGUES board. "There's been an accident. He's in the hospital in LA."

"What kind of accident? He'll be okay, though, right?"

He reached for me, his skin worryingly pale. He shook his head. "They're not sure whether he's going to make it."

THE END

Wanted: Companion for reclusive billionaire. Apply online now.

It should be so easy. A twelve month contract with a fat bonus at the end—providing I don't quit.

Except when something looks too good to be true, it usually is.

Little did I know how interwoven my life is with his.

Saving him might cure my own crushing guilt.

Or it could break us both.

The question is—am I brave enough to find out?

Ebook available to preorder on Amazon

ACKNOWLEDGMENTS

I owe so much to my wonderful team who cheer me on, encourage me every step of the way, and challenge me to dig deep to make every novel I release the very best it can be.

I love you all - and in no particular order...

To hubs - my love and gratitude forever.

To my critique partner, Incy... Thank you so much for your critique as always. I'm so glad you loved Garen as much as I did.

To my gorgeous, big-hearted, wonderful PA, Loulou. Thank you for always being in my corner. I promised you an asshole and I hope you think I delivered.

Emmy - thank you for your brilliant editing as always. I appreciate the heck out of you and am so glad you're my editor.

Katie - gah! I love you and appreciate you so much. Sorry about the cliffy!

Jenn - thank you from the bottom of my heart for reading Entrapped and making sure I had the Canadian voices just right - and thanks for the weather report!

Jean - I love you. Love love love. I'm still chuckling at your "You're going to leave it THERE!!!" comment. Oops...

Jacqueline - Thank you for reading, as always. You're awesome.

To my ARC readers. You guys are amazing! You're my final eyes and ears before my baby is released into the world and I appreciate each and every one of you for giving up your time to read —and point out the odd errors that slip through the net!

And last but most certainly not least, to you, the readers. Thank you for being on this journey with me. It still humbles me to think that my words are being read all over the world.

If you have any time to spare, I'd be ever so grateful if you'd leave a short review on Amazon or Goodreads. Reviews not only help readers discover new books, but they also help authors reach new readers. You'd be doing a massive favor for this wonderful bookish community we're all a part of.

ABOUT TRACIE DELANEY

Tracie Delaney realized she was destined to write when, at aged five, she crafted little notes to her parents, each one finished with "The End."

Tracie loves to write steamy contemporary romance books that center around hot men, strong women, and then watch with glee as they battle through real life problems. Of course, there's always a perfect Happy Ever After ending (eventually).

When she isn't writing or sitting around with her head stuck in a book, she can often be found watching The Walking Dead, Game of Thrones or any tennis match involving Roger Federer. Coffee is a regular savior.

You can find Tracie on Facebook, Twitter and Instagram, or, for the latest news, exclusive excerpts and competitions, why not join her reader group.

Tracie currently resides in the North West of England with her amazingly supportive husband and her two crazy Westie puppies, Cooper and Murphy.

Tracie loves to hear from readers. She can be contacted through her website

www.authortraciedelaney.com

Printed in Great Britain
by Amazon